The Life
She Chooses

A GRANITE SPRINGS NOVEL

Maggie Christensen

To my lovely granddaughter, Lara, whose help and assistance with current teenage slang was invaluable.

Also by Maggie Christensen

Prologue

Something wakened her.

Kay Jackson reached across the bed to touch her husband, only to find her hand encounter a cold, empty space. Her eyes shot open as she surveyed the vacant spot where David should be lying. She started up, then fell back, her mind going around in circles. He was probably in the kitchen. Since the rumours had started – four weeks ago – he'd had trouble sleeping, often getting up to drink whiskey and gaze unseeingly out into the darkness.

The first few times she'd found him like that, she'd coaxed him back to bed, but now she knew it was best to let him be, to face whatever demons he had, alone. There was nothing she could do to help him, try as she might.

She knew the rumours were untrue. They had to be. Her David was a gentle creature. They'd been married for over thirty years. She knew him inside out. There was no way he was a child molester. She couldn't even utter the word paedophile. It was a mistake. It had been someone else. Or the girl had some grudge against him. She tried to ignore the fact that, in the past few days, other girls had come forward to tell the same story.

But David was a respected member of the community – the local dentist, a friendly figure to the girls in the netball team he'd coached for what seemed forever. They'd realise their mistake, and life would go back to the way it had been.

Kay closed her eyes again, but sleep eluded her. She got out of bed, pulled on her soft blue robe and slid her feet into her sheepskin slippers. It was cold at this time of the morning, and the kitchen tiles were unforgiving on her bare feet.

In the kitchen, Milly, their old cat, stretched in her basket by the Aga which kept the room warm all night. But she knew it was too early for her breakfast, so immediately curled up again, purring loudly. It was a comforting sound, and Kay needed comfort. She filled the kettle and measured the tealeaves into the teapot she and David had chosen together in better days – days when the dental practice was growing, and the future looked bright.

There was no sign of David. Kay assumed he'd gone for an early morning run. He'd be back soon.

She stood, staring out the window watching the sun come up. She used to love this part of the day, but now it filled her with apprehension as to what the rest of the day might bring.

When the rumours first began, when the first girl made her accusation, David had brushed it off as the wild imaginings of overactive teenage hormones. But as those rumours grew, it had become more and more difficult to dismiss them.

Despite Kay's suggestion they take time off, go away till it all died down, David had been unyielding. He'd gone into the surgery each day, regardless of the cancelled appointments, the sly whispers. And she'd been there beside him, receptionist, wife and supporter, putting on a brave face and offering a tight smile to the critics.

She sighed, slid a slice of bread into the toaster and took a tub of butter and a jar of marmalade from the fridge while she waited, though she had little appetite.

Breakfast over, Kay gazed anxiously out the window, but there was no sign of her husband. He was usually back by now, ready for a second or third cup of coffee. He wasn't eating much either, a sign the gossip was affecting him more that he was willing to admit.

By the time she was ready to leave, David still hadn't appeared. Now Kay was really worried. She opened the garage door and gave a sigh of relief. His car was gone. He must have decided to go in early. Maybe today would be different; there would be no more cancellations; the rumours would die down; they could get on with their lives. But, deep down, Kay knew life could never be the same again.

To Kay's surprise, the office door was locked. David wasn't there. A curl of fear flickered in the pit of her stomach making her fingers clumsy as she fitted the key into the lock. But, once inside, the morning routine took over. She greeted David's partner with a smile, managed to make civil conversation with Denise and Alanna, the two dental hygienists, as they arrived, and to welcome the first patients of the morning.

A check of the diary revealed David had no appointments till close to lunchtime, so maybe he'd gone for a drive to *get his head together* as he put it.

The door opened. Kay glanced up, ready with a welcoming smile, only to have it disappear when she saw the sombre face of a police officer.

'Mrs Jackson, is there somewhere we can talk?'

Kay felt her head spin. She could barely breathe. She thought she was going to collapse.

'Are you all right, Kay?' Denise emerged from behind her.

'No, yes. Can you take over for a bit, Denise? The officer wants to…'

She led him into the small staff-room.

'I think you should sit down,' he said.

She did, clasping her hands tightly in her lap and trying not to imagine the worst. Had David had an accident? Was he badly injured? Why was she sitting here when she should be rushing to hospital?

'I'm sorry to tell you, Mrs Jackson, Kay, that early this morning, your husband's car was found on the outskirts of town. It appears he took his own life.'

One

The pall of smoke from the recently extinguished bushfire hung over the town as Kay made her solitary way to the cemetery. It was three years since David died, and each year on the anniversary of his death, she'd made this lonely pilgrimage. It would have been nice if her children chose to accompany her, but Adam, her son, lived in England, having taken a position there over ten years ago, and her daughter...

Zoe lived in Brisbane, had rejected her dad as soon as the rumours started, and refused to return for the funeral or to visit his grave. It was up to Kay to make the trek to Brisbane if she wanted to see her grandchild.

She knelt on the parched grass in front of the simple stone to lay flowers on the grave, her eyes filled with tears. Why couldn't he have stuck it out? But, despite all her denials, in her heart Kay now knew David had been guilty of everything they'd accused him of. That was why, after his death, she'd left the practice, had practically become a recluse. Granite Springs was a small town in New South Wales and, like all small towns, had a thriving gossip mill. She couldn't bear the pity, the words of sympathy, the way people whispered behind her back.

She sighed as she made her way back to the car and drove home, the house enveloping her in its warmth. Milly, the black cat who'd been her sole companion for the past three years, was lying in a puddle of sunlight and opened one eye when she walked in.

The message light on the phone was blinking. Kay debated ignoring it, but suspecting it was her good friend, Jo, she pressed *play*.

She was right.

'Hi Kay. I know this is a difficult day for you. I just wanted you to know I'm thinking of you.' There was a pause, then, 'If you'd like to meet for coffee, I'm available all day, but I understand if you want to be alone.'

The message ended with a silence that filled the room. Kay slumped into a chair. Did she want company? Even the company of the friend who'd supported her through her grief might prove too much to bear. She knew Jo thought that, after three years, she should be making a life for herself. She just didn't understand.

The trouble was, Kay knew, Jo understood all too well. She'd lost her own husband through divorce six years earlier and a good friend to cancer over a year ago. But Kay felt her own grief to be unique.

As if sensing her dilemma, Milly stretched and sauntered over to jump up on her lap, kneading it with her tiny paws. Kay's fingers automatically reached down to scratch the cat's soft fur. Milly strained upwards into her hand.

'Oh, Milly. What would I do without you?' But, of course, there was no reply.

Kay sat like that for a few minutes before deciding what to do. The lonely day stretched out before her. There was still another week of holidays before she was due back at the university. The job she'd taken there a year earlier had been a godsend. Getting back into the workforce had been an impulsive decision, but a good one. She enjoyed the day-to-day buzz of the university office, the demands of the staff and the liveliness of the students. It was only here, at home, that the loneliness set in.

She rose, the sudden movement forcing Milly to tumble from her lap with a loud meow. Coffee with Jo seemed like a good idea.

*

'How are you, really?' The woman sitting opposite fixed Kay with concerned eyes as she held her coffee cup in both hands, her elbows on the table.

'Okay.' Kay brushed a strand of hair out of her eyes wishing she'd taken time to do something more with it. Maybe she should get it cut, but David had liked her shoulder-length dark hair. She gave herself a shake. David was gone. 'I am. Really. It's just this time of year. It all comes back.'

Jo's hand reached across the table to cover hers. 'I know.'

The two sat in silence, then Jo asked, 'When do you go back to work?'

'Next week. I'll be better then. The office is busy; the faculty is busy. I don't have much time to think.'

'It's been three years, Kay.' Jo's voice was gentle, but Kay was aware of the implicit criticism. In her friend's mind she should be moving on.

'I'm not ready.'

Kay wondered if she'd ever be ready in the sense Jo meant. Unlike her friend's new husband who had got together with Jo only a year after his wife's death; there were extenuating circumstances there, she allowed. And men were different – they needed a woman in their lives. *She* couldn't imagine sharing her life with anyone else.

'How's Col?' she asked to change the subject.

'Good. Did I tell you we're talking about taking back the far paddock, and Col has it in mind to plant lavender? He's full of ideas. A lavender farm one day, a pig farm the next. I was worried he'd have time on his hands after retiring, but it's lovely having him around all day. Now I'm worried he's trying to do too much.' She laughed – an indulgent laugh.

'And the grands?'

Jo's face broke into a wide smile. 'They're wonderful. Lottie and Livvy are excited to be going into grade one. They're hoping Allegra will be their teacher. Did I tell you she's been offered a position at Granite Springs Primary?' she asked, referring to the girl who, in her final year at university, had been babysitter for Jo's twin granddaughters the previous year. 'And Emily Rose, she's growing so fast. It's difficult to believe she's only three months old. What about your little Noah? How was Christmas in Brisbane this year?'

Kay sighed. She worried about Noah. A lovely little boy, now almost five, her grandson was alert, curious and turning into the image of his dad, but Kay was concerned his mother regimented his life too much. Surely at his tender age, he should be allowed more independence?

'Zoe hasn't changed,' Kay said. 'I was glad to get home. I don't know how Eric puts up with her. She seems to forget she's not a manager when she gets home from work and wants to organise all our lives. I suppose he's used to it, and he's not home much. His work keeps him busy. Nan's lovely though – his mum. She was there too this year. She's a widow like me. We...' she paused, about to say they had a lot in common. But had they? Nan Bailey's husband had died after a lingering illness, mourned by friends and family, neighbours and former workmates. He was still spoken of highly by Zoe and Eric. How could that experience compare with the rejection and humiliation Kay had suffered?

'It's good to have you back.' Jo's gentle voice was reassuring. Here was someone who understood what she had been through, was still going through.

'And you're still thinking of moving?'

Kay hesitated. She'd mooted that idea with Jo before leaving for Brisbane, but since coming back the idea of packing up the house she and David had shared, the one they'd moved to after Zoe and Adam had grown up and left, all seemed too hard.

'I've been too busy to think about it.'

'Maybe you should.' Kay saw Jo bite her lip. 'I know I fought against leaving Yarran when Danny and Kylie had their eye on it, but it's different for you.'

She didn't need to say any more. Kay still had nightmares about the media frenzy outside the house.

'Maybe,' she said, picking up her cup and finishing the now cold coffee. She grimaced.

But Jo wasn't prepared to leave it at that. 'It's not as if you raised your family there. And surely the memories...' She buttoned her lip as if knowing she'd said enough.

'I should go.' Kay ostentatiously looked at her watch, as if she had some pressing engagement. She could see from Jo's sympathetic expression she hadn't fooled her friend for one second.

But Jo made ready to leave too. 'Remember,' she said as they hugged before parting, 'You can always call me if...'

'Thanks.' Kay turned away and hurried off. Jo's sympathy was more than she could bear. Maybe Zoe had been right when she suggested

Kay should see someone, that she was clinically depressed, that by now – three years later – she should be getting over David's death.

Two

'Damn!'

Nick Kerr stood watching helplessly as the bulky bundle of papers slid to the floor and scattered. He thrust a hand through his short thatch of thick greying hair, tugged at his beard, and scowled. He should call it a day. Dean of the School of Education at William Farrer University, he'd been in his office since the crack of dawn, pretending he needed to prepare for the start of semester. It was past six o'clock. He should go home. But there was nothing for him there.

When his wife had left the day after New Year, she'd taken their teenage son and daughter with her, along with half the furniture. The house now had an unlived-in appearance without the dining table, one of the sofas and the widescreen TV. He knew he should get around to replacing them, but it was easier to spend his time here in the office and pretend it hadn't happened.

At least Sam would be back in time for school to start, but that was weeks away. At seventeen, she'd refused to make the move with her mother, demanding to know why she should be disadvantaged and separated from all her friends in her final year of school just because her parents couldn't see eye-to-eye. Never mind that it was Michelle who'd chosen to move north with the man Nick deridingly referred to as her *toy boy*.

He checked his computer again, hoping he'd misread the email that had appeared in his inbox that morning. As if his personal life being in chaos wasn't enough, Fran, his trusted personal assistant, had been summoned to her mother's bedside in the UK and needed to take leave for the entire semester. Where would he find someone to replace her? He supposed one of the office staff could be seconded to fill the position on a temporary basis. He sighed. This was going to be a difficult year.

Unable to contemplate the empty house that awaited him, Nick drove instead towards the river, coming to a halt in the carpark of The Riverside, the restaurant owned by Steve's partner. Steve was one of the few on the faculty who'd shunned the annual rush to the coast by most of the other staff. It would be quiet there at this time midweek, and Nick would be sure of a good meal.

As he pushed through the glass doors, Nick was met with an assortment of delicious aromas, and greeted by the tall broad-shouldered man he was more accustomed to seeing in the university hallways or presenting the union's case in faculty meetings.

'Good evening, Prof Kerr. Table for one this evening?' Steve glanced behind Nick as if expecting to see Michelle, impeccably made-up, chestnut hair sweeping her shoulders.

'Yes.'

So the word hadn't yet got around about Michelle's leaving? It wouldn't take long. Granite Springs might be becoming a larger regional centre, but the gossip mill was still as effective as it ever had been.

Shown to a corner table already set for two, Nick studied the menu before ordering a Cascade Light and a dish of lamb shanks. While he was waiting for his meal, he checked his phone to find two texts from his daughter.

Yeppoon sucks. And Terry's a wanker. Cn I cum home? Samx

Can't stand it here much longer, Nick. Cn u talk to Mum? Samxx

Nick gave a wry grin. In the past year – since turning seventeen – Sam had decided she was grown up enough to drop the *Dad* and call him *Nick*. He missed the little girl who'd called him Daddy and hung onto his every word, and was finding it hard to come to terms with the stranger who'd taken her place. Now he sighed and rubbed the back of his neck.

Poor Sam. Although he dearly wanted to give in to her plea, he'd made a deal with Michelle and the deal was that both Samantha and

Ryan would stay with their mother until the end of January. Then Ryan, who was only fourteen, would start school up there while Sam would return to finish school in Granite Springs. Who knew what would happen then? He'd like to see his daughter follow her parents into teaching, perhaps even enrol in the education program right here at William Farrer. But he knew that wasn't likely to happen. This coming year would most likely be the last he'd have with his daughter before she headed off to another university and greener pastures.

'Evening, Nick.'

He looked up. Standing by the table was a woman he had every reason to dislike. A good friend of Michelle's, Nick was pretty sure Faye had conspired with his ex on more than one occasion to give her an alibi, pretending the pair were out together when the deceitful minx was otherwise engaged with her new partner.

'Hello, Faye.'

'Happy New Year! Heard from Michelle?'

What was happy about it? But Nick put a smile on his face and replied, 'You're more likely to have heard from her than I am.'

'Don't be like that.' She pouted – not an attractive look on someone who'd never see fifty again – and took the seat opposite him. 'I thought you might be a tad lonely. I heard the kids are spending the holiday with their mum. You must be rattling around in that big house without them. Maybe you'd like some company?' She gave him what he assumed she thought was a winsome smile, which only served to alienate him further.

Was the woman really suggesting…?

Fortunately, he was saved from replying by the arrival of the waiter with his meal. 'Would madame like to order?' he asked Faye, who was making herself at home opposite Nick.

'Madame was just leaving,' Nick said, glaring across the table. 'Sorry, Faye, I can't help you,' he said, hoping she'd understand his meaning.

Not now, not ever. He was done with women for good.

Three

At last the holidays were over! Kay found herself humming along to the tune on the radio as she dressed. It was an oldie – *I am woman* sung by Helen Reddy. Before her time, really, but it expressed how she was feeling. She'd wakened this morning with the sense that she was about to enter a new phase. Having a job made such a difference. Even Milly seemed to sense her change of mood.

The mood lasted till she parked in her usual spot outside the Education building, then a sense of despair began to seep in. What could possibly be different this year? As she made her way up the pathway, she recognised the back of the dean, Professor Nick Kerr, striding ahead of her. She barely knew the man. As a mere admin assistant in the faculty office, their paths rarely crossed. She thought she'd heard some rumour about him and his wife during one of the pre-Christmas events, but it didn't affect her, so she hadn't paid any attention.

'Kay!' Ann Baird, the office manager, greeted her as soon as she walked through the door. 'I need a word. Grab a cuppa and come into my office.'

Kay's heart sank. This didn't sound good. What if she was about to lose her job? She'd heard there were some financial constraints, which usually meant budget cuts. This wasn't how she expected her day to start. She'd been thrilled to be offered this job a year ago. It had given her something to live for – a reason to get out of bed every day. Ever since coming home from Brisbane, she'd been looking forward to getting back into the routine.

Trying not to think the worst, she made a cup of coffee – extra strong – and went back to knock tentatively on Ann's door.

'So you'd be doing us a big favour if you agree.' Ann finished speaking and looked at Kay expectantly.

Kay stared back at her. What was Ann thinking? She'd only been there a year. Surely there were others better qualified? She started to speak, but Ann held up a hand to silence her.

'I know what you're going to say.'

She did?

'You're the latest addition to our little office unit, and you're still relatively new to us. But that's exactly why I think you're perfect. As I said, Fran's been called away and will be gone all semester. The others are all familiar with the needs of our lecturers – and the students. And, efficient as they are, they're all very young.'

That, at least, was true. At fifty-eight, Kay was by far the oldest of the group.

'What Professor Kerr needs is someone mature enough to understand the role, someone who won't...' she coughed, '...get the wrong idea. Between ourselves,' Ann lowered her voice, 'the professor's wife has left him. It's a difficult time for him. And the last thing he needs is some flipperty-gibbet gossiping and making eyes at him in his office. Also,' she said, in a more normal tone of voice, 'I'm aware you ran a busy dental practise for many years. I've been watching you. You're careful and efficient – meticulous. You can do this standing on your head. What do you say?' She cocked her head to one side, the action making her look like an overfed budgerigar.

'I need to think about it.' Kay remembered the slightly forbidding back view of the dean in the car park that morning. What would it be like to work for him, instead of spending the day in the noisy atmosphere of the general office? Could she cope with the added responsibility it would bring? Fran Reilly had been the dean's PA for years. Kay only knew her slightly. They belonged to the same choir and it was Fran who'd suggested the position in the education office to Kay just a year ago. For that, Kay would be forever grateful. It had brought her out of her self-imposed exile. But this was completely unexpected.

'Don't take too long,' Ann said, rising to show the discussion was over. 'I need someone in place immediately. I can give you till tomorrow to decide.'

When Kay returned to the main office, she found the place abuzz. They were all wondering who'd be chosen to "move upstairs" – the dean's office was on the upper level of the building. It seemed the gossip mill had been active while Kay was ensconced with Ann, and there was much speculation both about who'd be Fran's replacement and the rumoured break-up of Professor Kerr's marriage.

Ignoring the whispers, Kay settled down to complete her routine tasks which today entailed organising the timetable for the semester based on drafts from each of the staff. It was a task she normally enjoyed, but today she found it difficult to concentrate. Her mind was going around in circles. Here in the office, it was easy for her to remain anonymous, but if she was sitting in an eyrie on the top level of the building, at the desk outside the dean's office, she'd be more visible, more of a target. There would be people who'd remember David. She didn't think she could do it.

*

Kay made it through the day without making any real decision. The smile and nod from Ann as she left made her stomach lurch. Why couldn't things just stay as they were? They could, she realised. All she had to do was to refuse. Ann would find someone else, and Kay could go on as before. But a tiny part of her felt flattered to have been singled out this way. If she was honest with herself, the idea of having more responsibility, of seeing what went on at the top of the faculty, did have some appeal. She was torn.

Getting into her car, Kay made a sudden decision. Taking out her phone she called her friend, Jo.

As she drove out towards Jo's, Kay passed paddocks of red dust parched from the drought. Here and there a windmill rose up into the sky, a reminder that there was no water to feed the dry land. She thought of the time, a few days after David's death. Consumed with grief, she'd driven out of town. She wanted to see where it had happened, where he had spent his last minutes on this earth. She'd got out of the car and stood leaning on a gate, the metal of the frame warm and smooth under her fingers, and she'd sobbed her heart out. There had been a windmill there too, and she'd wondered if that was the last thing David had seen – the windmill, its tall frame stark against the blue sky.

Half an hour later she was driving across Yarran's cattle grid.

'Lovely to see you,' Jo greeted Kay with a warm hug, followed by Col who gave her a peck on the cheek. The pair seemed so happy and content together that, for a moment, Kay envied them. Then she shrugged it off. This sort of companionship was something she'd never experience again. She had to get used to it. All of that had disappeared from her life with David's death.

'A glass of wine?' Col asked, brandishing a bottle of red.

'And you'll stay to dinner,' Jo added. 'I made a chicken casserole and there's plenty for three.'

'Thanks,' Kay accepted gratefully.

'She's been slaving over a hot stove all afternoon,' Col said, filling three glasses with wine, 'I'm glad there's someone else besides me to appreciate it.'

Kay saw the pair exchange a tender glance. She'd been wrong a year earlier when she'd told Jo it was too soon after Col's wife's death for him to be forming a new relationship. They were happy together.

'Now,' Jo said, 'What's up? You started back at uni today, didn't you? Has something happened to upset you?'

Kay ran a finger round the rim of her glass. 'Not upset exactly. I've been offered a different position.' She paused.

'Yes?' Jo's eyes brightened.

'The dean's personal assistant has taken a semester's leave and Ann, the office manager, has asked me to step in.' Saying it out loud like that, it didn't seem so bad.

'Sounds like a good opportunity. No?' Jo asked as Kay's face clouded over.

'I don't know. It was so unexpected.' Suddenly Kay felt foolish. 'I don't know,' she repeated, tucking a strand of hair behind one ear and taking a sip of wine. 'Do you really think so?'

'I do. It's Professor Kerr, isn't it? But you'll already know him. Steve has only good things to say about the dean.'

For a moment, Kay wondered who Jo was talking about. Then she remembered. Of course, Steve Henderson one of the education lecturers, was the partner of Jo's son, Rob. She'd often seen him around the campus.

'Not really. I know who Professor Kerr is, of course. But that's about all. It's just that…' She twirled a lock of hair round one finger.

'What are you afraid of? The guy's not going to proposition you. He's married, isn't he? And it would get you away from all the gossip you say sometimes drives you mad.'

Col cleared his throat. 'I've heard his wife left town with the two teenagers – just after New Year.'

Kay turned to face him. 'Ann said that too. Not about the children, but about his marriage. She said I'd be a more appropriate person for the role as I wouldn't expect anything from him. As if!' Kay snorted.

'Well. What's stopping you?'

Kay couldn't articulate exactly what worried her, why her stomach churned at the thought of moving from her comfortable spot in the main office to the more visible – and important – one outside the dean's office.

'I don't know.'

'Well, let's have dinner and talk about other things. Everything may become clearer after you've eaten.'

Kay doubted it, but agreed, knowing her friends only had her best interests at heart. At least she knew Jo wouldn't try to make something of her working so closely with a man who was so recently out of a long-term relationship. And he must be at least five years younger than she was.

Kay managed to avoid any further discussion about the matter, pleading a headache as soon as the meal was over. But on the drive home, she considered her friends' words. She had to give Ann a decision tomorrow.

What should she do?

Four

'Professor Kerr!'

Nick glanced up from the computer screen to see Ann, the office manager, accompanied by an attractive tall and slim woman with dark hair. She looked to be in her fifties and was wearing white pants and a blue floral shirt. They were standing in the doorway and from the dark-haired woman's expression, she'd rather be somewhere else.

'This is Kay Jackson. She's agreed to stand in for Fran this semester. She's fairly new to the faculty – only joined us a year ago – but I have every confidence she'll prove to be as efficient as Fran, though it may take her some time to come to grips with the nuances of working with you.' Ann smiled and gestured to the woman to come forward.

'Hello, Kay.'

'Professor Kerr.'

Nick's face broke into a grin. This was the first good thing to happen in two days. The woman looked like a scared rabbit. He wondered what Ann had told her about him. Sometimes she could be a bit too officious. 'If we're going to be working together you should call me Nick – when the others aren't around, at least.'

He saw Ann's lips tighten. Despite the fact she was only in her forties, the manager liked to keep things on a more formal footing than he preferred.

'Will that be all, Ann?' he asked pleasantly. 'I can take Kay through the ropes and show her how Fran left things. I'm sure you have a lot to be getting on with.'

Ann's lips tightened again, but she merely said, 'As you wish,' and left.

'I'm not really the ogre Ann probably painted me out to be. I'm actually quite human.' Nick smiled and saw Kay relax. 'Why don't you take a seat and I'll try to fill you in. I'm afraid I tended to leave a lot to Fran's discretion – she's been here longer than I have and is a bit of a law unto herself. But I'll do my best.' He pulled on his beard and grinned, realising it made him look like a naughty little boy asking to be forgiven. 'Tell me a little about yourself.'

Nick saw Kay tense. *What had he said?* Then he remembered something he'd heard a few years ago about a local dentist who'd committed suicide after a number of allegations. Hadn't his name been Jackson? Could this be his widow? If that was the case, then he'd just put his big foot in it.

'You've been with us a year already, so you'll be familiar with the operations of the university in general and this faculty in particular. It may be best if you ask me what you want to know, and we can start from there.'

Kay, who'd been perching on the edge of the chair, sat back and seemed to take a few seconds to consider before replying, 'Well, I am pretty familiar with the way the faculty and most of the staff operate, but I assume this role covers aspects of the operation with which I haven't become acquainted and requires some more confidential handling.'

Nick steepled his fingers and observed her more closely. She was more intelligent than he'd anticipated. Maybe this one would work out okay. He was so accustomed to Fran doing much of the thinking for him – allowing him to get on with his writing and minimising his participation in the never-ending university politics – that he'd been dreading the arrival of some fresh-faced young thing with a brain like a sieve.

'You're right, of course. The problem is...' he dragged a hand across the top of his head, feeling at a distinct disadvantage, 'I'm not really sure where Fran's got to in organising this semester's faculty meetings and my calendar. These are probably the most important things to start with. Could you...?'

'Maybe if you show me how to get into her computer, I could make a start, and…' She glanced around the office, her eyes falling on the pile of papers still lying on the floor where he'd stacked them the day before, unsure where they should be filed.

Nick gave an embarrassed laugh. 'I'm not usually so untidy and I certainly don't expect you to clear up my mess. But I never did master Fran's filing system.' He shrugged.

'Maybe I can be of help there too?' She seemed to be trying not to laugh.

Nick returned to his own office feeling confident he could leave his new PA to get on with it. He was glad Ann had chosen a mature woman to take Fran's place. It would save any wrong impressions. He didn't want to be conceited – he was no more attractive than any other man – but the exchange with Faye at The Riverside had left him apprehensive. Were there so few available men in Granite Springs that one whose wife had recently left was considered fair game?

His mate, Mark, seemed to think so.

Nick thought back to their conversation over dinner the previous evening. The pair had been sitting in the Leagues Club enjoying a beer with their burger and chips, when Mark had leaned over the table and said confidingly, 'Now Michelle's gone, you can have your pick. It's not only the single ones who're looking for someone to warm their bed.' He'd winked, causing Nick to wince and flush with embarrassment.

He wasn't like Mark.

His friend had been divorced for a number of years and joked that he couldn't keep up with the ladies who were keen to fall into bed with him. He bragged about his conquests the way a fisherman would brag about the size of his catch, and how he practically had to fight them off. Until now, Nick had always considered he was exaggerating.

What if he wasn't?

But the last thing Nick wanted was to be seen as *a catch* – as someone to be pursued. He pictured Faye again. And she'd been a close friend of Michelle's. Heaven help him if there were more like her out there.

Nick forced his mind back to the task in hand. He knew he should make a list of all the committees, their membership, and how frequently they met. That would help his new assistant and give her a feel for the overall operation of the faculty. Then, he needed to work on preparing the submission for a new degree they planned to offer the following year.

By the end of the day, Kay sent through a spreadsheet with suggested dates and times for all the meetings and, when he walked into her office, he could see she was making progress with the filing which had built up. There was a lot of talk about the paperless office, but Fran still preferred to maintain hard copies of important documents and he tended to agree. He was glad Kay hadn't disputed that practice, as someone younger might.

'Thanks,' he said. 'Looks like you've made a good start. I think we'll rub along well together.'

Kay blushed, gave a nervous smile and a slight shake of her head.

What had he said? Although obviously competent, she was as nervous as a kitten. Life obviously hadn't been kind to Kay Jackson.

Nick determined to find out more about the woman who he'd be working closely with for the rest of the semester and vowed to do what he could to make her feel appreciated.

Five

'It's as if you've always been here. I don't know how I'd manage without you.' Nick stood in the doorway between his office and Kay's and rubbed the back of his neck.

It had been two weeks since Kay had taken on the role of his personal assistant, and already she couldn't imagine going back to the office she'd worked in before. Although she didn't feel she knew much more about the man she spent all of her working days close to, she knew she loved her new role and the insights it gave her into the political manoeuvrings of the university – things she'd never been aware of before.

'I need to leave early today. I have to pick up my daughter.' He smiled and his face lit up. He must love her a lot, Kay thought, seeing his often-sombre face so changed with that smile.

'No worries. I should have the proposal you gave me completed by tomorrow. Would you like to see it before it goes to the committee?'

'Yes. Good idea. And why don't you get off early yourself? It's Friday and you've been working flat out since you moved up here. You must need some time to yourself to...' he cleared his throat in embarrassment, '...do those things women like to do. You know – hair appointments, massages, nails. I'm sure the weekends aren't enough. They weren't enough for Michelle.' The tips of his ears turned red as if he suddenly realised he'd said something personal. 'Anyway, I'd best be going.'

He left before Kay had time to reply. If she had, it would have been to say she didn't need time to herself; the weekends dragged, only punctuated by the odd coffee or lunch with friends who were few and far between, most having abandoned her even before David's death. But it was kind of him to think of her.

Nick Kerr was a kind man. That was one thing she'd discovered about him in the past two weeks. Another was that he was a workaholic, as keen to spend time away from home as she was. Maybe that would change with the arrival of his daughter. She hoped so. It wasn't healthy for him to be so focussed on his work.

Kay gave a grim smile at the thought. Why wasn't it healthy for him, but okay for her? She didn't have an answer to that.

When she finished the proposal sooner than anticipated, Kay had time to spare. She tidied her desk, then filed away some documents, peering into the mirror perched precariously on top of the filing cabinet as she closed the top drawer.

Maybe she should take Nick's advice. She gazed at the stray grey hairs starting to show. She was beginning to look older. Older than her fifty-eight years? Perhaps. There were a few more lines there now, too. But what did it matter? There was no one to notice besides herself. Still, it wouldn't do any harm to make a hair appointment, and it would fill up some of the rest of the day. She picked up the phone.

Back home, Kay admired her newly trimmed and chestnut-tinted tresses. Not bad. The slightly lighter shade seemed to brighten her skin. She grimaced. Why was she bothering? Though there was Jo's birthday do this weekend. She and her husband shared a birthday – and Australia Day – and the celebration would be a fun evening.

She had kicked off her shoes and was pouring the one glass of wine she permitted herself each evening, when her mobile buzzed. Seeing Zoe's face on the screen, Kay sighed, pulled out a chair and sat down, prepared for a long chat. Zoe didn't call often, so when she did, Kay liked to hear all the latest news about her grandson. Her daughter was less forthcoming with news about her own life, probably assuming Kay wouldn't understand the challenges of her position of HR manager in a busy health service. It saddened Kay that Zoe chose not to share her life with her, but she'd long since given up trying to elicit information her daughter didn't want to reveal.

She sometimes wondered if David had ever... with Zoe... No, it was too awful to contemplate. But it would help to explain why she refused to mention him, had refused to come to his funeral, refused to visit. What if Kay's own humiliation was nothing compared to the embarrassment Zoe felt? She hadn't been able to broach the subject with her daughter who'd kept Kay at arm's length each time she visited.

Kay remembered how so-called friends had turned away, staff at the clinic had avoided conversations, how acquaintances had grown silent when she appeared on the scene. It seemed as if people believed she'd known about and condoned David's behaviour, as if she was guilty by association. Nothing could be further from the truth, but she'd felt ashamed to have been so ignorant of the man she'd married, the man she still loved.

Had she been so wrapped up in her own agony, she'd ignored her daughter's anguish?

'Zoe, darling. Lovely to hear from you,' she said, curling one leg under her, beset with fresh guilt.

'Mum!' Zoe said without any preamble, her voice sharp. 'I've just booked a flight. Noah and I'll be arriving tomorrow. I'll hire a car at the airport, and we should arrive around lunchtime.'

Kay gasped. 'What...?'

'Can't talk now. I'll explain when we arrive.'

She finished the call abruptly, leaving Kay staring at a blank screen in a state of shock. Then anger set in. It was just like Zoe to make arrangements this way – with no thought for whether or not it would suit her mother. Although it would be lovely to see her and little Noah, it would be nice to know how long they'd be staying.

She thought of her scant food supply. Living on her own, she'd become accustomed to eating sparingly and rarely kept a stockpile of food. She'd need to do a major shop and plan menus for the weekend. Maybe she could do a quick dash to the supermarket before their flight arrived?

Surely they wouldn't be staying longer? She'd love to have her grandson for a lengthy period, but Zoe could be wearing. She hadn't visited since David died, and would no doubt find fault with everything about how Kay was choosing to live.

Six

Nick couldn't wait to see Sam again. The house had seemed so empty without Michelle and the two kids. At least with Sam back, there would be music and chatter, and no doubt she'd fill the place with her coterie of friends. He sighed. Did he really want his home filled with their teenage angst?

The answer was a resounding "yes". Anything but the dead silence he'd been coming home to throughout the holidays. He wished Ryan was coming home, too. But he'd have to wait till Easter to see his son.

Michelle had rung the night before to let him know the time of Sam's flight – despite the fact Sam had already texted him all the details.

It had been strange to speak to his wife again after all those weeks. The joy he used to feel at the sound of Michelle's voice – Chelle as she now liked to call herself – had gradually died over the past year. She'd distanced herself from him, noticeable in the way she'd broken from his embraces, disappeared for hours at a time, pretended to be asleep when he came to bed and, finally, admitted to seeing someone else.

But that was behind him now, and he was ready to set the divorce proceedings in motion. He looked forward to being a free man – though free to do what? He had no inclination to make the same mistake again.

The small country airport loomed ahead, and Nick turned into the carpark just as the Qantas-link flight was touching down on the tarmac. He locked the car and sauntered into the terminal, knowing it would take some time for the plane to unload. But it wasn't long before he saw the leggy teenager striding across the tarmac, her long chestnut hair flying behind her in the breeze, a wide grin on her face.

'Dad!' Any attempt to appear cool was lost in her joy at being back home, Sam fell into Nick's open arms.

'Sam. Good to have you back. I've missed you and Ryan so much.'

'Not so much you couldn't let me come home earlier.' Sam drew out of his grasp.

'Your mum…' Nick started to say.

'Yeah, yeah. But I'm here now, though I had a long wait in Sydney. About an hour!'

'That's what comes of living in the country,' Nick replied. 'Let's pick up your luggage and get out of here.'

'There's only one bag. Here they come now,' Sam said, as the luggage cart made its way into the terminal.

Once in the car, Sam was silent, only twisting and turning when they drove along Granite Springs main street.

'There's Jackie,' she said, 'and Ruby. 'Can we stop, Dad?'

'Not now, honey. Let's get you home first. You can call your friends then.'

But Nick saw Sam was madly texting and he tried to hide a sigh. How could he have forgotten the young's complete disregard for their parents' feelings? Was this how it was going to be? Was he continually going to be beating his head against a brick wall trying to get through to his seventeen-year-old?

Back home, Sam ran around the house as if to make sure nothing had changed. 'Where's the TV, Dad? And what happened to the sofa? Where am I supposed to sit? At least my room is the same,' she declared, running upstairs, pushing open her bedroom door and throwing herself on the bed.

Nick followed her in, lifting her case onto the foot of the bed. 'Your mum took a few items. Remember? You've no doubt been enjoying using them up north.'

'Oh right.' That didn't seem to have occurred to her.

'I thought,' Nick said, suddenly having an idea, 'we could look for replacements together. What do you think?'

But Sam was already checking her phone and replying to what appeared to be a host of messages.

'Okay if I go out for a bit, Dad?'

'Okay. But back for dinner. I thought we could go out somewhere to celebrate your homecoming.'

'Cool.' She jumped up, kissed him on the cheek and was off, the door banging shut behind her to leave Nick in a house that no longer seemed so empty. Sam's brief presence had changed it back into the family home he thought had disappeared forever.

*

Nick walked into the restaurant, Sam dragging behind him. He'd planned this as a treat, a welcome home for her. The Riverside was regarded as one of the best restaurants in town and its setting, right on the banks of the river, was nothing short of spectacular. But Sam hadn't been impressed when he told her where they were going. He sensed she'd have been happier dining in one of the fast food joints that had sprung up in recent years to cater to the ever-growing number of students in the town.

He sighed inwardly. At least he'd enjoy the meal.

'Professor Kerr!' Steve greeted them inside the door.

'Let me show you to your table. For two tonight?' He smiled at Sam who was beaming at him and flicking her hair back flirtatiously.

Steve showed the pair to a table overlooking the river and handed them menus. 'One of the waiters will be with you shortly,' he said.

Sam's gaze followed him. 'You know him, Dad?'

'One of my staff. He's way too old for you, Sam. And he's in a relationship. His partner, Rob, is part-owner of this place.'

'Oh.' She pouted.

'How were things in Queensland?' he asked when they'd placed their orders. 'Is Ryan liking it up there?'

Sam shrugged. 'You know Ryan,' she said. 'He doesn't give much away. He seems to like it okay. I think he's made a few friends. But he tends to keep out of Terry's way.'

Nick's ears pricked up. He'd wondered how his sensitive son would cope with Michelle's new partner. Terry Wilson was in his thirties, almost twenty years younger than Ryan's mother and around the same number of years older than Ryan. He hoped neither of those things would make life difficult for Ryan who'd be trying to settle into a new community.

'And your mum?' he asked, with a false smile.

'Oh, she's loving it. She and Terry run along the beach in the mornings, and they've joined the local tennis club. She's made a lot of friends already. They're all just like her,' Sam said bitterly. 'And she's found some part-time work in a local school.'

'And Terry?' Nick could barely bring himself to say his name.

'His family are all there. He's working with his brother in some business or other.' Sam gave a heartfelt sigh. 'Bo…ring! What's been happening here while I've been gone?'

'Same old, same old. It's good to have you back, possum,' Nick said, using her childhood nickname.

Sam winced, but smiled. 'I'm glad to be back, Dad. I've missed you.'

And Nick was glad she'd reverted to calling him Dad.

Their meals arrived at that point, and it wasn't till they were about to leave that Sam said, 'It's odd without Mum, isn't it? Do you miss her?' She put her head on one side and gave Nick an intense look.

Miss Michelle? He supposed he did. He missed her presence around the house, missed the meals she cooked, missed having his laundry done. But actually miss her as a person, as his wife? She'd given up her right to that role in his life long before she left town with Terry.

'Not so much as I missed you and Ryan,' he said honestly. 'Will you miss her now you're back home?'

'I guess.' Sam twirled a lock of her hair. 'It'll be odd without her. But it was odd up there without you. And Terry can be a real idiot. I don't know what she sees in him.'

You and me both.

They drove home in silence, punctuated only by the pings of texts coming into Sam's phone and the clicks of her replies.

'Can I have a sleepover at Jackie's tomorrow?' she asked as he turned into their driveway and pressed the control to open the garage door.

'Tomorrow? I thought…' Nick had hoped, now that Sam was home, they'd spend some time together – some father-daughter bonding, anything to make the house feel like a home again. He hadn't bargained on her being so keen to catch up with her friends. Though he supposed he should have. He tried to remember what he'd been like at her age. Probably not much different, he guessed. Friends were your whole life. You never thought how much things would change in the next few years. He could barely remember his high school buddies now, the guys he'd thought would be his mates forever. University had changed all that.

'Da…ad!'

He realised he hadn't given Sam an answer. 'I thought we might spend some time together,' he said.

Sam sighed. 'You're going to be just like Mum. We're living in the same house. We can't spend every waking hour together. I *do* have a life.'

Nick refrained from reminding her he was gone all day, and that he had a life too, one he hoped she was part of. 'Okay, I suppose. Though you've only just got back.'

'Duh! That's *why*. I've missed the entire summer. I need to catch up.'

'Well, I'll just call Jackie's mother to check.'

'What? I'm not a kid, Dad. I'm seventeen. Some girls of my age are living away from home. Surely I can stay over at my best friend's house without you getting all angsty?'

Suitably chastised, Nick agreed, closing the car door with more force than was necessary and following Sam into the house.

As he undressed and made ready for bed that night, he reflected he had a lot to learn about teenage girls. He hadn't realised how much of the children's upbringing he'd left to Michelle.

Was he really up to being a single father to a teenage girl – one who looked and acted as if she was twenty-one and considered herself to be an adult?

Seven

'Grandma!'

Kay bent down to take the little boy into her arms as he rushed towards her. She hugged him, savouring the feel of the soft flesh of his cheek against hers. She closed her eyes, inhaling the little boy aroma of chocolate and a tangy soap which reminded her of when her own children were little. She opened them again to see Zoe struggling with a large case.

'Let me help your mummy,' she said, releasing the child who immediately ran past her into the house, forcing Milly to scamper out of his way.

'Welcome, honey. Can I help?' she asked, aiming a peck on the cheek Zoe offered.

'There's another one in the back seat,' Zoe said, indicating the open car door.

Another case? This looked like more than a weekend visit.

'I'll get it. We can have lunch, and you can tell me what's brought you here.'

'*Pas devant*,' Zoe said, gesturing towards Noah who had reappeared carrying a struggling Milly.

'Nana has a cat!' he announced. 'What's its name?' he asked Kay, his chin almost hidden in the cat's fur.

'Not near your face!' Zoe yelled. 'Sorry, Mum. But Noah's not used to animals. He doesn't realise…'

Ignoring Zoe's comment, Kay replied to her grandson, 'The cat's a girl and she's called Milly. She won't like it if you hold her too tightly, but, if you put her down and sit beside her, she may allow you to pat her. She likes to have her ears scratched.'

'I didn't know you had a cat,' Zoe complained as she hefted the case through the door.

Kay dropped the other smaller case on the floor and closed the door. 'Why don't we leave these here for now? You can get settled in after lunch. Do you want to freshen up, first?'

'Yes. Thanks,' Zoe agreed, though she looked as if she'd like to get settled in first. 'Noah, leave that cat alone. You need to wash your hands before we eat.' She took his hand and led him to the family bathroom, leaving Kay gazing after them.

Her head was pounding already, and Zoe was barely through the door. What would it be like when she'd been here for a few days?

And... how long did she intend to stay?

*

'Muuum!'

What did Zoe want now? Kay was trying to get ready for work. But her normal morning routine was being disrupted by her daughter's demands.

Zoe was sitting at the kitchen table with her iPad, her forehead creased in thought.

'What is it, Zoe? I need to leave.'

'I don't know why you took on a job at your age. Surely you don't need the money?' She didn't wait for a response. 'School starts here tomorrow, and I wondered if I should enrol Noah now or wait till he turns five. I've just been looking up the regulations and he's on the cusp.'

Kay stopped in her tracks. *Noah? School?* There had been no mention of that over the weekend. Just as there had been no mention of the reason for their visit or how long it was to last.

'You're intending to stay a while, then?' she asked, dropping her bag and taking a seat next to her daughter.

'Well, yes. Unless we're not welcome.' Zoe's voice held a hint of uncertainty.

'Of course you're welcome. It's just that I didn't expect…' Kay thrust her fingers through her hair. 'You haven't said how long you intend to stay,' she finished weakly.

'As long as it takes Eric to come to his senses,' she said. 'And I don't know how long that will be.'

Kay surreptitiously checked her watch. This was a conversation they needed to have. But she had no intention of being late for work. Nick Kerr might be a kind man, but he was her employer. And she was loving her new role. This would have to wait till later.

'We need to talk, but now isn't the time. Tonight. When I get home. When Noah's in bed. And with regards to school. For what my opinion's worth, I think he's ready for the sort of challenges it would provide. See you later, sweetheart. Have a good day.'

*

Kay felt flustered when she finally reached her office only ten minutes later than usual. Seeing Nick Kerr's door was still closed, she breathed a sigh of relief. Maybe he was running late, too.

Settling down at her desk, she turned on her computer and checked her boss's diary – her first port of call every morning. He had an early meeting – a faculty heads meeting with the vice chancellor in the main building. That would probably go on all morning, so she'd have time to get through her morning's tasks before he returned.

This new role was proving to be more challenging than Kay had anticipated, but she was loving it and would be disappointed when Fran returned, and she was sent back to the general office.

As she worked, Kay's mind wandered to Zoe. What had caused her sudden departure from Brisbane? Zoe's oblique reference to Eric this morning was disturbing. Although Kay had often wondered how her mild-mannered son-in-law put up with Zoe's high-handed behaviour, they'd seemed happy enough when she'd stayed with them at Christmas. Or had it all been an act – put on to fool the two mothers?

She determined to get to the bottom of it that evening. As soon as Noah was in bed, she'd sit down with Zoe and demand an explanation.

As Kay surmised, it was close to lunchtime when Nick bustled in carrying a sheaf of papers.

'Did the meeting go well?' she asked. She recalled seeing the agenda, one of the items of which was Nick's proposal to set up a sister relationship with a university in Canada, and another, less contentious one, to send a cohort of students to complete one of their practice teaching assignments in New Zealand.

Nick grunted and went straight into his office. Kay heard the papers thump down on a hard surface – most likely his desk – and his chair screech across the parquet floor. Not well, then.

It was almost ten minutes later when he appeared in the doorway.

'Sorry. I didn't answer your question,' he said, pulling on his beard – something Kay had noticed he often did. 'As you might have guessed from my abrupt manner, they voted down the Canada idea.' He brushed a hand over his close-cropped hair. 'But they did go for our New Zealand proposal, so we can move ahead on that one. Can you...?'

'I'll make contact today. I think you said you have a former colleague who'd be our first point of contact?'

'That's right. I'll let you have his details.'

But instead of returning to his office as Kay expected him to do, Nick stood in the doorway. He swayed from one foot to another.

'Is there something else?' she asked.

'I... I need some advice. On a personal matter.'

Advice? On a personal matter? Kay wasn't sure what sort of advice she could offer this man; a man who kept his personal life almost as carefully buttoned up as she did hers. She raised one eyebrow, pushed her chair back and turned slightly to meet his gaze.

'You're a woman, a mother,' he began. 'Sam arrived last week and... We went out to dinner. It was good. I was glad to have her back. The house has seemed empty without her. I guess you've heard my wife left me,' he said ruefully.

Kay nodded. And she knew all about empty houses. Except hers wasn't anymore – that was *her* problem.

'I suppose it's just her being a teenager. But, whereas I was hoping we could spend some time together, she just seems to want to spend it with her mates. Am I doing something wrong?'

Kay gave what she hoped was a sympathetic smile. 'A teenager? How old?'

'Seventeen.'

'Almost grown-up then. Seems it's natural she'd want to be with friends.'

'I guess. And should I be worrying about sleepovers? I know she's practically grown up but to me she's still my little girl. She flew off the handle when I suggested contacting her friend's mother. It's just… you hear such dreadful things happening.' He exhaled loudly.

'In Granite Springs? I think she's pretty safe here.'

Though Kay thought of the girls who'd accused David. They'd thought they were safe in Granite Springs too. She quickly suppressed the thought, seeing Nick's expression change to one of sympathy. Well, she'd asked for that. Would the memory of what David had done ever leave her?

'Right.' He wheeled round and went into his office, only to return a few seconds later, a card in his hand.

'This is Ted – my New Zealand contact. He'll set you in the right direction. I think I'm right in saying our prac coincides with their student break – though the schools will already be in session – so our guys can stay in their halls of residence. Then you can pass it on to Phil Little. He'll organise the student group, but I need you to make all the initial contacts, travel etc., and maybe throw in a bit of sightseeing for the students on the way. It's not till the beginning of next year but the boss wants us to have everything in place this financial year so he can finagle the budget.' He grinned. 'As ever. Nothing changes.'

Kay smiled to herself as he left and closed the door between them. She was gradually learning more about the man she worked for – and about the ins and outs of the university. Nick, who'd originally seemed unapproachable, was proving instead to be shy and often unsure of himself, despite the confident image he projected to staff and students. The university itself was another matter. Rumour had it that the vice chancellor was, among other things, a whiz with the stock market, using university funds to make a killing. He did siphon it all back into the general coffers, but Kay wasn't sure how legal it all was. Still, it was none of her business.

Kay had managed to put Zoe out of her mind throughout the day, glad to have plenty to keep her occupied. But as she slid into the car to drive home, her daughter's predicament raised its head again. She sighed. Life had been dull, the house empty. But she'd been managing with only herself to consider. Now there was Zoe and Noah for goodness knows how long.

When she walked into the house, it was to discover Zoe on her iPad again. Had she even left it? Noah was kneeling on the floor engrossed in a jigsaw. When he saw her, he jumped up.

'Grandma, you're back!'

'Hello, little man.' Kay bent to hug him and whirl him around.

'Don't do that, Mum. He'll get dizzy and overexcited and won't be able to eat his dinner.'

Kay halted and Noah slowly slid out of her grasp. She took a deep breath, opened her mouth to protest, then closed it again. This wasn't the time. She'd wait, find out what was eating Zoe then… then what, she wasn't sure. But she knew that, if her daughter and grandson were to live with her for any length of time, it had to be under her rules.

She chatted inconsequentially with Zoe about her day, discovering Zoe had taken Noah to the library and joined them both up, then driven past several possible schools.

'I've decided, Mum,' she said. 'I've enrolled Noah in Granite Springs Primary. I enjoyed my time there and it still looks much the same, though parts have had a facelift. We bought his uniform today and he'll start tomorrow.'

Trying to hide her shock at Zoe's sudden decision, Kay said, 'I have a friend whose grandchildren go there.' She thought of Jo and her twin granddaughters who'd started school a year earlier. 'They love it.'

Zoe nodded, as if that confirmed her decision, but Kay was still no wiser as to why they were here.

While Zoe was bathing Noah and putting him to bed, Kay poured two glasses of wine and settled down in the living room to wait for her daughter.

'Now,' she said, when Zoe had taken a seat and curled her legs under her. 'You have some explaining to do.'

Eight

After Zoe had gone to bed, Kay sat gazing into space. She didn't know what she'd expected to hear from Zoe, but not this. Her daughter had revealed that Eric wanted another child; insisting that Noah needed a sibling, while she was adamant one child was quite sufficient if she was to continue in her career.

Kay had always known Zoe was ambitious but had never considered it would lead to this sort of stalemate. Zoe had demanded Eric have a vasectomy, as she didn't want to take the pill for the next twenty years, or to go under a general anaesthetic to have her tubes tied and run the risk of an ectopic pregnancy.

Sighing, Kay wondered where she'd gone wrong. How had she and David produced such a selfish child – though Zoe was far from being a child. Had she always had these controlling tendencies or were they a result of David's behaviour? Kay's head ached as she tried to remember if and when Zoe had changed.

It was such an irony. Gordon, the ex-husband of Kay's best friend, Jo, had a vasectomy only a year ago and kept it secret from his young wife who desperately wanted a child. He'd come clean since and the marriage was still intact, but both Jo and Kay wondered for how long. That Kay's daughter was the one demanding it of her husband was difficult to countenance.

Eric had Kay's sympathy. She'd love to have another grandchild – maybe a girl next time? And Noah would benefit from a sibling. A second child might also make Zoe less controlling. Couldn't she remember her own childhood? How close she'd been to her big brother? Until Adam had gone overseas, the pair had been in frequent contact.

As if sensing her mistress's disquiet, Milly jumped onto her lap and pushed her head against Kay's clenched fist, forcing her to open her fingers to stroke the cat. 'Oh, Milly! Why does life have to be so difficult?' she asked. While every part of her sympathised with her son-in-law, Kay knew she had to handle Zoe carefully lest she antagonise her. As an adult, Zoe was just as temperamental as she had been as a teenager and would take offence if Kay uttered one word which could be construed as criticism.

Thinking of the teenage Zoe brought back the conversation Kay had with Nick earlier in the day. It sounded as if he was going to have his work cut out. Looking at him ruling the roost as dean of the faculty, it was difficult to imagine him being mastered by his teenage daughter.

But we are all the same when it comes to our children.

Rising carefully so as to dislodge Milly gently, Kay made her way to bed, hoping Zoe's news wouldn't prevent her sleeping. After David's death, it had taken her months to get a decent night's sleep, only managing to sleep through the night after she started working. Zoe didn't understand what a lifesaver for Kay the job had been. It gave her something to fill her mind – as well as her days. Though Zoe's unexpected arrival was managing to do that quite satisfactorily, too, if not as pleasantly.

*

Kay couldn't wait till Saturday when she'd arranged to have coffee with Jo. She was dying to share Zoe's news and to unload all her worries onto her friend's capable shoulders. But there were still three days to get through.

Zoe and Noah were already eating breakfast when Kay entered the kitchen next morning.

'Don't you look smart?' Kay ruffled Noah's hair.

The little boy wriggled away from her hand and gave her a grin. 'I'm a big boy now. I'm going to school.'

'Yes, you are.'

Zoe frowned. 'I hope I've made the right decision,' she said, biting into a piece of toast, spread with only a sliver of marmalade – she attempted to avoid anything which might contain sugar and insisted Noah did the same. 'But Noah seems happy enough about it.'

'And what about you?' Kay could see Zoe might be regretting the fact she'd have less control over her son's actions once he mixed more with other children.

Zoe misinterpreted the question. 'I'd like to check out what's changed in Granite Springs and maybe see what I might do here.'

'Do?'

'Well. Mum,' Zoe sounded as if she was speaking to an intractable child. 'I can't sit around all day now Noah's started school. I may have taken leave from my job in Brisbane, but that's no reason why I can't find something to occupy me in Granite Springs.'

'Right.' Kay hadn't considered how Zoe might spend her time. 'When did you last walk down Main Street?'

'It's been years. Not since…' she closed her eyes '…not since Noah was born. When we came to visit you and Dad, we never took time to venture farther than the front yard.'

'There have been lots of changes since then. You'll be surprised.'

'Mmm.'

Kay nodded to herself as she cleared away the breakfast dishes. Noah slid down from his chair and, with a wary glance in his mother's direction, wandered off to find Milly who was sunning herself by the dining room window, while Zoe immersed herself in the local paper. What did she hope to find there, Kay wondered, surprised when Zoe let out a yelp of surprise.

'Eve's Fashions. Is that Eve Slater? She's now Eve…?'

'Tait. She married the Tait boy.'

'So she did. And stayed here in Granite Springs,' Zoe said in a derogatory tone.

'She has twin girls just a year older than Noah and a baby, Emily Rose, born last year.'

'A glutton for punishment.'

Kay felt her lips tighten. 'Not everyone thinks as you do. Eve's children are lovely. The twins, Lottie and Livvy, are the girls I mentioned who attend Granite Springs primary, and Eve manages her shop on a part-time basis. *She* manages a family and career without too much trouble.' Kay couldn't resist putting the emphasis on *she*.

'She has a mother close by to babysit,' Zoe retorted. 'It didn't occur to you to move to Brisbane, then…'

'That's not fair, Zoe. My life's here. You know that.'

Though it had occurred to Kay. When David died in such a dreadful way, her first thought had been to distance herself from the whole debacle, and moving to Brisbane, closer to her daughter and grandson, had presented itself to her as a solution. It had been her friend, Jo, who'd counselled her not to do anything rash while she was grieving, reminding her of the difficult relationship between her and Zoe.

Kay was glad she'd listened. Zoe had only been back in Granite Springs for two weeks and she was already managing to get under Kay's skin. What would it be like if they lived in the same city?

Nine

'I thought I might leave Noah with you this morning,' Zoe said, as they were eating breakfast on Saturday morning. Noah had already left the table and was playing with Milly. He'd settled in well at school, and already Kay could see he was becoming more independent, much to his mother's dismay. 'I have the possibility of a job.'

'A job?' Kay was too surprised to say she had plans for the morning.

'Mum! I told you I was looking for something to do while Noah is in school. There's not much for me here.' She looked around the room disdainfully. 'I've made a few contacts – people I knew when I lived here.'

'Right.' Kay hadn't considered how Zoe might have been spending her time in the last couple of days and this was the first she'd heard of these *contacts*. 'Well, not this morning. I'm meeting a friend for coffee.' Then, seeing a pout begin to form on Zoe's pretty face, added, 'maybe this afternoon. We could go to the park. Would you like that, Noah?'

'Are there swings?' the little boy asked with a cautious glance at his mother.

'Swings and a climbing frame and a slippery slide.'

'Yes, please.' Noah ran to hug Kay.

'I suppose that'll have to do,' Zoe muttered. 'I'll have to make some calls.' She disappeared into her bedroom, leaving Kay to surmise that she wasn't to be party to any further information.

*

'Am I glad to see you,' Kay greeted Jo when she joined her at their usual table in Mouthfuls, the coffee shop by the library. The two friends had been meeting here for coffee for years. Before Kay started working at the university, they'd met during the week, but now Kay only had Saturdays free. It suited them both to combine coffee with a trip to the library.

'That bad?' Jo's face held a concerned expression.

'Let's get our coffee in first, then I'll fill you in.'

Once Kay had her flat white and Jo her skinny cappuccino, Kay launched into a retelling of Zoe's story, finishing with, 'I'm not sure what to do about it.'

Jo laughed.

'It's no laughing matter.'

'I know. It's just that Gordon...'

'I know. You told me. And Carol has accepted it?'

'That's the strange thing. At first, she was clearly resentful, but recently Eve – who sees them fairly often now she has Emily Rose – says Carol has seemed happier. No idea why.'

'Maybe Carol's just decided to accept the inevitable, make do with visiting Emily Rose, and she loves Gordon enough to put up with it.'

'Mmm.' Jo seemed doubtful. 'Difficult to believe. Anyway, that doesn't solve your problem.'

'No.' Kay sighed. 'I'd like to talk to Eric, hear his side of the story, but...'

'I know. You don't want to upset Zoe any more than you have to.'

'No. And I'm not her favourite person right now.' Kay heaved a sigh. 'Oh, Jo. I don't know how long I can put up with her meddling. I'm beginning to feel my house isn't my own. And now she's talking about getting a job here.'

'Look on the bright side. She won't be there forever. Your Zoe likes the bright lights. She's a city girl. She may have grown up here in Granite Springs, but as soon as she finished school, she couldn't wait to brush the dust of this town from her shoes. Granite Springs isn't big enough for her. Oh, she may stay for a bit but mark my words, as soon as that husband of hers agrees to her demands, she'll be off again back to Brisbane.'

'You're right about Zoe. Even as a young girl, she hankered for more than this town could offer. But what if Eric doesn't *see sense* – her words. What if this is one matter on which he digs in his heels?'

'Then she'll have to make a decision, won't she? Either way, there's nothing you can do about it.'

'I suppose not.' But Kay wasn't convinced. 'You're lucky with your crew.'

Jo gave a wry grin. 'Lucky? Now, maybe.'

'You didn't think that last year.'

'True.' Jo laughed as they both remembered the previous year when Jo's children had caused her many sleepless nights – her son and his wife angling to move into her home and her daughter trying to take over her life. 'But everything passes. Just remember that.'

'Mmm. Well at least I'll have little Noah to myself this afternoon while Zoe *checks out* some job opportunities. What she hopes to find here, I can't imagine. She's already dismissed Granite Springs as the back of beyond. But Noah's a honey.'

'You're minding Noah? I have the twins this afternoon. Why don't you bring him over for a swim? They're around the same age.'

'Good idea. I had planned to take him to the park, but in this heat, a swim is a much better option. And if Zoe intends to stay for some time, it'd be good for Noah to make friends.'

When Kay returned home, Zoe was sitting on the back veranda while Noah was throwing a ball against the fence. Milly was lying in a shady spot eyeing them both with a jaundiced expression.

'You're back!' Zoe greeted her.

'I said I'd be back for lunch.'

'We've had a sandwich. I wanted to get off.'

Kay checked her watch. It was only quarter past twelve. She bit her tongue. 'You'd best go, then. Where will I find Noah's swimmers? You did bring them, didn't you?' she added, seeing a blank look on her daughter's face.

'Where will you be swimming?' Zoe asked. 'He's only had a few lessons. The river…'

'I'm not stupid.' *As you seem to think.* 'Jo's invited us to Yarran for a swim. She has a lovely pool there and Eve's twins will be there this afternoon, too. You'd like that, Noah wouldn't you – two new friends to play with?'

Noah's face brightened, but he glanced towards his mother before replying. A frown creased Zoe's otherwise perfect face.

'Jo and I will go in with them, of course. You don't imagine we'd let three four and five-year-olds into the pool by themselves?'

Zoe's face cleared. 'Well, in that case… I'll fetch his swimmers.'

She dashed off, leaving Kay counting to ten.

By the time Kay's car bumped across the cattle grid at Jo's gate, she was feeling more relaxed. She had joined Noah in singing along to his favourite songs on the way and it had succeeded in melting the anger she felt at her daughter's unwarranted concerns. As if she'd do anything to harm a hair of her grandson's head. He was such a dear.

'You made it. I was beginning to wonder,' Jo greeted her, two identical blonde girls at her heels. The girls were wearing bright pink swimsuits with matching rashi vests, while Jo sported a fitted black one-piece, a towel wrapped around her waist.

'Wow! Look at you!' Kay exclaimed.

'Don't!' Jo attempted to hide herself with the towel. 'When I bought this, I only intended to wear it when I was alone. But since being with Col… He says I look good in it – womanly, if you can imagine?' But she smiled as if remembering when he said it.

'Well you put my old cossi to shame. Let's get changed Noah.' But Noah was gazing wide-eyed at the twins.

'There's two of them,' he said, blinking as if he was seeing double.

'We're twinnies,' one of the girls said giggling. 'I'm Lottie and this is Livvy. And Gramma said your name is Noah. That's the same as the man who built the ark. We learned about him in school.' She was hopping on one leg as she spoke. 'Are you going to swim with us?'

Noah nodded, unused to such an onslaught of chatter, then followed Kay into the house.

Depositing the three children to splash around in the spa section of the pool where it was shallow. Kay and Jo sat on the wide steps. They watched Noah gradually open up to the girls when he discovered they also went to *his* school.

'It's so lovely here,' Kay said to Jo when they were towelling the children dry. 'And you're lucky you and Col…'

'You didn't think that this time last year,' Jo chuckled. 'Your reaction to us quite upset me.'

'Sorry. I was thinking of myself. I spoke out of turn. You and Col are good together. You've both benefitted from having each other in your lives. I couldn't imagine…'

'Don't be too sure. If the right man came along, you'd do the same.'

'No!'

The three children, who'd been chatting together, looked startled.

'It's okay,' she reassured them. 'Sorry, Jo. That came out wrong. I didn't mean to yell. But there's no way I'd ever start another relationship. What happened with David has cured me of men for good.'

'Never say never,' Jo said with a smile.

'Oh, I am! Never! There, I've said it.'

Jo let the matter drop.

But as she drove home, with Noah fast asleep in the child seat behind her, Kay thought of Jo's comments.

She thought Jo understood her.

How could she imagine Kay would trust a man ever again?

Ten

Zoe was sitting on the back veranda with a glass of wine when Kay and Noah arrived home. Noah rushed to greet his mum.

'There were two of them!' he announced. 'Lottie and Livvy. They match!'

Zoe looked at Kay in surprise.

'The twins,' Kay explained. 'Identical. I have trouble telling them apart. I think Jo does, too. Eve delights in dressing them in the same outfits. I have no idea how they manage at school.'

'They had my teacher last year,' Noah continued, 'but now they have Legra, but they have to call her Miss Moretti.' At that point, he caught sight of Milly, who was trying to sneak out of reach, and ran after her.

'Sounds like he had fun,' Zoe said. 'Legra?'

'Allegra did a child-care stint with them last year when she was in her final year at uni. She's just taken up a position at the school. I don't expect she'll be there for long. She wants to travel but needs to save first. Seems she liked the town while she was studying here so opted to stay on.'

'Hmph.'

Kay smiled to herself. Her daughter had trouble accepting anyone would *want* to live here.

'How was *your* afternoon?'

Zoe lifted the glass of wine she was drinking. 'Productive. When we were at the library earlier in the week, I bumped into Donna. Remember her? We were in the same year at school but were never close friends.'

Kay nodded, remembering the rather shy bespectacled girl who'd always seemed to be on the outer of the group of popular girls Zoe hung around with. Donna had studied at the local university, married a local boy, taken a job at the local library and was now in charge of the historical archives for Granite Springs. She regularly ran sessions on searching for ancestry which Kay had been meaning to attend but had never got around to.

'Well, she's now what's called the heritage coordinator and has six month's funding for someone to help with a local history project and guess what?'

Kay could guess, but all she could think was *six months*.

'You're it?'

'Right on. It's perfect. I can fit the interviews around school times, and it'll make use of my interviewing skills.'

'Donna's lucky to get you.'

'That's what I think.' Zoe preened herself. 'Of course, it doesn't pay much. But I won't need much living here with you, and it'll mean I can save my long service pay in case...' She bit her lip and a shadow flitted across her face.

'I'm sure it won't come to that. You and Eric will find some common ground.'

'Common ground? What do you mean? How can there be common ground when he wants another child and I don't? I don't want to turn into a hausfrau like Jess,' she sneered.

'Jessica is happy being a mother.' Kay's daughter-in-law, in far-off England, had given up work when she had their first child. Adam junior was now eight, his brother four and, as far as Kay knew, Jess had no intention of returning to full-time work.

'Fine for her. It's not for me. Anyway, Adam...'

'Leave your brother out of this.'

Zoe calmed down. 'Sorry, Mum. It's just that...'

Kay saw a bead of moisture in the corner of her daughter's eyes. She leaned over to hug her. Regardless of all the irritation she caused, Zoe was her daughter and she loved her. She just wished there was something she could do to help.

*

Sunday dawned as a glorious day, a heat haze on the back lawn promising another scorcher. Kay was looking forward to a quiet relaxing day. She'd loved Noah's company yesterday but had to agree with Jo that caring for grandchildren was a tiring business. She showered, slipped on a favourite sundress and went into the kitchen. It was too early for Zoe and Noah to be around, so she fed Milly and let her out into the yard, then made herself a cup of tea.

Taking her tea out onto the veranda, which was shaded at this time in the morning, she settled back into one of her cane chairs, enjoying the silence, broken only by the sound of a whip bird in the distance. No kookaburras this morning. She breathed in the familiar scent of her garden – lavender mixed with jasmine and honeysuckle. She loved this place and would be sorry to leave. But she knew the time had come. The house was too big for her and when Zoe and Noah left – please God they would – it would seem empty again. She knew enough time had passed since David's death. She was ready to move on.

Suddenly, her peace was shattered by her daughter's voice.

'There you are!' Zoe emerged, fully dressed and made up, followed by a smiling Noah who was grasping a wriggling Milly.

'I found Milly, Grandma,' he said proudly. 'Can I give her something to eat?'

'She's already had her breakfast, honey.' Kay stood up, wondering how Milly had allowed herself to be picked up. The cat was usually adept at avoiding Noah's little hands. 'But I expect you're ready for yours?'

'Stay where you are, Mum,' Zoe said. 'I can fix up Noah. What about you? Have you eaten?'

'Not yet. I was just enjoying the morning.'

'It's after eight.' Zoe sounded reproving as if everyone should be active by this time of day. 'I'll make us all breakfast, then I thought I'd take Noah to the park before it becomes too hot. Will you join us?'

Kay thought quickly. It would be lovely to join them. But, since they'd arrived, she had scarcely had a minute to herself. A morning on her own to catch up on her life, maybe even have time to read, would be welcome. 'Maybe not. I have a few things I need to do.'

'Why don't we go out to lunch? My shout. I noticed a new restaurant on the river that looks nice. What do you say?'

Surprised, Kay took a few moments to respond. 'That would be lovely, dear. The Riverside is owned by Jo and her son, Rob. Remember him? Eve's little brother, though not so little now. Jo isn't there so often these days and Rob's partner, Steve, often helps out when he's not working.'

'Yes. I'd heard. A lot of girls had a crush on Rob when we were at school. What's Steve like?'

'He's a lovely young man – lectures in the school of education. He and Rob are planning to marry now the laws have changed.'

'Mmm. I'll make a booking. You say it's called The Riverside?'

'That's right.'

Zoe disappeared inside and Kay could hear her on her mobile. It would be nice to have lunch at The Riverside, but if she wasn't careful, Zoe would have Kay's life organised as much as Noah's. She sighed and hoped Zoe and Eric would soon resolve their differences and she could have her life back again.

*

Sitting at a table overlooking the river, Kay allowed her daughter's chatter to flow over her, thinking instead of how she and her friends used to spend their summers below this very spot, swimming, swinging from the overhanging branches of a tree on a rope which had long-since disappeared, and daring each other to dive from the bridge. That's where, one hot summer like this one, she and David had met.

He'd come to live with his grandparents, and the locals had drawn the city boy into their circle. He'd asked her to the drive-in and the rest was history, as they say.

'Mum!'

Kay realised Zoe had asked her a question.

'What, dear?'

'You haven't heard a word I've been saying.'

'Sorry, sweetheart. I was remembering. Down there,' she pointed out the window, 'was where your dad and I met. He was such a handsome boy. He…'

'I don't want to know.' Zoe's face turned red. 'I don't know how you can…'

'He was your dad, Zoe. Whatever he may have done – or not done – he was a good husband and father for many years. You can't just wipe that out.'

'I can. I don't want to talk about him.' Her lips formed a tight line.

Kay wondered again if she should ask Zoe about her dad, if he'd… But she couldn't bring herself to believe he'd… not with his own daughter. Surely she'd have known, there would have been some sign? She suppressed the image that rose up unbidden.

'You were asking me something?' Kay tried to change the subject. It upset her when Zoe took this line with her dad, but there was nothing Kay could say to change her mind.

'What do you want to order?' Zoe handed her the menu.

Kay glanced at it briefly, before choosing the warm smoked salmon salad.

'It looks good. I think I'll have it too,' Zoe said, 'And Noah can have the children's serving of krispie fish fingers with salad. At least it looks semi-healthy,' she fussed. 'Would you like something to drink? Wine?'

'A glass of white would be nice, thanks.' *And might make you more bearable.*

Their drinks were served first and Kay took a grateful gulp of hers.

'Mum, who's that? There's a man over there looking this way – the one sitting by the wall with the young girl. Don't let him see you're looking.'

How could she turn without seeming obvious? But, after a few moments, Kay turned slightly to see Nick Kerr sitting with a girl she assumed was his daughter. He nodded and smiled in her direction. Reddening with embarrassment, she turned back to face Zoe. 'It's Professor Kerr, my boss,' she said.

'He doesn't look like a professor. He's younger than I expected… and quite good looking, if you like that sort of thing.'

Kay almost choked on her wine. She was saved from replying by the arrival of their meals and Noah complaining he didn't like cucumber. She was able to regain control as Zoe moved the offending cucumber from Noah's plate to hers, while telling him it was good for him. Stealing another glance across the room, Kay had to admit Nick Kerr was looking good today. Away from the university and dressed in a tight-fitting tee shirt and jeans instead of the business suit she was accustomed to seeing him wearing, he looked years younger – almost too young for the responsible position he held.

But Zoe wasn't finished. 'I didn't know you were working for such a hunk. If I didn't know you better, I'd be telling you to watch yourself. Who's the girl he's with?'

'I presume that's his daughter.' Kay busied herself with forking up a mouthful of salmon and hoping Zoe would change the subject. She didn't want to discuss Nick Kerr with her.

Eleven

'Who's that, Dad?' Sam pointed across the room with her fork to the table that was the focus of Nick's attention.

Nick quickly withdrew his gaze, a flush flooding him. 'That's Kay, my new PA. I may have told you Fran had to go to England suddenly, so I have a new lady from the education office.'

'Maybe.' Sam didn't sound sure. But she rarely paid attention to him, and the goings on at his office were of no interest to her. 'She looks a bit upmarket for you.'

Upmarket? Nick considered. He glanced across again to where Kay was now glancing in his direction. She did look pretty good. Out of her everyday office outfit, wearing a strappy low-cut sundress, her hair swept back from her face, she looked like someone he'd like to know better. But he wouldn't describe her as upmarket. Attractive, sexy even, with that slight glimpse of cleavage. She seemed…

Embarrassed, he nodded and smiled, then turned back to his daughter, taking a long draught of his beer before replying, 'Oh, I don't think so, Sam. I hadn't noticed her appearance. She's a good worker.'

'Dad?'

'What?'

'Now that Mum has Terry, will you…?'

Nick was startled. Was his daughter suggesting he have a love life?

'One woman in the house is enough for me,' he said drily. 'And I have no intention of replacing your mum.'

'But,' Sam persisted, 'if you met someone, would you, you know?'

Nick had no desire to discuss his sex life – or lack of it – with his teenage daughter. 'I don't, and it's not something you should be thinking about – or discussing with me.'

'Mum said you would. She said there would be a rush to see who'd snare you.'

Damn Michelle! How dare she have a discussion like this with their daughter!

Seemingly sensing his thoughts, Sam added, 'I heard her and Terry talking. I was lying on the sofa reading and they didn't know I was there. I thought they might be going to discuss me.' She picked at a piece of lettuce and put down her knife and fork. 'I don't want any more of this. Can I have dessert?'

Nick agreed and picked up the menu again, stunned and somewhat amused by how quickly Sam had moved from such a sensitive issue to dessert. But that was teenagers for you. She probably had no idea how much it annoyed him to think of Michelle and Terry discussing him like that. He wondered what else they had to say, but there was no way he was going to ask Sam, who was now trying to decide between lemon cheesecake and chocolate mousse, her previous comments forgotten.

*

Back home again, Sam disappeared into her room saying she had homework to complete, but the noise of the double bass from upstairs didn't sound conducive to study. This time, Nick chose to ignore it. He didn't want to be on her back all the time. Even though this was an important year for Sam, with the leaving certificate looming in October, she needed to do well if she wanted to have a choice of courses and universities for the following year. At this stage she seemed unclear what she wanted to study – environmental science one day, English literature the next. He wished she had more focus, then wondered if he'd been the same at her age. He seemed to recall having some idea of going into the forces, but his best mate said he was going to the Australian National University in Canberra, so Nick decided to join him and chose to study history. What he learned about the conflicts Australia had been engaged in over the years put all ideas of becoming a member of the defence forces out of his head for good.

Deciding to make use of his unexpected privacy and having left all of his urgent work at the office, Nick resisted the temptation to fire up his computer and make a start on a paper for the annual conference of the Australian Association for Research in Education to be held in Brisbane. The conference itself wasn't till December and the Queensland location might give him an opportunity to catch up with Ryan. He knew there were some who wouldn't see it appropriate for someone in his position to be still attending what could be considered to be a grass roots conference, but he liked to keep his hand in and the conference was a good place to find out what was going on in other institutions – and to catch up with colleagues from interstate.

Instead he took his current read – a Michael Connelly thriller – outside with a can of beer to while away the afternoon. But he had trouble concentrating. Sam's words kept coming back to him. He cursed Michelle for putting ideas into their daughter's head. As if he'd be interested in another woman after the appalling way she'd treated him.

He remembered how Kay Jackson had looked – very different from at the office. She'd been with a younger woman and a small boy. That would be her daughter and grandson. He seemed to recall her mentioning something about them coming to stay. He'd thought she meant for the weekend, but that had been – he scratched his chin through his beard – at least a week ago. It had been around the time Sam arrived. Just before school started. He hadn't paid much attention. The personal life of his staff was none of his business. Kay was good at her job, efficient, didn't enquire into his life, so why should he enquire into hers? But he began to wonder about her, trying to recall what he'd heard on the university gossip mill.

It took Nick several minutes, then he remembered. She was a widow whose husband had committed suicide after... he racked his brains... hadn't there been something about unsubstantiated rumours of some sort of sexual abuse? The poor woman, having to live that down in a town this size.

He was drawn out of his musings by the realisation he'd been daydreaming all afternoon and it was almost five o'clock. Since Michelle left, he'd made it his habit to call his children at this time every Sunday. He knew, if he left it to his wife, any calls would come as it occurred to her. He was more of a creature of habit and liked to think they – now only Ryan – looked forward to his weekly news bulletins as he liked to call them. Picking up his empty can and closing his book, Nick went inside, calling through the now silent house to alert Sam it was time.

'Do I have to, Dad?' she asked, sauntering in holding her mobile – a clear indication not much homework was being done.

'You do. Your mum will want to talk with you now school's started. Ryan, too. Don't you want to talk to your brother?'

Sam shrugged, but joined Nick on the new sofa they'd purchased the day before. It wasn't a patch on the one Michelle had gone off with, but the best they could get without going to a major centre and having to await delivery. The local store had been happy to deliver straight away along with a flat-screen television, large enough to satisfy Sam's viewing needs.

Nick patted Sam's knee as he pressed the speed dial for the Queensland number, relieved when it was Ryan who answered the phone.

'How are you, son?' he asked, a break in his voice. Although glad to have one of his children home, he missed his son.

'Good, Dad.' Ryan was a boy of few words.

'How's school?'

'Okay.'

Nick tried to encourage more conversation by telling his son what he and Sam had been doing, ending with, 'We miss you, Ryan.'

'Miss you, too.' Nick could almost see his son shrugging – just like his sister.

'Is everything okay up there? How are you getting on with Terry?' Nick held his breath waiting for Ryan's response.

'I suppose.' Ryan's voice gave nothing away.

Nick sighed. He should have known better than to ask. But he worried about Ryan, who was a sensitive soul. How was he coping in a new town, a new school, and with his mother's new partner? Realising Ryan wasn't going to say any more, Nick nodded to Sam and said, 'I'll put your sister on.' He handed over the phone and went back outside, leaving the two of them to talk without him listening.

'I'm done, Dad.' Sam appeared in the doorway and handed back the phone. 'I'm going over to Jackie's for a bit?' She started to leave, then turned her head and added, 'Okay?'

'Dinner at six-thirty. Be back by then and I expect you to stay in afterwards. You didn't get much homework done this afternoon if the noise from your room was anything to go by, and tomorrow's a school day. This is an important year, remember.'

'Yeah, yeah. Jackie's parents aren't always on her back like you are. I wish…'

Nick was tempted to tell her Jackie's parents might not envisage her going to university but decided to remain silent. Sam would work out soon enough that she was both brighter and more ambitious than some of her school friends.

Then Sam surprised him. She stood in the doorway, hopping from one leg to the other. 'Ryan,' she said, 'I don't think he gets on too well with Terry.'

'What did he say to you?'

'Nothing, really, but… It's like… When I was up there… He always tried to stay out of Terry's way.'

'What did your mum say?'

Sam grimaced. 'Mum's mad about Terry. She does everything he says. She wouldn't notice Ryan or know what he's feeling.'

After she left, Nick poured himself another beer and sat down, the weekend papers open on the kitchen table in front of him. But all he could see was his son's face and the weeks stretching out till Ryan came to visit at Easter.

Twelve

Kay took one last glance in the mirror before heading into the kitchen. She hadn't deliberately taken more care with her appearance that morning, but was wearing her smartest powder blue linen dress and had popped on a pair of silver earrings to match the chain around her neck.

She was feeling good until she felt Zoe's assessing gaze on her.

'You look nice, Grandma,' Noah said, running over for his morning hug. He sniffed. 'You smell nice, too.'

Kay flushed. She'd sprayed herself liberally with her favourite Vera Wang scent – perhaps more than usual. Had she overdone it?

'Trying to impress someone?' Zoe asked, raising one eyebrow.

'I'm going to work. I need to look smart. It's only a couple of weeks till start of semester and the lecturers will be beginning to filter in.' Kay fell silent, wondering why she felt she had to explain herself to her daughter.

'If you say so. Will you be able to pick Noah up from school today, Mum? I have a meeting with Donna after lunch and I'm not sure how long it'll last.'

Kay didn't reply immediately, taking a deep breath and pouring herself a cup of tea. It wasn't till she was seated opposite her daughter and spreading some thick orange marmalade on a piece of toast that she said, 'I'm sorry, Zoe. My working day doesn't finish till five. I can sometimes get away a bit early, but that depends on my workload.' *And the generosity of Nick Kerr.* It was strange. Although she called him Nick to his face, Kay always thought of her boss as Nick Kerr, as if somehow that lent distance to their relationship – made it more professional, which it was, of course. But she couldn't help remembering how much more approachable he appeared in the restaurant the day before.

'Surely Donna will understand? She knows you have a child in school, doesn't she?'

Zoe wriggled in her seat. 'Yes, but… I don't want her to get the impression I'm tied to school hours. I'll need to be available when the interviewees are.'

'Won't they all be older people – retired? If you're working on local history, I can't imagine you'd be interviewing anyone who's still in full-time employment.'

'You don't understand.' Zoe pursed her lips. 'But I suppose I'll have to work it out. Maybe there will be after-school care or something if I have any that go past three o'clock.'

Kay raised her eyes to the ceiling. Poor Noah. It seemed he was going to be palmed off to whoever or whatever Zoe could find so she could pursue this new project.

'What did you do in Brisbane? You were working full-time there, and Noah wasn't at school.'

'There was a pre-school and childcare at the health service. It was perfect.' Zoe's forehead creased and, for a moment, it seemed to Kay that her daughter was regretting her precipitous move to Granite Springs. Then her face cleared. 'I'm sure I can find something,' she said, determinedly. 'But not for today. Are you sure…?'

'I'm sure. And I'm equally sure Donna will understand,' she said at the risk of repeating herself.

'Maybe you're right.'

Kay could see Zoe wasn't convinced, but she refused to feel guilty. It had been Zoe's decision to leave Eric and Brisbane, and to immediately take on this role with the library. It was up to her to work out her own solution.

*

Kay knew nothing had changed but, when Nick appeared in the doorway between his office and hers, leaning against the doorjamb, ankles crossed, a winsome smile on his face, her stomach did somersaults. Was it because she'd seen the more private side of him the day before? Surely not? And not because of Zoe's heavy-handed comments either. The strange thing was that, in a town this size, their paths had never crossed outside the university before now.

'Can you come in for a moment?'

Kay rose to her feet.

'Better bring your notebook.' He sounded amused.

'Of course.' Flustered, Kay picked up the book which always lay on her desk and followed him in. About to take her usual seat opposite the large glass-topped desk, Nick surprised her, gesturing instead to one of the two low chairs by a strategically placed coffee table. Then, instead of taking *his* customary place behind his desk, he fetched two cups of coffee from the Nespresso machine in the corner and joined her.

'Did you enjoy your meal?' he asked. 'I assume that was your daughter and grandson with you. He looks like a nice little guy.'

Kay gulped at these unexpected remarks. Up till now, their communications had been on a strictly professional level – apart from him asking for advice regarding his daughter. 'Yes. Thanks,' she said.

'You must be proud of them. That was Sam with me.' He sighed and drew a hand across the top of his head. 'Children, eh?'

'You have a son, too?' Kay wasn't sure if she was being too personal, but he *had* started this conversation.

'Ryan. Yes. He's with his mother in Queensland. I don't know...' he pulled on an earlobe. 'Sorry. You don't want to hear about my problems.'

Kay was interested. There was more to this man than she'd imagined. From what he hadn't said, it sounded as if things weren't too good with his son, and he'd already confided problems with his daughter. Thank goodness her children's teenage years were far behind them.

Though was it so different now? Zoe's life seemed to be on hold while she and Eric tried to sort out their differences – even though she was at pains to fill every minute with some sort of activity – and Kay had little idea of Adam's life in England. The odd phone or skype call, the texted photos, gave only a vague impression of time passing and her grandsons growing up. She'd dearly love to see them in person. Maybe when this semester was over and Fran returned, *she* could take a trip to the UK. But why, instead of filling her with pleasure and anticipation, did the thought summon up a sense of dread?

'Now, to business.' Nick put on his glasses, picked up a folder and began to speak. For the next half hour, they were all business, then, Nick removed his glasses, pinched the top of his nose and said, 'Thanks, Kay.' He fiddled with the leg on the spectacles for a moment then cleared his throat. 'I wonder,' he said, then paused.

Kay looked up expectantly.

'No.' He shook his head.

'Will that be all?'

'For now. Yes.' He appeared relieved. Kay walked back to her own desk, wondering what he had been about to say before he evidently thought better of it.

The remainder of the morning passed swiftly as Kay worked on yet another course proposal and managed to make contact with the New Zealand friend of Nick's to set up the proposed practice teaching trip. She made a note to check with Phil Little as soon as he appeared on campus, aware that, although some staff were already in their offices and hard at work preparing for the semester ahead and writing conference papers to further their careers, others were taking advantage of the flexibility of their roles to extend their holidays by "working at home". Kay suspected that many of the *homes* were located on the coast, many kilometres from the campus, and not much work was being done.

'I'll be gone for the rest of the day.' Nick closed his office door, carrying his briefcase and laptop. 'I have a meeting with the finance committee,' he grimaced, 'then I propose to go home to see if I can get this damned paper written without being interrupted by the phone.'

'I could…' Kay began, but it was too late. He'd disappeared.

Deciding to fetch a sandwich for lunch and eat at her desk, Kay was about to leave when her phone buzzed with a text.

Big news. Skype tonight at 7.30 your time? Adam

Kay smiled. Just as she'd been thinking of him. Maybe there was something in ESP. It was early morning over there, so Adam was having an early start. She wondered what the big news was – a new baby, a promotion at work, some new achievement of one of the boys? Whatever it was, he was going to call mid-morning his time, considerate as usual. Unlike his sister, Adam always took Kay's life and circumstances into consideration. He knew Zoe and Noah were staying with her. She'd already texted him about their arrival. But she didn't know if Zoe had also been in touch with her brother, giving him her tale of woe and soliciting his support. Kay didn't expect she'd get much of that from Adam, who'd no doubt come down firmly on Eric's side.

Kay set off to buy her lunch in a happy frame of mind, looking forward to talking with Adam that evening.

*

Kay cleared away the dinner dishes and loaded the dishwasher, glad Zoe had taken an exhausted Noah to be bathed and put to bed. Hopefully his bath and demands for a story would keep Zoe occupied so Kay could enjoy Adam's call in private. It wasn't that she wanted to keep their conversation secret from her daughter, but she knew if she was in the room, Zoe would want to be included. Adam's calls were so infrequent, Kay, perhaps selfishly, wanted to keep them to herself.

At twenty-five minutes past seven, she settled herself in the study and fired up the computer. Almost immediately, there was the familiar ping and Adam's face appeared on the screen.

'You've grown a beard!' Kay couldn't help exclaiming.

Adam fingered his new addition. 'Haven't shaved properly since Christmas,' he said. 'What do you think?'

Kay considered. She'd never gone much for men with beards, except… An image of Nick Kerr appeared behind her eyes. She dismissed it. 'It looks very nice,' she said. 'What does Jess think?'

'She's getting used to it.' He laughed. 'We had a deal. If I grew a beard, she'd cut her hair. She knows how much I like it long, but…' He shrugged and laughed again. 'And how's it going with my dear sister? Is she being her usual handful?'

'Zoe is Zoe. She doesn't change. But I'm loving seeing more of Noah. I just wish I wasn't missing out on so much of your boys.'

'That's what I wanted to talk with you about.'

59

A curl of excitement began to twist in Kay's gut. *Was he going to say what she longed to hear?*

'How would you like some more visitors?'

'You…?'

'Jess is pregnant again and we've decided we should make the Australian trip before we're inundated with nappies.'

'Oh, Adam!' Kay could scarcely keep the emotion out of her voice. She felt herself tear up.

'How does April sound to you? We were planning to take a summer holiday, but Jess will be too far gone by then.'

'April? That's only…'

'Two months away. Can you cope with an influx of your UK family for Easter?'

*

'Bad news?' Zoe asked, meeting Kay in the hallway as she was patting her eyes with a tissue.

'The opposite. Adam, Jess and the boys are coming for a visit. They'll be here for Easter. And they're having another baby.'

'My brother! Can't Jess keep him in order?' Zoe pushed past Kay into the kitchen. 'Tea or coffee?' she asked.

'I think I'd like a glass of wine,' Kay said. 'It's good news. A fourth grandchild – and, if you're still here, Noah will be able to meet his cousins again. Family is important.'

'Well, you'd better enjoy Adam's lot. *I* won't be having any more,' Zoe said as she took a bottle of white wine from the fridge. 'This do?'

'Thanks, honey.' Kay accepted a glass of the chardonnay. She couldn't imagine why Zoe was so determined to make Noah an only child – even at the expense of her becoming a single parent. But surely it wouldn't come to that?

'So, what else did my dear brother have to say? I'm sure he made some remarks about my staying here.'

'Actually, he didn't. He was too full of his own news. The world doesn't revolve around you, Zoe, no matter what you think.'

'Hmm. You haven't asked me about my day?' she said, ignoring Kay's comment.

'Sorry, dear.' Zoe would never change. Kay took a sip of her wine, enjoying the slight buzz it gave her. 'How did you go with Donna?'

'It's really interesting, Mum.' Zoe held her glass in both hands and curled her legs under her. With the go-ahead to talk about herself, she was in her element. She chatted on, explaining the project and the people she'd be interviewing.

It did sound interesting – something Kay wouldn't have minded doing herself, if she hadn't already been employed.

'So, you had no problem in picking up Noah?' she asked.

'Not today, no.'

Zoe seemed to be considering something. Kay could almost see her mind working.

'I asked at the school, and they do have an after-school program. I saw Eve's two girls in the playground. Noah recognised them. They *are* alike. I don't know how she manages. And you said she has another one, too?'

'Yes. Emily Rose must be around six months now.'

'I didn't see Eve. The girls were with a young woman who looked like a student?'

'Maybe their teacher? Allegra Moretti who was their child carer last year is their teacher now. But I think I told you that already.'

'She didn't look like a teacher.' Zoe frowned.

'Well, I don't know who she is then. Unless Eve has found another student to fill in when she or Jo isn't available. Though, the students wouldn't be back yet. I don't know.' Kay took another sip of her wine. 'Does it matter?'

'It occurred to me as you were speaking that,' Zoe waved her glass in the air, almost sending wine all over the carpet, 'if Eve has a babysitter, child-carer – whatever you call it – then, maybe we can share her.'

Zoe didn't miss a trick.

'I'll pop into her store tomorrow, catch up and find out.' Zoe nodded as if pleased with herself. 'Think I'll have an early night, Mum.' She yawned, drained her glass and went off in the direction of the kitchen.

Kay heard the dishwasher open and close, then the bathroom door. After several minutes, she heard the door again, then the sound of Zoe's bedroom door closing. She heaved a sigh of relief.

Seemingly prompted by the sound of the door closing, Milly

appeared meowing loudly. Kay picked her up, her hand automatically dropping to stroke her pet. 'It'll be good to see Adam and his two again, Milly. It's been too long. And just as I was thinking of making a trip over there.' But Kay knew she couldn't have gone if Zoe and Noah were still here. She'd never leave her home to Zoe's tender mercies. Goodness knows what she'd manage to *improve* if Kay wasn't there to stifle the worst of her organising tendencies.

Thirteen

Nick gazed out of his office window, seeing the campus filling up with young bodies. Cyclists jostled with each other on the pathways, a few brave souls skidded past on skateboards, and the car parks were full of cars entering, reversing and being unpacked. The air was bursting with happy voices and loud music. Semester was due to start on Monday and the students were filtering back. Those living in the specially-designed student residences were moving in – first-years accompanied by worried parents, the more senior eager to reconnect with friends. It was a time of year he loved – a time pregnant with new beginnings.

But his joy was clouded by an underlying concern. At the meeting of faculty heads that morning, the finance officer had made no bones about the fact that the budget was in dire straits. He had instructed all deans to examine their respective budgets carefully to determine where cuts could be made. Nick turned away from the window, his forehead creased in thought. He had to report back next week and had no idea what he was going to do.

'Something wrong?' Kay walked in with a bundle of letters and documents requiring his signature. Since the Sunday he'd seen her at lunch, he'd felt awkward in her company. It was nothing he could put his finger on – just an awareness of her as a woman that hadn't been there before. *She* hadn't changed. If anything, she'd been even more professional in her approach to her job. But there was still something…

He thought back to the occasion a few weeks ago – the day after he'd seen her in the restaurant. He'd been on the point of inviting her to lunch when he got cold feet. It would have been a working lunch, but he was worried she might get the wrong idea. And after Sam's reporting of Michelle's comments, he knew he had to be even more vigilant. If Granite Springs was a small town with its characteristic gossip mill, it was nothing compared to that of the university. Reports of him lunching with his PA would be around the place in no time.

Despite that, Nick knew he still wanted to get to know his new employee better. Maybe he could invite her to dinner. He realised she was looking at him in surprise. 'Sorry. I was thinking.' He brushed a hand across the top of his head. 'I've just come back from the budget meeting.'

'Not good?'

Her face was so full of concern he had an impulse to hug her. *Where had that come from?*

'No. We've all been asked to identify how we can cut costs. Cut costs! We've pared down to the bone already. I don't know what else we can do – apart from cutting staff. And that would mean those left would have larger workloads.' He shook his head. But thinking aloud – talking about it with Kay – seemed to help. He'd never been able to do that with Fran.

'Are you thinking redundancies?'

The very word sent a chill through him. He'd almost faced redundancy himself in his last position and knew how terrifying the prospect could be. 'Not if I can help it,' he said. 'I'll think of something. Meantime, what have we here?' Nick took the sheaf of papers from Kay, their hands touching slightly as he did so. A jolt of something akin to desire flashed through him.

Shocked, Nick glanced at Kay to see if she'd noticed – if she'd felt it too. But her expression hadn't changed, though the air felt charged with something unidentifiable.

Why now? Why today? Surely they'd touched before?

But they hadn't. Thinking back, Nick realised Kay had been very careful to avoid all physical contact, almost as if she wanted to evade touching him – or anyone else. *What made this woman tick?*

Before either of them could say anything more, Ann appeared in the doorway. She coughed, breaking the tense atmosphere. 'Professor Kerr, Kay... We wondered... The girls and a few of the lecturing staff are planning a small get-together in the staffroom this afternoon before semester starts in earnest. Would you care to join us? Just a few drinks and nibbles.' She paused, looking from one to the other.

Nick glanced at Kay to see her hesitating. 'That's a lovely idea,' he said. 'I'd be delighted to join you and I'm sure Kay would too. Kay?' He raised one eyebrow.

'Ye…es,' she said. 'But I won't be able to stay for long. My daughter…' her voice trailed off.

'I'm sure everyone has to get home,' he said, trying to sound hearty. This could give him the opportunity he wanted, a chance to speak with Kay in a less formal setting; a chance to find out more about the woman who now intrigued him.

'Four-thirty then.' Ann withdrew, and Kay returned to her own office, busying herself with the computer, her eyes focused on the screen.

What was she thinking as she busied herself on there?

It was some time before Nick could get his attention back to his work. When he did, he had barely begun to examine the faculty financial projections when his mobile rang. Seeing Michelle's number, he cursed and contemplated ignoring the call. She should know better than to call him at work. But he knew from experience that, if his wife wanted to talk to him, she wouldn't give up till she succeeded. With a heavy sigh, he pressed to accept the call.

Usually Michelle got straight to the point. But today she hedged, asking how Sam was doing at school, complaining about Ryan's indifference, saying how much she was enjoying life in the tropics.

Get to the point, Nick thought. *You didn't call me in the middle of a workday to make small talk.*

He heard her take a deep breath then, 'We want to get married.' There was a silence during which Nick tried to work out how he felt, realising he felt nothing, nothing at all. If the woman he'd been married to for all those years, the woman who was the mother of his children, wanted to throw herself away on a wastrel almost young enough to be her son, it was her lookout. He realised that was a gross exaggeration, but it felt good.

'So, what do you need me to do?' he asked, hearing a relieved exhalation of breath.

'I've spoken to a solicitor here and she'll be sending you some papers. I suppose you need to find one in Granite Springs.' There was a pause. 'I don't want to make things difficult, Nick, but I need…'

Nick sighed. He could guess what was coming. Michelle would want her share of the house, at least. Surely she couldn't demand anything more? He'd heard of cases where, when a couple split, the wife laid claim to half of everything, superannuation included. But Michelle had been the one to leave, and she was earning money – as was her toy boy. They'd already come to an agreement about custody. No, it should be fairly simple.

'No problem,' he said. 'I'll do that. I've always dealt with Slater and Ford here in town, though,' he scratched his head, 'I think Col Ford has retired. Can I let you know?'

'Don't take too long. Terry and I would like this settled as soon as possible.'

I just bet you would.

Nick hung up and sat staring into space. In a way it was a relief. With a divorce, he'd really be free of Michelle for good. An image of the woman in the office just outside his door floated into his consciousness. For the first time he had a reason to want his freedom.

With a grin he picked up the phone to dial his solicitor's number.

Fourteen

The afternoon drinks in the education staff-room started out as the usual collection of lecturers and office staff, with the latter standing awkwardly to one side while the academics stood in another. After a few drinks the two groups managed to mingle, but Kay still felt uncomfortable. She wasn't used to social occasions. Since David's death, she managed to avoid this sort of situation which might encourage others to remember her humiliation.

But it was interesting to see those she considered to be stuffy academics letting their hair down and proving they were human after all.

Taking a glass of wine, she sidled past a loud group of staff and took a seat on one of the soft chairs by the coffee table, hoping to become invisible.

She was surprised when Nick sat down beside her.

'Mind if I join you?' he asked.

She did mind. What on earth would they talk about? But he was her boss. She could hardly refuse, ignore him, or move away. 'No,' she said, taking a small sip of her drink. She intended to make hers last, unlike some of the others who were milling about, chatting in loud voices and consuming wine and beer like it was going out of fashion.

'Looks like we both feel the same way about these affairs,' he said, with a wry smile. 'But you seem to have found a good spot.'

Kay looked down into her glass unsure how to respond and wishing herself somewhere else, anywhere else.

They sat in silence for a few moments, then Nick said, 'Ann made a good choice. I'm pleased with your work, but I don't know much about you as a person. Is it being too intrusive to ask?'

Kay shifted awkwardly in her seat. With the others all on their feet, it was as if she and Nick had been trapped in their own little cocoon. It was a strange feeling, as if they were in a private place and that anything they shared here would be their secret.

Nick was looking at her reassuringly. 'As you've no doubt guessed, I've heard the gossip,' he paused, 'about your husband. I understand if you don't want to talk about it but sometimes… I've found… it helps.'

Kay put her glass down and twisted her hands together. What could she say? How could she put into words what David's death had done to her? Until now, she'd only ever talked about it with Jo. But she'd already decided Nick was a kind man. Maybe it *would* help.

'Your husband,' he prompted.

'David…' Somehow, saying his name to Nick felt right. 'He was my first love, my only love. We had a happy marriage, two lovely children – they're both grown now. Then, out of the blue, the rumours began. You've no doubt heard all about them. At first, I didn't believe them, couldn't believe them. How could I? Then, when it became obvious, when he… I knew it must be true.' Kay took out a tissue and patted her eyes. 'Sorry.'

'No, I'm sorry. I shouldn't have asked, shouldn't have brought it all back to you.'

'No,' Kay said, suddenly feeing stronger, 'I'm glad you did. It helps to talk about it to someone who's completely divorced from the situation. I've heard your marriage isn't so good either,' she said, not caring that she might be accused of listening to gossip, too, but he had told her he was separated.

'Divorced is an apt word,' Nick said, rubbing his fingers through his beard. 'Michelle – my wife – wants to get married again, so I'm starting divorce proceedings. She's found a younger model.' The bitterness he felt for the woman who was still his wife was apparent in his voice. 'It's not easy, but nothing like what you've gone through. Your children? How did they cope?' he asked.

'Adam seemed to handle it. It may have been easier for him being in England. But, Zoe…' Kay drew in a breath, a wave of guilt almost overwhelming her. 'I don't know. Maybe I should have talked about it more with her. It's as if she refuses to accept it has anything to do with her. She didn't come home for the funeral, doesn't want to talk about it, hasn't come back to Granite Springs till now. I don't know if…' Kay bit the inside of her cheek, her worst fears coming to the fore.

'You wonder if she too…?'

Kay nodded, unable to speak.

'I doubt it. Of course, I don't know your family, but you strike me as a very perceptive person. I'm sure you'd have known.'

'I didn't know about the others,' Kay said bitterly. 'People thought I should, that I must have, and I'd protected him.' There, she'd said it – the suspicion that had nagged at her for three years, the explanation for why she felt she'd been so vilified.

'They weren't your friends.'

'No. Thanks.' Kay sensed Nick had some understanding of what she'd been through.

She was glad he didn't offer any false sympathy. She'd had plenty of that, enough to last a lifetime. It made it easier to talk to him.

Nick told her of his two children, the daughter about whom he'd already asked her advice, and the son who lived with his mother.

Kay was glad her own children were now past their teenage years. She might find Zoe a problem, but at least she was grown-up and no longer Kay's responsibility, though did parents ever relinquish responsibility for their children?

When she finally rose to leave, Kay adroitly evaded Nick's outstretched hand, reminding herself of the need to maintain a professional relationship with him, and that he'd merely been kind to a new employee and trying to set her at ease by this conversation. Though it had become more personal than she'd anticipated. It had something to do with their being cut off from the rest of the room.

Kay drove home in a daze. What had made her open up so much to Nick?

Nick!

Kay could still feel the shock when their hands accidentally touched that morning. Had he felt it too? It had been difficult to remain impassive when her entire body was in the throes of sensations she'd never expected to experience again. He was her boss, for God's sake, *and* younger than her, *and* still married. She had no business feeling that way. There and then, she made the decision that, if she was to remain as his PA, she'd have to be more careful, and had managed to keep out of his way for the rest of the day.

She reached home to see a strange car in the driveway and no sign of the one Zoe had been driving.

'Zoe?' she called as she entered, going straight through to the kitchen from where she could hear Noah's voice.

'Mum!' Zoe looked up from where she was trying to persuade Noah out of his sports uniform. The little boy was grimly hanging onto his muddy soccer shirt, his stubborn expression very similar to his mother's.

Kay glanced around but couldn't see the owner of the red car in the driveway. 'Who does the red car belong to?' she asked, setting her bag down on the table and pulling out a chair.

'Do you like it? I decided I couldn't rent if I'm going to be here for long, so I bought the one out there.'

'Oh!' Kay's heart sank. One more sign Zoe intended to stay for some time. Although Zoe had made it clear she wasn't in a hurry to return home, Kay had been hoping her daughter and son-in-law would soon find some common ground. Eric rang every evening to speak to Noah, and the small boy seemed puzzled when his mother silently handed over the phone. He clearly missed his daddy, and often resorted to tears when the call was over.

'It's a great little runabout and was a good price. Second-hand, of course, and I won't lose much on resale.'

'Right.' That was something. At least Zoe was considering a return to Brisbane at some stage in the future.

'And I have more good news. I've talked with Eve. The girl I saw with her two *is* a student. Her name's Amber something. She's local. And Eve'll be happy for me to share the cost when needed. So that's a weight off my mind.'

Kay wished Zoe had taken her advice to ensure all her interviews took place during school time, but when had Zoe last taken her mother's advice about anything? She pressed her lips together.

'What's up, Mum?' Zoe peered at her mother. 'Have you been drinking? On a work day? It's only...' she checked the time, '...six o'clock!'

'I had a glass of wine. There were a few drinks for staff. Semester starts next week,' she explained. 'I'll get dinner started in a few minutes.'

'No need. We stopped off on the way home and bought some fresh salmon and salad veggies. *I'll* do it. You look as if you need a shower or something to freshen yourself up. Why don't you do that while I make dinner, then I can tell you about *my* day.'

Relieved to be excused the chore of cooking dinner – if she'd been alone, she would have settled for cheese and biscuits – Kay headed off to the shower. But as she stood under the blast of cool water she felt, not only refreshed, but surprised at the way her body had reacted to contact with Nick Kerr's hand. She'd believed herself immune to a man's touch, that the business with David had immured her to all sexual feelings. She gave a smile at the memory of the early years of her marriage, times when she and David couldn't get enough of each other, times before the children had been born when they'd chase each other around the house to finish in each other's arms.

She sighed. It had been a good life, a good marriage, until it was all spoiled. 'Damn you, David Jackson,' she said aloud, the tears running down her cheeks mingling with the shower water. 'Damn you to Hell if that's where you ended up!'

By the time she returned to the kitchen, Kay had recovered her equilibrium. She found a peaceful scene. There was the delicious aroma of salmon cooking on the stove, and Noah was happily reading aloud to his mother. In the short time he'd been attending school, the little boy had really progressed, seemingly having gained confidence almost overnight. He'd always loved having books read to him and now delighted in reading for himself, stumbling over the words he couldn't pronounce but determined to try.

Kay had also noticed a tendency in him to rebel against his mother's over-protective behaviour and over-controlling attitude, and could foresee battles ahead. But tonight, all was serene as Zoe listened proudly to Noah's eager voice gleefully reading from her own battered copy of an old favourite – Dr Seuss's *The Cat in the Hat*.

Over dinner, Zoe gave Kay details of the two interviews she'd conducted that morning – one with a lady who'd been married for years to a local doctor and had stories to tell of days when the town was much smaller and the only shopping centre for the surrounding properties. 'Such an interesting lady,' Zoe said. 'Maybe you even know her – or her husband. Her name's Val Brennan, so he'd have been...'

'Dr Brennan. Yes, he was my doctor up until he retired. And I believe Jo still sees Val, delivers library books to her.'

'She does?' Zoe seemed put out to have her thunder stolen.

In the break in conversation which followed, Noah regaled them with a report of his sports afternoon after which his class had joined with the year one class in the school vegetable garden. 'And I saw Livvy and Lottie,' he said, 'and we planted carrots and cauliflower and picked tomatoes. Little ones – not like these.' He speared a slice of tomato from his salad.

'So that's why your uniform was so muddy,' Zoe scolded. 'Were you playing in the dirt?'

'Nooo.'

But from the gleam in his eye, Kay knew that was exactly what had happened. 'Boys will be boys,' she said. 'Be grateful if a bit of mud and dirt is the worst of your worries. Adam...'

'I remember the troubles Adam got into,' Zoe said raising her eyebrows. 'Don't mention it. Little ears...'

Kay chuckled. Zoe had been a handful too. Especially in her teenage years. She didn't envy Nick Kerr still going through that stage, though at least he only had one of his children to worry about.

What was it about her tonight? It seemed she couldn't get her boss out of her head.

As if reading her mind, Zoe suddenly asked, 'What about your professor? Was he at the drinks session too?'

Kay felt herself blush as she replied, 'Yes,' hearing her voice come out as a squeak and seeing her daughter's eyes widen.

'You're not thinking...?'

'What? Of course not!' Kay tried to sound indignant. But Zoe was right. Kay was thinking about him *in that way* – a term used in a favourite television programme which she and David had laughed about.

No more was said on the subject but, once Noah was in bed and she and Zoe settled down to watch television, Kay could feel her daughter's eyes on her.

It would never happen, of course. It couldn't, for all sorts of reasons.

But Kay couldn't help imagining what it would be like to be the object of Nick Kerr's affection.

Fifteen

It had been a long day, interrupted by an angry call from Michelle. When Nick had finally managed to get to an appointment with Gordon Slater – he'd been right in thinking Col had retired – he learned there was no fast track to the divorce he and Michelle were seeking. Her own solicitor should have told her that. They had to be separated for a full twelve months before the process could be started and, although they'd lived separate lives for longer, they'd been sharing a house until she finally left on January second.

Now the die had been cast, he didn't want to wait till next year either, but the law was the law and they had to accept it. In the meantime, he'd agreed to examine the documents her woman had sent down. Maybe they could at least make a start on *the division of assets* – a cold-hearted term for the disposal of goods from a marriage of over twenty years. So far, Nick hadn't been able to bring himself to open the bulky manila envelope. It was sitting on his office desk at home like a large spider ready to strike.

Nick gathered together a few papers and stuffed them into his briefcase, promising himself that tonight he'd take a glass of something into the office, and at least take a look at what Michelle and her solicitor were suggesting.

Heading out to the car park, he saw a figure bending down beside a white Hyundai Accent. Wasn't that Kay's car? What was she still doing here? And it looked like she was in trouble.

Ever since the drinks session, he'd been trying to pluck up the courage to invite her to lunch – or dinner – or something. But the opportunity had never arisen. Every interaction between them had been professional, detached. It was as if Kay was deliberately finding ways to avoid any more personal contact. With any other member of staff, he'd have welcomed the impersonal manner, but with Kay he had this strange desire for more.

'Having trouble?' Nick dropped his briefcase and leant down, putting a hand on her shoulder.

Kay leapt away as if she'd been scalded and stood up. 'No. Yes,' she said ruefully. 'Seems I have a flat tyre.' She reached into her pocket. 'I'll just call the NRMA.'

'Maybe I can help.'

She blushed, the rosy hue making her look much younger and more vulnerable. 'I don't want to trouble you.'

'No trouble. Do you have a spare?'

'I think so.' She popped open the boot where, under a collection of books, a tartan travelling rug and a pair of gumboots, rested the necessary spare tyre.

Nick set to, feeling her amused and grateful eyes on him while he worked. Finally, he stood up and stretched. It was some time since he'd had to do a job like this and was glad he hadn't lost his touch. 'There. That's it. You should be right now.'

'How can I thank you?'

Kay's grateful smile was all the thanks he needed, but Nick found himself saying, 'Why don't you let me buy you a drink – or dinner?' He didn't know which of them was more surprised.

'There's no need… I don't think…'

Nick saw Kay hesitate then she nodded, 'That would be lovely,' and took out her phone. Nick tried not to listen but couldn't help overhearing her clearly overcoming her daughter's questions and objections as she explained she'd be late as she'd agreed to have drinks and possible dinner with *a friend*.

'Are you sure about this?' she asked as she slipped the phone back into her pocket. 'I mean we… You're the boss, so…'

'So, you have to follow my directions,' Nick said, suddenly feeling as if a whole new world was opening up for him.

Why had he thought his life was over when Michelle left, decided to eschew women and concentrate on his career? How could he have forgotten the thrill of beginning a new relationship? Was that what this was? Maybe, maybe not. There were a lot of obstacles in the way of any relationship he might want to have with his PA, not least of which was his daughter, never mind the university hierarchy who would no doubt frown on fraternising between staff. And, if it extended beyond tonight's dinner, there would be little chance of escaping the gossip which would ensue.

He was drawn out of his musings by Kay saying, 'I'd better take my car and follow you. Where did you have in mind?' She stood, one hand on the door of her car, waiting for his response.

Where? Nick hadn't thought that far ahead. Hadn't thought at all, really. 'That little Italian on Main Street – Pavarotti's. Do you know it? It's…' Nick stopped short. It would be highly inappropriate to say it was where he and Michelle had chosen to dine from time to time – when they did dine out together, which hadn't happened for several years.

Tony, the waiter at the restaurant, greeted Nick like a long lost friend.

'You come here a lot?' Kay asked with a smile.

'Not recently.' Nick drew a hand through his hair, unwilling to explain he'd never been here since Michelle left, rarely been anywhere but home and the office till Sam returned. 'But I can vouch for the food. Sorry, you probably know that as well as I do.'

Kay smiled again. He could get used to that smile. It lit up her whole face.

'Now, what'll you have?' he asked. 'I can recommend the special gnocchi…' He saw her expression, and grinned. 'Sorry, I'm doing it again.'

'That's okay. I love the Gnocchi Pavarotti, too. Maybe with some garlic bread? They do a nice unleavened one here.'

'*Touché*! And some red wine?'

He saw her hesitate for a moment and wondered if he'd made a mistake. He seemed to recall she'd only had one glass of wine at the staff do. Maybe she wasn't into wine.

'That'd be lovely thanks.'

Nick breathed a sigh of relief. He'd need at least one glass of wine to get through dinner. He'd been thinking about inviting Kay to dinner, to seeing her outside the office and this opportunity seemed too good to miss. But now they were here, he wondered if he'd overstepped the mark.

One glass into the meal, the conversation became easier. They laughed together over some of the foibles of several of the senior administrators at the university, discovered a common dislike of artifice, and despaired of a mutual fondness for black comedy.

The evening passed pleasantly, and Nick was surprised when after sharing the bottle of Ciao Bella Sangiovese with the meal, Kay refused coffee and looked at her watch with a grimace.

'I didn't realise how late it was,' she said. 'It's been lovely. I don't know when I was last able to relax so much. Thank you. I must be off. I'm not in the habit of going out in the evening and, although I rang to explain, Zoe will be wondering what's happened to me.'

Nick asked for the bill. He'd enjoyed Kay's company and the time had flown. He'd been right. There was more to this woman than she revealed as a university employee. The wine had allowed her to drop her guard, and she'd proved to have a wicked sense of humour.

Nick knew he couldn't let her go without making arrangements to see her again outside the confines of their workplace association.

Walking towards their cars, Nick tentatively reached out to take Kay's hand. He felt her fingers curl around his for a moment, before she drew them away and began fossicking in her bag muttering, 'My keys... I know they're here somewhere,' and the contact was lost.

'Thanks, again.' She smiled – a smile that lit up her face – and started to open her car door.

'I... Can we do this again sometime?' Nick felt as awkward as a teenager on his first date. 'Have dinner – or a movie – or...'

Kay looked amused. 'That would be very nice,' she said politely. 'If you're sure it would be appropriate.'

Appropriate! Probably not – for all the reasons he'd enumerated earlier. But, somehow, he didn't care.

Sixteen

Kay's mind was in a whirl, her fingers still tingling from Nick's touch. She couldn't believe it. She'd had dinner with Nick Kerr – Professor Nick Kerr – and he wanted to do it again. She hugged the knowledge to herself, determined not to share it. What if it got around the faculty, the campus, the town? She, of all people, knew how the gossip mill worked in Granite Springs. She'd been the target of it before. Could she risk falling foul of it again?

'Have a good night?' Zoe was slouched in front of the television, watching a documentary about drought in central Australia. She muted the sound when Kay walked in.

'Yes thanks. Everything all right here?'

'No probs. I was just going to make a cup of tea. Want one?'

'Thanks.' Kay dropped her bag onto the coffee table and sank into a chair, remembering the way Nick's fingers on hers made her heart leap.

She was still thinking of him when Zoe returned with two mugs of camomile tea.

'Thanks, honey. Just what I need.' Cradling the mug in both hands she took a sip of the soothing tea, leant her head against the back of the chair and closed her eyes.

'Who was the friend you had dinner with? Jo Slater rang when you were out, so it wasn't her. She seemed surprised to hear you were out to dinner.'

'Oh! Just a friend from work. What did Jo want?'

'She didn't say. You're to ring her back. Mum! You're blushing! What's up? Who *did* you have dinner with?'

Kay cursed her face for giving her away. She held her cup in her lap, running her finger around the rim. 'It was Professor Kerr. I had a flat tyre. He helped me change it, then asked me to dinner. It would have been rude to refuse.' She held her breath, hoping Zoe would leave it at that.

She didn't.

'Professor Kerr? Your boss? That dishy guy we saw at the restaurant? The one who was staring at you?'

Kay shifted uncomfortably in her seat and took another sip of tea. She nodded.

'And does he make a habit of rendering aid to damsels in distress then taking them to dinner?'

Almost choking at the thought of being called a damsel in distress at the ripe old age of fifty-eight, Kay tried to read the expression on her daughter's face. Was it amusement, shock, or disgust?

'I'm sure I don't know.' She finished her tea and rose. 'I'd better return Jo's call.'

'Well, go you! I knew it was only a matter of time...'

Kay stared at her daughter who was now looking at her with something resembling admiration – or was it satisfaction? 'A matter of time?'

'Before you found someone. After Dad...' she paused, cleared her throat, then continued, 'You went into your shell, wouldn't let anyone else in – apart from your friend, Jo. Adam and I hoped...'

Kay froze. She stared at her daughter who'd suddenly become a stranger. Zoe and Adam had discussed her, had talked about her future – about her finding...

'It's none of your business. I'd have thought you and your brother would have more to do than to discuss my sex life or lack of it.'

Her hand rose to cover her mouth as she realised what she'd said. Zoe hadn't mentioned her mother's sex life. It had been Kay who'd put her own thoughts into words. If she'd been blushing before, she knew her face must now be beetroot. After deciding to keep her dinner with Nick a secret, she'd now revealed her innermost feelings about him to Zoe.

'You'd better call Jo,' was all Zoe said, but Kay could see her surprise. Well, it wouldn't do her any harm to realise her mother could have a sex life. But *could* was the relative word. There was no way she was going to have a sexual relationship with her boss, was there?

Moving quickly, Kay made her way to the phone in the kitchen, taking a deep breath before dialling Jo's number.

'Jo,' she said when her friend answered, 'Zoe said you called. Sorry I missed you. I was…'

'Out to dinner,' Jo said. 'I'm so glad you're beginning to have more of a social life again. You've been behaving like a hermit for too long. Someone from work?'

After a moment's hesitation, Kay said, 'Yes.'

That moment alerted Jo who knew Kay so well.

'Don't tell me. It wasn't… was it?'

'I don't know what you're talking about.' Kay sat down with a thump. *Was she so transparent?*

'Granite Springs is a small town, and the university campus is even smaller. We had dinner at The Riverside tonight and Steve just happened to mention he'd seen your professor changing a tyre for you in the education car park. It *was* him, wasn't it?' Jo's chuckle echoed down the phone.

'Well, if you must know, it was. Professor Kerr is a gentleman. He saw I was in trouble and helped me out. You know I've never been much good with mechanical things. David always…' She swallowed remembering how David had always taken care of the cars, telling her that was his job.

'But dinner?'

'I asked how I could thank him, and he suggested a drink, which…'

'Segued into dinner. I know how it goes. Remember?'

Kay did. She remembered how Jo had found love again with her old friend, Col, after his wife's death – and how she'd tried to dissuade Jo, telling her it was too soon. She bit the inside of her cheek.

Jo seemed to understand what Kay was thinking. 'It's been three years, Kay. It's time.'

Kay sighed. 'So you keep telling me, but…'

'What does Zoe have to say about it?'

How did Jo know she'd told Zoe?

'She thinks like you do – that it's time. Evidently she and Adam have been discussing it – me!'

Jo chuckled again. 'That's what children do. We all have your best interest at heart, you do know that?'

'I guess so. It's just so uncomfortable knowing they've been discussing me behind my back and…'

'And?'

'I got angry and accused her of discussing my sex life with Adam.' This time Jo laughed loudly.

'Your sex life? I thought you only had dinner?'

'Not you too!'

'Sorry, I couldn't help it. So was this a one-off thank-you dinner or…'

'He wants us to do it again.' Kay couldn't keep the excitement out of her voice.

'So maybe sex is on the agenda?'

'You have a one-track mind. Chance would be a fine thing. He has a teenage daughter and I have a grown-up one living with me.'

'Where there's a will…'

'It's one dinner – and he's my boss!' But by this time, Kay was laughing too.

'I'll have to drop over to campus and check out this demigod.'

'He's just a man.'

'A man who seems to have got your knickers in a knot. I haven't heard you like this since… since we were teenagers and you spied David Jackson by the river.'

Kay was silent, remembering.

It had been the middle of summer, around this very time of year. She and a group of friends had gone to the river to cool off. There had been a group of boys from the local catholic school annoying them, splashing and throwing handfuls of wet sand. David and a couple of his friends had been taking turns to swing from a rope someone had fixed to an overhanging branch.

Dressed in only a pair of board shorts, with a tanned body sporting more muscle than the others, his hair just a little longer than was typical, David had been every girl's dreamboat. Like a modern Tarzan, he'd swung over to rescue Kay and her friends, chasing off the annoying bunch and winning their heartfelt thanks. To Kay's surprise and delight, she was the one who caught his attention and that was the beginning of their romance. Since then, she'd never looked at another man – until now.

The fact that Jo was right didn't make Kay feel any easier.

'So…?' Jo was waiting for an answer.

'Maybe. Let me think about it. I don't want him to…'

'Coffee as usual tomorrow? You can tell me all about him then.'

'Coffee? Yes. See you then.'

Kay hung up. She ran her hands through her hair. Jo hadn't said why she called. She looked at the phone, wondering whether to call back, then shrugged. They'd see each other tomorrow. She'd find out then. She just hoped she wasn't in for an interrogation about Nick Kerr.

She rolled the name around in her mind. A strong name for a strong man. She wondered what it would be like to… before stifling the thought.

Seventeen

Two weeks. That's all it had been since their first dinner together, but already Kay knew she and Nick had found something special. Of course, there could be no future in it, and it hadn't progressed beyond a few dinners and one chaste kiss on the cheek. But she felt she'd found a good friend, and those were in short supply. Her experience after David's death had shown her that. Women she'd considered friends, had grown up with, parents of her children's friends, had shunned her, even crossing the street to avoid her. No wonder it had taken her so long to recover.

She checked the time, tidied the papers on her desk and turned off her computer. 'Okay if I go out for a bit?' she asked, popping her head around the door which separated Nick's office from hers. 'I arranged to meet a friend for coffee. But if you need me for anything...'

'No, on you go. You spend too much time behind that desk of yours. It's good to see you take some time for yourself,' Nick said with a warm smile.

Kay felt her heart melt. They might only be friends, but Nick Kerr had brightened up her life – a life that had been on the verge of despair.

As she made her way across campus to the Banjo Patterson Café, she began to doubt the wisdom of meeting Jo here on campus. Despite her friend's urgings, she'd managed to delay this meeting. But she'd finally had to give in, could put it off no longer, and today was the day. Kay knew Jo wanted to cast her eyes over Nick – the man who'd engaged her friend's affections. There, Kay had said it, albeit silently and to herself. She might pretend, even to herself, that she and Nick were only good friends, but deep down she knew she wanted more.

When Kay arrived, Jo was already seated on one side of the café surrounded by groups of chattering students. 'I hope you haven't been waiting long,' she said, plopping down into a chair opposite, and pushing back a strand of hair which had become loose. 'Maybe I should get this cut,' she said, 'Or try putting it up like you do.'

Jo regarded her carefully. 'It looks good on you like that. At least you've kept to your natural colour.' She indicated her own silver hair, currently wound up in a bun on top of her head with only a few tendrils framing her face.

'With help from my hairdresser,' Kay laughed.

'I ordered for us both,' Jo said as a waitress appeared carrying two cups of coffee – cappuccino for Jo and a flat white for Kay, and a plate containing a slice of banana bread cut into two. 'I thought we deserved a treat, too. You'll have some, won't you?'

Kay looked at the sweet confection, patted her flat stomach, and said, 'If you insist.'

'You're not the one who has to lose weight. I swear I only need to look at something like this and I add kilos. But Col says he likes me the way I am.' She laughed again, and Kay felt a twinge of envy for her friend's obvious happiness.

'Now, tell all,' Jo said, when they'd both taken their first sip of coffee and their first bite of banana bread. 'Mmm. This is delicious.'

Kay hesitated. She hadn't seen Jo for a couple of weeks. She hadn't been deliberately keeping out of her way, but Zoe had a habit of making arrangements without consulting her mother, and her recent planned Saturday excursions had interrupted Jo and Kay's regular coffee mornings.

The excursions themselves had been fun – a time to bond further with Noah. It had been good to renew her acquaintance with the local beauty spots – and Kay hadn't been averse to missing her meetings with Jo, knowing a grilling was on the cards.

'There's not much to tell.'

Jo's eyes widened. 'That's not what I hear.'

Damn! Kay should have known news of her dinner with Nick at The Riverfront would get back to Jo. 'I suppose Rob told you.'

'He might have said something, but it was Steve who reported that the prof and his PA seemed to have more than a professional relationship.'

'Oh, hell. If Steve knows, I suppose the entire faculty does.' Kay blanched at the thought of being the focus of gossip yet again.

'Not necessarily. Steve can be particularly perceptive. Surely you'd be aware if it was common knowledge?'

Kay considered. 'Maybe,' she said slowly. She hadn't noticed any sly looks, any whispers which died down when she appeared.

'So?' Jo held her cup in both hands and gazed eagerly across the table.

'We've had dinner a few times, that's all. I feel I've found a friend. He's… going through a difficult time.'

'Mmm?'

'He's still married, Jo. There's nothing more going on. Friends, that's all. It's good to have a friend who's a man. It's…'

'Sure.' There was a wicked twinkle in Jo's eyes. 'And I suppose you'll be telling me you haven't had any other thoughts about him of a more intimate nature?'

'Jo!'

'Well, it's been a dry old time for you, and I know…'

Kay could feel her face redden and, just at that moment, who should walk into the café and stop by their table, but the man in question.

'Hello, Kay. Are you going to introduce me to your friend?' Nick leant on the table with one hand and smiled.

'This is Jo,' she managed to stutter.

'And you must be Professor Kerr.' Jo gave Kay a smug glance and looked up into Nick's eyes which were twinkling with amusement.

'Pleased to meet you,' he said. 'I just popped in for a takeaway coffee. No need to hurry back,' he said in Kay's direction, and walked off to place his order.

'Well!' Jo stared after his receding back. 'You didn't tell me he was such a looker. Nor did Steve,' she said thoughtfully.

'You see why I don't imagine he's looking for anything other than friendship, then,' Kay said. 'He's at least five years younger than me. His children are still teenagers. And he's married, for God's sake.'

'Didn't you say he was separated? That makes him fair game. Methinks the lady doth protest too much.'

'Fair game!' Sometimes Jo exasperated her, but Kay appreciated her friendship. She'd been one of the few who'd stood by her when all the rumours about David began to circulate. 'You know why I feel I can never trust another man.'

'Hmm.' Jo seemed undeterred. 'Have you met his… it's his daughter who lives with him, isn't it?'

'Yes, it is – Sam, Samantha. And no, I haven't met her and don't expect to. I'm not privy to that part of his life, although he has asked for the odd bit of advice about teenage girls.'

'See!'

'No, I don't see, and I don't think I can be of much help in that direction. It's a long time since Zoe was a teenager. Times have changed a lot.'

'But teenagers not so much. They probably still lie to their parents about what they're doing and where they're going, and hide their consumption of cigarettes and alcohol. Bet you're glad those days are over.'

Kay rolled her eyes. 'A thirty-year-old Zoe is bad enough. I don't think I could cope with a teenage Zoe in this day and age. Anyway, his daughter'll be out tomorrow night.'

'What's happening tomorrow night?'

Damn! Kay hadn't meant to let that slip. 'He's invited me home for dinner. He's going to cook.'

Jo's eyebrows rose. 'A man who can cook, too! A teenager-free house. And you don't think…?'

'Of course not!' But Kay *had* felt a tiny sliver of anticipation mixed with curiosity when Nick invited her to his home. She was interested to see where he lived. A person's house always said a lot about them. For example, the wall of bookshelves in her own home was evidence of her love of reading, though the piano – a remnant from days when both Adam and Zoe had taken music lessons – might encourage the visitor to imagine she was more musically inclined. Membership of a local choir was as far as her musical ability went.

'Don't be too sure. It didn't take long for Col and me.'

'But you'd known each other forever,' Kay objected, to which Jo had no reply.

'I should get back,' Kay said, when they'd finished their coffee and all that remained of the banana bread were a few crumbs. 'Satisfied?' She didn't mean with the coffee.

'Very. I can now understand what it is about Professor Kerr that's brought you out of that bubble you'd wrapped yourself in. I approve.'

Kay knew it would be of no use to try to persuade her friend otherwise, so merely gave a small smile, not sure whether to be pleased or sorry he'd chosen to visit the café where they were having coffee, and suspecting it had been a deliberate act on his part.

Regardless, the conversation with Jo had forced Kay to consider whether Nick might indeed be planning more than a meal together when he invited her to dinner.

Although the idea scared her, she couldn't help a tiny glimmer of what might be hope.

Eighteen

"Bye, Dad! Have fun!' Sam winked. 'I wouldn't mind if you found someone, Dad. Really!'

She hoisted her bag more firmly on her shoulder, before slamming the door behind her. Nick winced. He didn't want to keep secrets from his daughter, so had told her he'd invited Kay to dinner, brushing it off as a routine sort of event. He didn't want her to get the wrong idea – or was it the right idea? Not knowing how Kay felt about him, he had no expectations for the evening, though maybe...

He hummed to himself as he prepared the salad to accompany the steak which was his *pièce de resistance*. Even Michelle had praised the way he cooked steak, which was something, coming from one who had graduated from a *cordon bleu* cookery course – one of the many distractions from their marriage.

It had been a long time since Nick had prepared a meal to impress a woman – not since he and Michelle had first dated, though back then, he'd have been more likely to have bought something from the local takeaway. He wanted tonight to be special; to find out if he'd been imagining things. He and Kay worked well together, had become friends, but could they be more than friends?

From what he'd heard around the traps, she hadn't looked at another man since her husband died – or before that. She'd married young and they'd been what the old-timers considered to be love's young dream. He wondered when it had all gone wrong. And it must have gone very wrong for him to have committed suicide.

The doorbell rang just as he'd put the steak in to marinate and had fired up the barbecue. He planned for them to eat outside though they might be deafened by the sounds of the cicadas who fed on the gum trees surrounding the yard.

Standing at his door, wearing a filmy dress in shades of cream and brown was a woman who took his breath away. For a few seconds, they stood staring at each other, then Kay broke the silence.

'I brought some wine. Red. I hope that's all right.' She held out a bottle of Wolf Blass Yellow Label Cabernet Sauvignon. 'I'm not much good on wines. David always...'

Nick saw her bite her lip and hastened to put her at ease. 'Looks great and will complement the steak I have marinating. I'm afraid my cooking talents are pretty limited, though Sam has been encouraging me to become more adventurous.' He grimaced. 'Come in.'

Nick moved aside to let Kay pass, inhaling a heady mixture of citrus, rose and musk as she did so.

Once inside Kay halted and looked around, her eyes roaming over the new sofa, the wide-screen television and the lack of ornaments or any other form of decoration. Suddenly, Nick saw the room through her eyes and became aware how bare the place must appear without the knick-knacks Michelle had always strewn around. The only other furniture was the wall of bookcases containing a mixture of academic texts and his recreational reading – mostly thrillers and the police procedurals which he devoured avidly.

'So, this is where you live?' she asked.

'It lacks a woman's hand,' Nick said ruefully, rubbing a hand over his head. 'I haven't spent much time here since Michelle left, and Sam...' He shrugged. 'I thought we could eat outside.' He led her through the house and out into the courtyard where he'd already set the table.

While Kay took a seat, Nick poured two glasses of wine and adjusted the barbecue ready for the steaks.

'A man and his barbecue,' Kay murmured, but her friendly smile took away any barb from her words.

Nick grinned. 'Just wait till you taste them. I've been told my steaks are pretty good. You do eat meat?' he asked, realising she could well be vegetarian.

'Love a good steak,' she said. 'And the salad looks delicious, too.'

She gestured to the large bowl sitting in the middle of the table. 'How long have you lived here?'

'As long as I've been in Granite Springs. Must be around...' Nick tried to do the mathematics, '...ten years now. The kids were still in primary school, and I came in as a senior lecturer. We'd been in Sydney before that and Michelle...' He bit his tongue. Now wasn't the time to talk about his almost ex-wife.

'It must have been a wrench for your son to leave.'

'Yes. Sam refused categorically, despite her mother's pleading. But I think the fact she was going into her last year at school held some sway in the argument.' Nick remembered those arguments – arguments that had gone on for days, with Sam yelling insults at her mother before disappearing into her room and slamming the door, leaving Michelle blaming Nick for their daughter's defiance. And poor Ryan. Nick thought he'd only agreed to go with his mum to avoid any further quarrels. Surely that must have been the reason? He couldn't believe his son had wanted to leave him, his friends, and the town he'd grown up in.

'I'm sorry. It must have been hard for you, too.' She put a hand on Nick's arm.

'Yes.' His forehead creased for a moment, then he shook off the memory of his despair at Ryan's decision. 'But he'll be back down in a few weeks for Easter. We just have to make the most of that. I'm going to take some time off to spend with him. What about you? You have another child, don't you – besides the daughter living with you?'

Kay's face broke into a smile. 'Yes. Adam lives in England. He'll be here for Easter, too. In fact, I was going to ask...' She hesitated as if unsure of what she was going to say.

'Yes?'

'I know I haven't been in the position for long, and I did have leave over Christmas, but I wondered if I could have a few days off while he's here.'

'Of course. Just let me have the paperwork. I'll clear it with Ann.'

'Thanks.' She rewarded Nick with another warm smile, making him wonder what else he could do to gain her approval.

'I'd better see to the steaks.' Nick emptied his glass before moving across to the barbecue and dropping the steaks onto the grill. While they were sizzling, he congratulated himself on setting up this dinner. When Michelle left, the last thing on his mind was the company of another woman, then Kay had appeared in his office. Her restful presence had been a balm to his troubled soul and now he was curious to know what made her tick.

'What does your daughter think of your having dinner with me?' Nick asked, when the meat was finally cooked to his satisfaction and they were enjoying the meal. He knew of cases where grown children didn't take kindly to their parent or parents seeing someone new. Though this was only dinner, he felt it could be the start of something more – he'd like it to be.

Kay seemed to consider the question before replying, 'I think she's pleased I'm making new friends. After David died, I hid myself away. You know what this town's like. No doubt you heard all the rumours, too. I felt as if everyone was looking at me, pointing and whispering. David was such a well-known personality around town.' She took a sip of wine before adding quietly, 'I told you, didn't I, that Zoe won't talk about her father, that she didn't come home for the funeral?'

Nick nodded. 'And your son?'

'Adam's quite different, always has been. He and Jess came all the way from England. I'm really looking forward to their visit – to seeing their two boys. I've missed so much of their growing up.'

'Will he be happy you have a new friend?' Nick wasn't sure if *friend* was the correct word, but it was the one Kay had used, and he didn't want to scare her off.

'I don't know. He and David were very close, and he didn't react like Zoe when it all blew up. He hasn't been here since.' She looked thoughtful. 'But what about your two?'

Nick laughed. 'I think Sam would be glad if I found someone to take my mind off her. She actually told me to have fun when she left tonight. I'd love you to meet her.'

Seeing Kay's sudden withdrawal, Nick knew he'd spoken without thinking. Of course, it was too soon to be thinking of introducing her to Sam. But he did feel relieved that it looked as if there would be no objection to any future relationship from their daughters, at least.

'Where is she tonight?'

'Sleepover at her friend's. They're at that age where they can't live without communicating with each other – texting or calling all the time. She'll be back in the morning, so we'll have the place to ourselves.'

Nick saw a strange look flicker over Kay's face. She didn't think… Hell, he could have chosen his words more carefully. He'd like nothing better than to carry her off to bed, but that wasn't his intention, wasn't why he'd invited her to dinner. *How was he going to retrieve the situation?*

He was saved by the loud ringing of the phone. Relieved, he rose. 'Better get this,' he said, going into the house.

When he picked up the phone, Nick was surprised to hear Tanya Wilson's voice. He and the mother of Sam's friend, Ruby, didn't know each other well. He couldn't imagine why she was calling.

'Sorry to bother you, Professor Kerr,' she said, 'but it's Ruby. She left without her new glasses, and I know she'll have trouble. I wondered if I could drop them round.'

'She's not here, Tanya. Sam said they were going over to Jackie's.'

'Oh! I must have got it wrong. I'll call there.'

'Right. Sorry I can't be of any help.' But Nick was perplexed as he hung up and went back outside.

'Problem?' Kay asked.

'I'm not sure. It's probably nothing.' But Nick couldn't dismiss a trace of apprehension. *Sam wouldn't have lied to him, would she?*

He shared his concern with Kay, who said, 'Why not call Jackie's parents if you're worried?'

Nick prevaricated. It was the obvious thing to do. But how would Sam react to his checking up on her? 'No,' he said at last. 'I have to trust her. Tanya Wilson must just have made a mistake.'

But Nick couldn't get the phone call out of his head. The evening was spoilt. It was no surprise when he received another call. This time it was Jackie's mother.

Kay's eyes met his when he returned. This time his heart was pounding and a vein on his forehead was twitching.

'I can't believe it,' he raged. 'Jackie told her mother they were coming here. Where the hell *are* they? They're only seventeen – young girls on their own. What are they up to?'

Kay began to laugh, quickly sobering up when she saw Nick's expression. 'Sorry, but we were teenagers once, and I've gone through two of them. I'd be willing to bet there are some boys involved.'

'Boys!' Nick raised his voice. 'But Sam has never…' Then he thought back through the weeks since Sam returned from Queensland. She'd been more secretive, but he'd put it down to Michelle and his separation, to the changes that brought to their lives. It hadn't occurred to him there might be another reason. It should have. He mixed with young people all the time. He knew how they were. He brought his fist down on the table with a thump that almost sent their glasses flying.

He saw Kay give him an odd look. 'What?' he asked.

'There's nothing you can do now,' Kay counselled. 'But you might want to have a chat when she gets home. You or her mother have talked with her about contraception, haven't you?'

'I left all that to Michelle. I suppose she has.' Nick blanched at the thought of having the sex talk with a teenager who might have a more active sex life than he had – and who was his daughter.

'I think something stronger than this wine is called for,' Kay said consolingly. 'I won't have any as I'm driving, but do you have any brandy?'

'In the pantry.' Nick pointed to the kitchen, too stunned by the direction of his thoughts to move.

Feeling more relaxed after the brandy, Nick leant his elbows on the table, face in his hands. 'Where did I go wrong?' he asked, not expecting a reply. 'Michelle and I gave her everything, encouraged her to share things with us. And until now, I believe she has. What's made her act like this?'

'I presume what she wanted to do tonight – where she wanted to go – was something and somewhere she knew you'd disapprove of. She's clearly not acted on impulse. It was carefully planned, right down to the switching around of locations. The good thing is, she's not on her own. From the calls you've had, it's obvious the three of them are in it together. That should give you some comfort.'

'Mmm.' Nick wasn't so sure. He exhaled loudly. His little girl was growing up. He just hadn't expected this part of it to come so soon.

'It's getting late. I should be going.' Kay made to stand up.

'Have some coffee first.' Nick didn't want to be alone. He knew he wouldn't sleep, worrying about where San might be, what she might be doing – and with whom.

'Okay.' Kay settled down again, and Nick went inside to start up the coffee maker, his anger with Sam making him handle the machine with more force than was necessary.

They made desultory conversation while drinking coffee, but Nick's mind wasn't on it. He kept imagining his daughter and cursing himself for being so easily fooled.

'You mustn't blame yourself,' Kay said, covering his hand with hers – a gesture which did offer some comfort. 'Teenagers can be very cunning when they want to be. She'll be back in the morning and you can read the riot act then.'

'You're right, of course. I'm sorry our evening was spoiled.'

'Not at all. I've enjoyed it. The dinner was lovely. And, if anything, it's made me realise I'm not the only one with a problem daughter – and grateful mine's no longer a teenager.' She laughed and Nick managed to join her.

They walked together to the door where they stood facing each other. There was a moment when neither moved then, as if propelled by some unseen force, they came together in an embrace, his lips searing hers as if they'd never let go.

'What's *she* doing here?'

The door flew open and a whirling dervish with flowing chestnut hair rushed past, almost causing them to lose their balance. Nick was first to recover.

'Sam!' he yelled.

But Sam had disappeared upstairs, the noise of the slam of her bedroom door echoing through the hallway.

'Maybe I should…' Nick began, starting towards the stairs.

'Leave her,' Kay advised. 'She's clearly upset. Her evening hasn't gone the way she planned. And seeing us together must have been a shock. It was a surprise to me, too.'

'A pleasant one, I hope.' But Nick was distracted, his focus on his daughter. It was as if those moments with Kay in his arms had never happened.

'Goodnight. I'll see you on Monday.' She left hurriedly, drawing the door closed behind her.

Nick went upstairs, stopping outside Sam's door. He could hear her sobbing. He knocked gently. 'Sam?'

'Go away!'

Nick stood there for a few more minutes as the sobbing continued, then shook his head and turned away.

Nineteen

The church bells wakened Nick next morning, followed by the cackling of a pair of kookaburras on the back fence. The sun streamed in through the white plantation shutters Michele had insisted on, claiming they were the only way to keep cool in this climate. She'd been right about that, though wrong about so many other things.

Nick had experienced a restless night – images of Sam with some longhaired lout interspersed with ones of him with Kay, both in equally compromising positions. He shook himself awake, dreading the conversation he knew he must have with his daughter.

Standing under a cool shower, Nick rehearsed how he'd handle the situation, planning to remain calm while ensuring Sam realised the seriousness of her behaviour of the previous evening. He was relieved to see her bedroom door was open when he passed. He peered in. The clothes she'd worn the night before were strewn over the floor and her bag upended on the bed, its contents scattered. He was unsurprised to see a half-empty packet of cigarettes. If that was all she'd consumed, he was grateful. At least she was prepared to face him.

'Morning,' he said to Sam who was seated at the kitchen bench, head bent over her phone, fingers busily texting, hair falling over her face.

At the sound of his voice she looked up and pushed her hair out of her eyes. 'I can explain, Dad,' she said, before he could speak. 'Jackie and Ruby texted me that their mothers spoke with you last night. We didn't mean…'

'You didn't mean to lie? Or you didn't mean to deceive us? Your behaviour was inexcusable.'

He finally wormed the story out of her over a few cups of tea and several pieces of toast liberally spread with her favourite crunchy peanut butter.

To his surprise, Sam began to weep. 'I'm sorry, Dad. It was horrible. We went to Declan's. He said there was a party. His parents were away.' She hiccupped. 'We knew you'd never agree when there were no adults, so we worked out something to say that would make it okay.'

'Okay? You thought it was okay to lie to your parents?' Nick could feel his anger growing again, then he saw how abject Sam looked. He remembered the state she'd been in when she got home. *What had happened to his little girl?* A curl of fear swept through him. If those boys had hurt her, they'd have him to deal with.

'Just listen! It was all right to begin with. The music was fire and Declan's friends were chill – some of them had already left school. We had a few drinks.' She shot a cautious look at her dad.

Nick didn't speak.

'We kept waiting for the others to arrive, for the party to start, but…'

'What happened?' Nick couldn't keep quiet any longer. He was imagining the worst.

'One of the guys had a bike. It was a Harley, Dad. Ryan would have loved it. Anyway, he offered to give each of us a ride. It sounded fun, and we were getting bored waiting for the others to turn up.'

'So, did *you* go for a ride on this bike?'

'No. It was Ruby's turn first. We all went outside to cheer them on. Declan lives outside town – on an acreage – and Jason – the guy with the bike – thought it would be exciting to take it for a spin across the paddock.'

Nick began to see where this was leading. He bit the inside of his cheek, glad it hadn't been Sam on the bike.

'They roared off. We watched, cheering. Then the noise from the bike stopped and the light went out.' She began to sob again. 'Jackie and I rushed to find out what had happened to Ruby. We met Jason limping back. When we asked about Ruby, he pointed back in the direction he'd come from.'

'And Ruby?'

'They'd both fallen off. She had a cut on her chin and was holding her arm in a strange way. I think it may be broken. The bike hit a tree stump. Jason didn't see it in the dark.'

'What happened then?' Nick was glad it hadn't been any worse, glad Sam was okay.

'We went back for our bags. The boys didn't want us to leave. But Jackie called a cab and we pooled our money to pay for it.' She paused. 'I don't think there was going to be a party,' she said sadly. 'No one else turned up. And it was late.'

Nick's anger dissolved. He hugged Sam. 'My poor baby. But you do realise it could have been much more serious?' There was a tightness in his chest at the thought of what might have happened.

'Yes, Dad. I'm sorry.'

'And have I your word you'll always be honest with me in the future? Tell me where you're going – even if you think I won't approve?'

'Yes, Dad.' This time, Sam sounded bored, but she was smiling. 'Anyway, what about you? I thought you'd invited your PA to dinner.'

'I did – Kay Jackson. That's who was leaving when you rushed past – and who you were so rude to,' he added, remembering Sam's comment. 'What was that all about?'

'That was your new PA? You said she was one of the women we saw in the restaurant. I thought it was the younger one. She looked more… more like someone you'd be interested in.'

Nick chuckled. 'Just because your mum's gone for a younger model, doesn't mean I would too.'

'But she's old!'

'Maybe a few years older than me. You didn't really think I'd be attracted to Zoe? She's young enough to be my daughter! She's Kay's daughter.'

'Whatever.' Sam shrugged, losing interest in her dad's affairs. Before long, she picked up her phone again, giving a whoop of joy when she read an incoming text. 'Ruby's okay. Her arm isn't broken. Can I go around to see her?'

'I suppose so,' Nick said, and Sam was off before he could blink.

Alone again, Nick made himself a strong coffee and picked up the weekend paper, wondering as he did so what might have happened last night if Sam hadn't returned home so unexpectedly.

Twenty

'Did you have a nice time last night?' Zoe was already having breakfast when Kay surfaced next morning and Noah was busily spooning up his Rice Crispies, Milly sitting by his feet in the certainty some milk would find its way to the floor. 'You must have got home late. You still weren't in when I went to bed.'

Did Kay detect a note of censure in her daughter's voice?

'Not too late, and I did have a nice time, thanks.'

'Mmm.'

Kay helped herself to coffee and slid a couple of slices of bread into the toaster. She wasn't really hungry this morning. She hadn't slept well, those last minutes at Nick's going around and around in her head – and that kiss! She'd been shaken to the core. It was the last thing she'd expected, and yet it happened so naturally. A pity his daughter had chosen exactly that moment to rush in. Or was it? Where would it have led otherwise? They were both too old to be unaware of the strong attraction, of the sexual tension building up. It was probably a good thing Sam had turned up when she did. Otherwise, who knows where it might have led?

Kay was so lost in her thoughts she didn't realise Zoe was talking to her. 'Sorry, darling, what did you say?'

'Don't you ever listen, Mum? I asked if you had anything planned for today. Eve Tait has invited me and Noah to lunch. He and her twins have become friends. But it means you'll be left alone.'

Kay couldn't help grinning at her daughter's concern. 'I'll be fine,

Zoe. I was on my own for three years before you arrived and managed not to go into a decline.' Though she had spent the first two years in a state bordering on that. Now, it would be nice to have the day to herself. Sometimes it seemed as if the house wasn't her own any longer.

'What will you do?'

Do? The thought of a free day stretching out ahead of her was like a treat to be savoured. 'Don't worry, I'll find something. I may drive out to Yarran to see Jo.' As soon as she said it, Kay knew that's exactly what she'd do. Since they'd had coffee on Friday, she and Jo had foregone their usual Saturday get-together and she knew her friend would be eager to hear how dinner at Nick's had gone.

*

'Good to see you.' Jo greeted Kay with a hug. 'Come on in. We're just about to have a glass of wine. You'll join us?'

'Yes, please.' Kay accepted Col's peck on the cheek and settled into one of the cane chairs on the veranda, Jo's old Labrador padding over to settle at her feet. 'Hello, old boy,' she said, ruffling Scout's ears.

'Don't let him bother you,' Col said, handing her a glass of white wine beaded with moisture.

'He doesn't. It's so lovely out here.' Kay gestured to the stretch of paddock reaching as far as the eye could see, the large pepper tree near the house and vegetable garden, and the grove of fruit trees by the fence line. As she spoke a flock of galahs flew down to feast on some seeds, their squawking blending with the screeches of the corellas feeding on trees in the neighbouring paddock.

'But not so peaceful,' Col commented.

'It's a different kind of peace,' Kay said, sipping her drink. 'You're so lucky to have all this.' But Kay knew it wasn't for her. She preferred to live in town, surrounded by other houses and neighbours. Although she loved solitude and valued her privacy, she liked the security of knowing she wasn't completely alone.

'We like it.' Jo linked arms with Col, and they smiled at each other. 'Now, I know Col has a few things to take care of before lunch, so why don't you tell me all about last night?'

As she spoke, Col disappeared inside the house, followed by the dog. 'Scout's changed his allegiance,' Jo said, her eyes following the pair. 'He was always a man's dog. He missed Gordon when he left but made do with me. However, as soon as Col moved in, Scout became *his* dog, He follows him everywhere. It's rather endearing to see them together. You never thought of getting a dog? They're such good company. I don't know what I'd have done without Scout those years I was here on my own.'

'As you know I'm a cat person.'

'But cats are so independent.'

'True, but I'm happy with my Milly and I dread to think how she'd react if I introduced a dog into the family.'

'Now, last night. How did it go?' Jo leant forward expectantly.

'Good. The house is a bit bare which I suppose is to be expected. It looks as if his wife took a lot of stuff with her and he hasn't bothered to replace it.'

'Men!' Jo agreed. 'Col didn't make any changes after Alice died, but at least the place was fully furnished. What did you have to eat? Did he make a move on you? Tell all!'

Kay laughed. She was usually the one asking the questions. It felt odd to be on the receiving end, though Kay knew Jo wouldn't be as judgemental as she had been over Jo and Col's relationship. She now regretted her remarks back then. Jo must have found them annoying, but she'd never said.

'I had a pleasant evening. Nick lives in that part of town near the old quarry. It's a nice house, two storeys. No animals there.' She could see Jo's impatience. 'He'd made a salad and cooked steak on the barbecue – rather well, actually. He'd marinated it in some nice herbs and spices. We talked.'

'And?'

'There was no "and".' Kay decided to keep the goodnight kiss to herself. 'Unless you count the arrival of his daughter as I was about to leave. She seemed surprised to see me.' Kay thought again of Sam's startling remark. 'I don't know who she was expecting to see. Nick said he'd told her I was coming to dinner.'

'Had she met you before?'

'Not met, exactly. They were at The Riverside when Zoe and I were there, and I assume he told Sam who I was.'

'You and Zoe?'

'Yes.' Kay stared at her friend. 'You don't think? No, she couldn't have imagined Zoe was his PA – that he'd invited Zoe to dinner.'

'Why not?'

Kay was silent, thinking about this, then both women broke into a peal of laughter.

'Anyway,' Kay said, sobering up. 'She seemed upset. She was supposed to be having a sleepover at a friend's, but they'd used the old switcheroo to fool their parents. I hope everything is all right.'

'You haven't heard from him this morning?'

'No. Why should I? I'll see him in the office tomorrow.'

And how awkward will that be?

Kay wondered how she was going to manage to maintain her professional manner after that kiss. Then it occurred to her she hadn't checked her phone that morning. She took it out now to see a missed text. She glanced at Jo who raised an eyebrow.

Kay looked at her phone again.

Sorry about Sam. We've had a talk. Case of mistaken identity. She had a bad experience. All good now. Nick.

'It seems you were right,' Kay chuckled, turning the phone round to show Jo. 'Though I've no idea how that could happen. I may be a few years older than him, but Zoe's twenty years younger.'

'Maybe wishful thinking on the girl's part. Zoe's the sort of woman she'd like to see her dad with.'

'Hmm.'

'So, no beating hearts, panting breaths, burning kisses? I'm disappointed.'

Kay blushed. 'We're not living in a Mills and Boon novel.'

'But don't you fancy him – even a little?'

'He's a nice man. But I've told you before, I'm not in the market for a man, nice or otherwise.'

'So you keep saying. Well, we'll see.'

Kay gave a heavy sigh and ran her fingers through her hair. Jo wasn't going to give up. But to her surprise, her friend changed the subject.

'Where's Zoe today? She's let you off the hook?'

'She's visiting with *your* daughter. You started something introducing Noah to the twins. They seem to have taken him under their wing at school and, in his eyes, Lottie and Livvy can do no wrong. Zoe has done a deal with Eve to share childcare arrangements, too. I worry she doesn't seem to want to spend much time with him, but what can you do?' She spread her hands, before picking up her glass again and taking a drink.

'I bet Eve wants her help with the birthday party,' Jo said. 'The girls turn six next weekend. I've always made them a cake, but Eve told me she wanted to do something different this year.' She picked at a piece of grass on the table, and Kay knew Jo wasn't happy about being cut out in this way.

'What has she in mind instead?'

'I've no idea, but I'm sure between them she and Zoe will come up with something – if they haven't already.' She sighed. 'Last year I worried she was trying to organise my life, now I'm upset she wants to do her own thing. We mothers are never satisfied, are we?'

'Have you ladies finished all your women's talk?' Col returned at that point, Scout lumbering behind him. 'Scout's been fed, but I'm getting a bit peckish.'

'Listen to him,' Jo said fondly, 'Don't let him fool you. He's the one who put the quiche together this morning while I was picking the salad veggies.'

Kay smiled at their friendly wrangling. She'd been so wrong a year ago. Col Ford was the best thing that had happened to Jo since Gordon had left.

It was when they had almost finished eating lunch that Col dropped his bombshell. 'I had a call from Gordon this morning when you were out in the garden.'

'What did he want?' Jo didn't appear overly concerned. Although Gordon was her ex-husband, he and Col had been best friends most of their lives and, until Col retired, had been partners in a local law firm.

'You won't believe it. He says Carol is pregnant.'

'What?' Both Jo and Kay spoke at once, then Jo shook her head. 'She can't be, unless... Oh dear. Has he been caught at his own game?'

'But I thought he had a vasectomy?' Kay asked.

'He did,' Col said with some relish. 'To avoid this very thing. But I don't think Carol ever gave up hope.'

'I did hear she was looking pleased with herself recently,' Jo murmured, almost to herself. 'Oh my. This will put a cat among the pigeons.'

'I don't think a cat had anything to do with it,' Kay laughed. 'Oh dear, I shouldn't laugh. It really isn't funny. What will they do?'

'Evidently they had a huge row. Of course, Gordon immediately accused her of having an affair which she vehemently denied. She says it must be his. He says not.'

'So?' Jo asked.

'I suggested he make an appointment with his urologist to make sure it wasn't a possibility. Meantime, I believe things are a tad tense in the Slater household.'

'Does Eve know?' Jo wondered.

'If she doesn't, she soon will. How will she take it?' Kay asked, patting Jo's shoulder.

Jo shook her head. 'I have no idea. When there was such a fuss about Carol wanting a child last year, Eve was distraught at the whole idea. But maybe now... Oh, I don't know. Is Gordon still adamant *he* doesn't want another child?'

'I think his main concern is Carol's infidelity,' Gordon said.

'That's rich, coming from someone who couldn't keep it in his pants when we were married. Sorry, but it's true. It would actually serve him right.'

'You don't mean that,' Kay said soothingly.

'You know, I think I do. Anyway, it's nothing to do with us. Are we all finished here? Coffee?' Jo gathered the plates and headed into the kitchen.

'It's bothering her more than she admits,' Col said, his eyes following Jo. 'Eve will be devastated. She thought this was all over and done with. Carol's child will be an aunt or uncle to her three and Emily Rose hasn't turned one yet. It's madness. And I don't think Gordon's any keener on the idea than he was a year ago.'

'It's so sad that the desire for a child can cause such upheaval,' Kay said. 'That's why my daughter has left her husband.'

'She wants another child?'

'Quite the reverse. She'd be delighted if he'd agree to a vasectomy. We never had problems like that in our day. We were grateful for the children we had and took care of contraception to prevent those we didn't want.'

Jo returned with the coffee and gave Col a glare. 'I hope you haven't been boring Kay with my family problems. She gets quite enough of that from me.'

'Not at all, honey. *She* was telling me about hers.'

Kay made an apologetic moue. 'Zoe and Noah will be home soon. I didn't mean to stay so long. But it's been good to see you both. I should go when I've had coffee.' But she felt no desire to leave. It was pleasant sitting here, in good company, with no daughter to worry her. She envied Jo and Col their companionship. It was at times like this she missed David most.

Last night had been good, better than good. But it could never come to anything. In this town she'd always be David Jackson's widow – the woman whose husband had been accused of those dreadful crimes and who'd committed suicide rather than face the courts.

Twenty-one

'This is crazy,' Kay told herself as she prepared to be picked up by Nick.

Zoe and Noah had disappeared earlier in the day to help set up for the twins' birthday party. Between them, Eve and Zoe had concocted the plan to hold it in the back room of The Bean Sprout, a local café. In recent years Marie Beattie had set up the back room, initially for cookery classes, but later branching out into children's parties which included baking fairy cakes plus the provision of other party food such as popcorn, fairy bread, and mini pizzas. At the last minute, it seemed that Eve had relented and given into her daughters' pleading for Jo to provide the cake, and Kay had been privy to her planning for the pirate theme chosen for this year.

Noah had been excited about the party for the past week, and it had been as much as Zoe could do to rein in his enthusiasm sufficiently to get him through the morning – his shouts of 'Isn't it time yet?' and 'Do you think they'll like my presents?' trying her patience.

Now Kay had the house to herself and was beginning to regret the impulse which had led her to accept Nick's invitation they attend a gallery opening in Canberra followed by dinner. His suggestion that they'd be less likely to meet anyone they knew in the capital had been what swayed her, but did that very reason make the whole thing seem underhand?

She heard his car pull up. It was too late to change her mind now.

As she peered out the window to watch Nick get out of the car, Kay's stomach did a somersault and she experienced an unexpected bolt of desire. Dressed casually in a pair of jeans and a white open-necked shirt, Nick looked even younger than the fifty-three her surreptitious examination of his CV had revealed. She glanced down at the cream linen dress she'd chosen. The colour suited her dark looks, but did it make her look old? Throwing a brown and cream scarf around her neck, she took a deep breath and opened the door.

Any sort of greeting was stymied by Milly choosing to wind herself around Kay's ankles, meowing piteously.

'Who's this?' Nick asked, as the cat decided to transfer her attention to him. He picked her up, scratching her ears and prompting the loud purring – a tell-tale sign of the cat's pleasure.

'That's Milly. Do you like cats?'

'Love them. This one's a real honey. We had a kitten when Ryan was small, but it ran under a car and Michelle decided it wasn't fair to get another when we were out all day. Shall we go?' he asked, setting Milly down gently. The cat scampered away.

Kay became more relaxed on the drive to Canberra. Nick was good company and entertained her with tales of his adventures as a student in the Australian Capital Territory when, if he was to be believed, he'd used his skills to achieve just sufficient grades to gain his bachelor and masters degrees while spending much of his spare time with a local gliding group.

'What did you do after uni?' she asked, curious to find out more about him. 'Did you teach straight away?'

'For two years,' he said. 'But I didn't enjoy the classroom. I decided to extend my career and spent a few years in further study in the States. It wasn't so easy to sail through a doctorate, so my social life was severely curtailed.' He grimaced. 'Then I returned to Australia, took a job in Sydney and met Michelle. We moved to Granite Springs around ten years ago – I think I told you that. What about you?' He threw a glance her way.

'Nothing as exciting. As I told you, I grew up in Granite Springs, met David, married young. He was a local dentist – came back right after uni to set up a practice – and I ran the practice for him right up till…' she swallowed, '…till it became unfeasible.'

'I'm sorry.' Nick put a comforting hand on her thigh.

Kay glowed. She was going to forget the past, forget her concerns and enjoy today. It might never be repeated. Nick might find her boring company. *She* might decide it was all too hard. But today, with their respective children otherwise occupied – Nick had said Sam was studying at a friend's home and this time, he believed her – they were just two people enjoying a pleasant day out.

'We're here.' Nick pulled up outside an innocuous-looking building in the doorway of which a collection of well-dressed people were milling around.

Half an hour later they stood looking at each other while people around them jostled to get a better view of what Kay thought were weird daubs.

'I'm afraid I don't understand what the artist is trying to say,' she murmured, hoping she didn't sound too unappreciative.

'Me neither.' Nick grinned. 'Let's get out of here and find somewhere we can get a drink. Saturday afternoon in Canberra, there must be somewhere open. I seem to recall when I was a student here… Though that was a few years ago.'

Feeling as if they were a couple of kids, they almost ran out of the building past couples commenting on the ingenious juxtaposition of shapes in this piece and the astute use of colour in that one.

'Phew!' Nick exclaimed when they reached the car again. 'I'm sorry I subjected you to that. I'd heard it was an exhibition by an up and coming artist and thought it'd prove interesting.'

'I can think of other words,' Kay said, chuckling, glad she wasn't alone in her opinion of the work. 'But some people seem to like it, so I'm glad for the artist.'

'Mmm, no accounting for taste. Now, I think we need a nice glass of wine with something to nibble. Or would you prefer tea or coffee?'

'Wine sounds good.'

'Okay. I've heard about this spot in Braddon. A good mate – Mark – talks about it. He's more *au fait* with the social scene than I am. He comes over here a lot.'

'Not Mark Coatts from the School of Business? He has quite a reputation.'

'That's the one. We met at uni and reconnected when I arrived in Granite Springs. He was the last person I expected to meet in a country town, but it seems to suit him.'

Kay pursed her lips. She'd heard all about Mark and his womanising. But Nick didn't seem at all like his friend.

They drove a little way, then Nick pointed to a much more salubrious establishment than the one they'd left. 'Hopscotch – that's it,' Nick said, pulling into a parking spot. 'Lucky to find a place to park. Canberra's not like Granite Springs. Mark says it's a bar and grill, so we should be able to find something. What do you think?'

For Kay, the day had taken on a surreal aspect. She allowed herself to be guided inside and to be seated facing Nick on a high stool at one end of a long table in a large barnlike room. Nick disappeared to return with a glass of white wine and one of beer.

'I've ordered a mushroom dish and calamari. I hope that's okay. Maybe I should have asked you first?' He brushed a hand across the top of his head and glanced around. 'This is more Mark's sort of place than mine. But at least it's not busy. I expect it starts rocking later in the evening. We'll be long gone by then.'

'That's fine,' Kay murmured, beginning to feel this was an adventure or a dream from which she might soon awaken. She took a sip of wine.

By the time their food arrived, the wine had relaxed Kay and she was beginning to enjoy herself. Nick was fun to be with, amusing her with tales of his time in Canberra as a student.

'But I always yearned to live in a smaller town,' he said. 'After the States, it seemed I fell on my feet with the Sydney job, but Granite Springs was everything I'd dreamed of – a good place to put down roots and bring up children. I even envisaged an acreage, but…'

'What happened?'

Nick stroked his beard. 'I suppose you could say Michelle happened. She seemed happy enough to move to the country with me when the job came up, but I don't think she ever really settled here. The very idea of living on an acreage was anathema to her, so we built the house I still live in. She was always more of a city person, I guess.' He sighed.

'You'd like Jo's place,' Kay said thoughtfully. 'She and Col live on twenty acres outside town. It's so peaceful there, I love to visit. You should come with me sometime,' she said without thinking.

'I'd love to. Is that the friend I met having coffee with you out on the campus?'

'Yes. Jo Ford; used to be Jo Slater. She…'

'Steady on. Not Col Ford's wife? He was my solicitor till he retired. Now I'm dealing with his partner.'

'Jo used to be married to Gordon Slater,' Kay said. 'She and Col married just before Christmas. It all seems a bit incestuous to me, but they seem to manage.'

Nick was silent for a moment, then changed the subject.

'Your daughter – will she be staying with you for long?'

'I hope not... I mean, she has her own life to live, and we'd drive each other mad before long.'

'And you said your son lives in England?'

'Yes,' she said. 'With his wife and two boys. They're coming to visit for Easter. They'll be arriving next weekend.'

'Yes, you said. That'll be nice for you, having both your children under one roof. I'm looking forward to having my two with me for Easter, too.'

'Right.' There didn't seem to be anything else to say. Was this his way of indicating they wouldn't be seeing each other outside work till after Easter?

But Nick had something to add. 'Sam will be going back up with Ryan for the last week of her holidays. Maybe...' he gazed into Kay's eyes, turning her knees to water, ...maybe you could come to dinner again when there's no danger of my teenage daughter barging in to disturb us?'

Kay swallowed hard. Was he suggesting what she thought he was? And if so, how did she feel about it? Her head warred with the other parts of her body that yearned for a more physical relationship. Taking a deep breath, she muttered huskily, 'That would be nice.'

Twenty-two

Kay was filled with excitement as she watched the small plane taxi to a stop just outside the passenger lounge at Granite Springs airport. The heat of the summer was a thing of the past and there was quite a nip in the air. She shivered slightly, wishing she'd thrown a wrap over her tailored blouse and pants.

The passengers began to stream across the tarmac, and Kay peeled her eyes, finally catching sight of the familiar figure of a tall lanky man, his dark hair flying in the breeze. Beside him was Jess, looking blooming and pregnant. The two boys, much taller than she remembered or had imagined, and more real than in their photos, were running beside them, waving madly.

She waved back, her heart thumping. Her big boy was home!

As they came closer, the boys slowed down, then all four were there, standing in front of her.

'Hi, Mum. You're looking good.' Kay was enveloped in a tight hug, Adam's arms almost lifting her off the ground. He was so like David had been at that age. It was like being back in time. For a moment, she forgot where she was and was eighteen again, feeling the warmth of her first love.

'Grandma?' a small voice asked, and she turned to receive an awkward hug from the older of her two grandsons.

'Adam, you look just like your dad,' she said, as the boy wriggled out of her grasp.

'And Luke,' she said, picking up the smaller one. 'Wait till you meet your cousin. Noah's been looking forward to you coming. He's just a little older than you are.' She rubbed her nose into his hair, loving the little boy smell, this time of apples and the remnants of two days in an airplane.

'Jess. Welcome.' Kay turned to her daughter-in-law who'd been silent during their greetings. 'It's so good to see you. How was the flight?'

'Tiring,' Jess said. 'It's good to be here at last. It's been a long time.'

'Three years,' Kay said. Adam and Jess had made a quick trip for David's funeral, leaving the boys behind with Jess's parents. 'How are your mum and dad?' she asked, remembering.

'They're well. They send their regards. They're getting older, of course.'

'Aren't we all?' Kay laughed, trying to recollect how old they were. Older than she was, she thought, recalling the wedding she and David had attended on their only trip to the UK.

'We should fetch our bags, Mum. Can you keep the boys with you?' Adam was eager to move on, never one for harking back to the past or stating the obvious.

'Zoe still with you, then?' he asked when they were on their way home. 'I heard you mention young Noah. He'd be what, now – four, five?'

'He'll be five in July, as you should know. He and Luke were born only a month apart. He started school this year. I expect Luke will start this year, too?'

'When we get back. Lukey's looking forward to it, aren't you, sweetie?' Jess asked. 'It'll give me time to prepare for the bub.'

'And how is my sister?' Adam asked, his voice heavy with sarcasm.

'Oh, Zoe doesn't change much. She's been trying – unsuccessfully, I might add – to organise me ever since she got here. Maybe your arrival will help her curtail her more sweeping reforms.'

Twenty-three

'Come on, Sam! We'll be late!'

'Okay, okay. I don't know why I have to come, too,' Sam grumbled, pulling on a worn-out hoodie and shrugging a bag over her shoulder, her hand grasping her mobile as if her life depended on it.

She probably believed it did, Nick thought. It was a pity the holiday in the two states didn't coincide. Sam still had a week of term to go while Ryan was already on holiday. Still, it meant they'd have a week together here, then another week together with their mother at the other end of Sam's holidays.

He hated how the decision he and Michelle had made resulted in their children being separated. But they seemed to be coping. At least Sam was. She had all her friends here. Hopefully, with Ryan here for two weeks, Nick'd be able to find out a bit more about how his son was doing. The weekly phone calls and the occasional skype didn't tell him much.

Despite Sam's delaying tactics, they arrived at the airport in plenty of time. They were walking into the terminal from the car when Nick saw a familiar figure walking in the other direction, accompanied by a younger couple and two small boys. He stopped in his tracks, wondering whether to call out to Kay, then Sam yelled, 'Da…ad!' and he followed her into the building. It was just as well, he supposed, as the door slid closed behind them. He could have precipitated an awkward situation. Kay might not have wanted to introduce him to her son and his family. And if she did, how would she introduce him?

As Professor Kerr her boss, or as Nick Kerr, her… friend? Is that what he was?

He hurried to follow Sam who was looking longingly at the display of drinks.

'Can I have a Coke, Dad?' she wheedled. 'Ryan's plane won't be here for ages.'

Checking his watch, Nick realised she was right and, fossicking for a few coins in his pocket, handed them to her. 'Off you go, and get me a coffee too, will you? Black.' He knew the coffee might be undrinkable, but it would help pass the time. He was scrutinising the arrivals board when he heard a voice behind him.

'Your boy coming down for the holidays?'

He turned quickly to see Faye Kershaw standing behind him, a satisfied smile on her face. Nick groaned. He hadn't seen the woman since that time at The Riverside when she'd made him feel so awkward.

'Hello, Faye. Yes, Ryan is coming down for a couple of weeks. What brings you here?'

'My nephew – Belinda's boy. He's coming to spend a few days with me. She moved to Brisbane when she married, and Tyler likes the country. He must be around Ryan's age. Maybe we could do something together?'

Wow, she's persistent.

'I think Ryan'll want to catch up with all his old friends down here,' he said politely. 'But I appreciate the thought.'

'Oh!' she pouted.

Nick remembered that pout. And, in this light, he could see the make-up caked in the lines around her eyes and mouth. An image of Kay came into his mind. She made no attempt to hide the signs of age, experience, and her suffering, and he respected her for it. She was so much more of a real woman than this painted doll.

But Faye didn't give up. 'I haven't seen you around,' she said. 'Have you been keeping out of my way? You naughty boy!'

Nick cringed. What had Michelle ever seen in this woman?

'Heard from Michelle recently?' she asked.

'No.'

Her face fell. 'She seemed to drop off the face of the earth when she and Terry headed north. Having too much fun, I expect.'

'Here's your coffee, Dad.'

Nick had never been so glad to see Sam. 'Thanks, honey.'

'Hello, Sam.'

'Hi, Mrs Kershaw.'

'Looking forward to seeing your brother?'

'I suppose.'

She tried again. 'You must miss your mum.'

'Mmm. Look, Dad. The plane's coming in now.' Sam pointed to where the Qantas-link was just touching down.

'So it is. If you'll excuse us, Faye.' Nick put a hand on Sam's shoulder and moved off.

'What did she want?' Sam wanted to know. 'I know she was part of Mum's group, but Mum never liked her much. She always thought she had the hots for you.' Then something seemed to occur to her. 'She hasn't... You didn't... ugh! Gross!'

'No. I don't much like her either, but I think she's a lonely woman,' Nick said, deciding to be charitable. And it was probably true. There were a lot of single women in Granite Springs, single men, too. But that didn't mean that they chose to pair up. Many of the men were single by choice, and there was no doubt a dearth of them in their age group. His thoughts turned to Kay again. She must have been lonely after her husband died, and that was three years ago.

'There he is!' Sam was pointing with her Coke can to where a lanky youth was descending the mobile stairway, a rucksack carelessly slung across one shoulder. He seemed to have grown in the three months he'd been gone. Nick knew from their phone calls that Ryan's voice, breaking when he'd left, was now almost as deep as his own, but he hadn't bargained for the spurt in growth.

'Hello, son.'

'Dad.' Ryan twisted out of Nick's hug. 'Can I have a slug?' he asked Sam, pointing to her drink.

'Get your own,' she retorted, before relenting and handing it to him.

'Hungry? Did you have anything to eat on the plane?' Nick asked.

'Starving,' Ryan replied.

'How about some lunch, then? The Bean Sprout do?'

Nick saw Sam and Ryan give each other a look.

'What?'

'The Bean Sprout, it's so…'

'Well, you guys choose.'

'Anywhere I can have a burger and chips,' Ryan said.

'Suit you too, Sam?'

'Whatever.'

'Okay, let's go.'

Once seated in one of the town's fast food eateries, Ryan began to open up. 'Everything looks the same,' he said. 'It even smells the same.' He sniffed appreciatively.

'Eeew! You're disgusting!' But Sam couldn't hide her smile. Nick relaxed. Everything was back to normal. Though it wasn't, was it? Michelle wasn't here. Things in this family would never be *normal* again.

'What's the matter, Dad?' Ryan asked, grinning like the Cheshire Cat when their burgers arrived, along with two thick shakes for the youngsters and a coffee for Nick.

He closed his eyes as he tasted the drink – much better than the one he'd hastily downed at the airport.

'Nothing, son. Just thinking. What do you want to do while you're down? I can take time off this week.'

Ryan's face took on a haunted look at the prospect of hanging out with his dad.

'Dunno. Chill out, I guess. School's still in here, Jake and Kyle said. We'll meet up after school, or they may ditch school and we can go down the river. I can catch up with them after this.'

Nick pursed his lips but didn't speak. It was too soon to come the heavy father.

'That's okay, isn't it?' Ryan asked, clearly seeing Nick's disappointment.

'Sure. It's your holiday. But I would like to spend some time with you.'

'Sure.' But Ryan didn't appear thrilled at the prospect.

'How's your mum?' he asked at last, after trying unsuccessfully to find out more about Ryan's life in Queensland. Hopefully he'd become more communicative as the weeks went on.

'All right, I think. She's always with *him*!'

The tone of Ryan's voice told Nick a lot, but he couldn't allow him to get away with disparaging his mother's new partner – regardless of what Nick himself might think of him.

'He's called Terry,' he corrected.

'Terry, then.' Ryan kicked the leg of the table, while Sam smirked and slurped up the last few drops of her shake.

Once home, both Sam and Ryan disappeared to catch up with friends, leaving Nick wondering what to do with himself. His children were home, but here he was all alone in the house again. He wandered around, noting once more how unlived in the place must have seemed to Kay, then on an impulse he headed out to drive to the nearest large store selling all sorts of decorative items.

Although feeling uncomfortable, he forced himself to select a couple of brightly coloured cushions he thought might look good on the new sofa, a coffee table and floor lamp, but he drew the line at choosing paintings, even though he knew the walls needed brightening up. Maybe Kay could be of help there? But, right now, she'd be busy with her own family. Although he'd only caught a glimpse of her at the airport, she'd looked happy.

Once home again, his new purchases spread around, Nick felt satisfied it was an improvement. He decided to fix himself coffee and spend the rest of the afternoon in the study trying to make a dent in the conference paper he now regretted having submitted. When the call for papers had come out, it had only been a germ of an idea. But now he had to put flesh on the bones of it if he was to emerge from the conference with his reputation intact. He'd never learn.

The noise of the front door slamming brought him out of his study to see Sam running upstairs.

'Sam,' he called. 'What's up?'

He received a mumbled reply that sounded like, 'Nothing', before her bedroom door slammed too. As he was debating whether or not to follow her upstairs, the front door opened again, and Ryan wandered in, whistling tunelessly. At least one of his children seemed happy.

'Hi, Dad. Is Sam home?'

'She just came in.'

'I saw her in town with those friends of hers and a group of boys. She seemed to be arguing with one of them, then ran off. I tried to catch up with her.'

'She's in her room. Best leave her for a bit. I think she's upset. Did you meet up with your mates?'

'Yeah. They're all going fishing at the river tomorrow. I said I'd go too.' He gave his father a pleading look Nick couldn't resist.

'Okay, I suppose. Are there any fish there?' Nick pictured the murky waters of the river which had been flowing sluggishly since summer, waiting for some good rain upstream.

'Dunno. Jake says there are.' He shrugged, giving Nick the impression *fishing* was a euphemism for some other activity. *Drugs? Alcohol? Girls? Or just tobacco?*

'Right, well, no monkey business. Your mum'll never forgive me if you get into trouble down here.'

'As if she'd care.' Ryan's voice was low, but the words were clear. 'And it's not *me*, you should be worrying about.'

'What do you mean?'

'I recognised those guys Sam and her mates were hanging around with.' Ryan's eyes refused to meet Nick's.

Nick exhaled loudly. This was supposed to be a relaxing two weeks – time he could spend with both his children, a happy family time.

'What's for dinner?'

Nick sighed. 'Pizza?'

'Good.'

'Want to help?'

But Ryan was already on his way upstairs.

Nick busied himself fixing a couple of large pizzas, finding unexpected pleasure in layering the tomatoes, olives, pepperoni, and mushrooms and topping the lot with slices of mozzarella.

'Dinner!' he yelled upstairs when he'd set the cooked pizzas on the table along with a bowl of salad and glasses of juice for Sam and Ryan. For himself, he'd poured a much-needed glass of cabernet merlot, having resisted the urge to have one while cooking.

Dinner was a pretty silent affair, both children rejecting Nick's attempts at conversation. Finally, Sam pushed away her half-eaten slice of pizza. 'I'm not really hungry,' she said, sliding her chair from the table and disappearing to her room again.

'Fancy a game of scrabble?' Nick asked Ryan when the pizzas had been demolished.

'Scrabble?' Ryan made it sound as if Nick had suggested something disgusting. 'I have my iPad upstairs. I just need to…' And he was off too.

Nick's phone pinged. The message was from Michelle.

Don't let Ryan have too much screentime.

Yeah, right.

He made his way upstairs determined to find out what was upsetting Sam. He knocked at the closed door. There was no reply. This time, he pushed the door open to find her sitting cross-legged on her bed staring at her iPhone, tears streaming down her cheeks. She raised her head as he walked in.

'What's wrong, sweetheart?' Nick moved toward her, but Sam shook her head. 'You wouldn't understand, Dad.' She dropped her eyes to focus on the phone again, shutting Nick out.

Walking heavily downstairs, Nick scratched his head. *What had he done wrong?* And neither of them had commented on his attempts to make the place more homely. *Had they even noticed?*

He poured himself a beer and sat on the new sofa. He could enjoy the improvements he'd made, even if his kids didn't. He contemplated the day, his disappointment in Ryan's desire to spend time with his friends rather than his dad, his comments about Sam's friends, her distress. What was going on? He was on the point of going up to her room again when there was a little voice behind him.

'Dad? I'm sorry. Mum said I shouldn't do that. I should share more. But, I don't…' She curled up beside him, just as she had when she was a little girl.

Nick's arm automatically went around her shoulders, his hand in her hair – hair so like her mother's. What's up, possum?' he asked, using the baby name she'd forbidden him to ever use again when she turned twelve. But tonight, it didn't seem to bother her.

Sam shook her head. 'Girl stuff. I can handle it. I wish Mum was here.'

Nick felt inadequate. He was a poor substitute for Michelle at a time like this. But he had to make an attempt. 'Try me,' he said.

Sam sniffed. 'We were in town and…'

'Is it something to do with the boys Ryan saw you with?'

'Ryan?' Sam drew away and glared at Nick. 'What did he say?'

'Only that he saw you and your friends with a group of boys, and you were arguing. Is that what this is about?'

'Sort of.' Sam sniffed again, then seemed to come to a decision. 'It was Brett Cooper. You know…'

Nick's lips tightened. He felt a vein pulse on his forehead. He knew exactly who Brett Cooper was. He was a local tearaway who'd escaped juvenile detention several times by the skin of his teeth. Good-looking, he always seemed to have a group of girls around him. Nick knew that drug dealing was the least of the suspicions the police had about him. But to say that wouldn't help Sam – or give her the confidence to trust her dad. 'I know Brett,' he said.

'He said I was...' she sobbed, '...he asked me to the disco on the weekend, then today... Dad, he said he'd changed his mind, that I wasn't smart enough, that he was taking Gai Andrews instead. He laughed at me.'

'My poor poppet. It sounds to me as if you're the smart one. I know it's not what you want to hear, but you're better off without him. I'm sure there are other boys out there who want to be your friend.'

'But...' She sobbed again, then pulled herself together. 'Thanks Dad. I'm going to bed now.'

Left alone again, Nick sighed. For the first time since she left, he missed Michelle. She'd have known what to say to Sam, what to do.

This single father thing wasn't going to be easy.

Twenty-four

'Hey, sis. This must be Noah?' Adam greeted his sister as they entered the house.

'Noah, this is your Uncle Adam and Aunt Jess and these two are your cousins – Adam and Luke.'

Noah hid behind Zoe as Kay made the introductions.

'Hi, Noah!' It was young Adam who spoke first, while Luke gazed at Noah, a surprised expression on his face.

'I told you Noah was your age,' Kay said, hoping the two boys would make friends.

'He's always a bit shy with strangers,' Jess said, hastily adding, 'I know you're not really strangers, but you are to Luke.'

'Give him time and you'll be wishing you had the shy version back again,' Adam said with a chuckle.

'I don't know how you managed the trip like that – and with two children,' Zoe said, glaring at Jess's pregnant belly with something akin to horror.

There was an uncomfortable silence, broken only by the sound of Milly mewing for attention. She'd snuck into the room when no one was looking and wanted to welcome the newcomers.

'It's a cat,' Luke said. 'Grandma has a cat.'

'That's Milly.' Noah found his voice and reached out to Milly who managed to evade his clutching fingers and leapt up on the sofa. 'He's *my* grandma's cat.'

'I'm Luke's grandma too, Noah,' Kay said gently. This wasn't how she'd envisaged their reunion.

'Luke loves cats,' young Adam told Kay in a serious voice. 'But Dad says we can't have one, not with a new baby.'

'You're having a new baby?' Noah's eyes widened. He turned to Zoe. 'Mummy, why can't we have one? Lottie and Livvy have Emily Rose and...'

'That's enough,' Zoe said.

Adam raised his eyebrows towards Kay, who shrugged. 'How about some tea?' she asked. 'Zoe, could you show your brother and his family to their rooms while I get it ready?'

'Let me help,' Jess said, following Kay into the kitchen, leaving Adam to his sister and the three boys to their own devices in the living room, where Milly was enjoying being the centre of attention.

'Sorry about Zoe,' Kay apologised. 'It hasn't been easy for her.'

'Or for you, I imagine.'

'No.' Kay filled the electric jug, sliced a banana and fig loaf she'd made earlier, and emptied a packet of biscuits onto a plate, embarrassed by her daughter-in-law's sympathy.

By the time they were all seated in the living room again, with Milly banished outside, the incident was all but forgotten. But Zoe's bitterness had laid a pall over what had been, for Kay, a joyous occasion. She just hoped her daughter wasn't going to allow her resentment over Jess's pregnancy to spoil their entire stay.

*

'It's good to be here,' Adam said, stretching out his legs 'But it seems odd without Dad.'

Kay nodded. The others had all gone to bed, Jess and the boys giving in to their jetlag, and Zoe taking Noah off with a murmured excuse. She and Adam were sitting out in the courtyard, the sharp scent of the tall lemon-scented gum in their nostrils as they enjoyed a last glass of wine. 'You're so like him, you know. When he was your age. He was a fine figure of a man.'

'Mum, you don't think... what they said about Dad... he couldn't have... could he?' Adam rolled the glass between his hands and gazed at his feet.

Kay stifled a sigh. This was something she and her son had never discussed. Adam had been long gone when all the rumours started. He remembered his father as a well-respected upright citizen, pillar of the community. What was she to say?

'I didn't believe them at first. How could I? David was the man I loved, had loved for most of my life. He was your dad, yours and Zoe's. I believed it had to be a vicious rumour. But when more girls came forward, when he withdrew more and more into himself, wouldn't talk about it with me, then...' She drew a ragged breath and put a hand over Adam's, taking strength from him. 'That morning, I think I knew. I knew even before the police told me. I think we have to believe the girls, Adam. They were telling the truth. But I still don't believe your dad was the monster he was painted. He was a good man – before all this happened. And he was a good father to you and Zoe. That's why it hurts so much that she won't talk about him, won't even mention his name.'

'Is that why, apart from that one with the four of us, there are no photos of him around – not even your wedding photo?'

'I hid them while Zoe is here. There was no sense in antagonising her,' Kay said, saddened by the loss of the picture she'd spoken to every morning. She'd bring them out again when Zoe left.

'Hmm. We have several sitting around at home – of Jess's family too, though we see them regularly. We want the boys to know their roots; to know who their grandparents are, even if...' Adam's voice broke too.

'And what is it with Zoe?' he asked. 'On the phone you said something about a disagreement with Eric over having another baby? Surely that's not worth leaving Brisbane for? What about her job? She's always been so proud of how she's climbing up the career ladder. How can she do that if she's stuck here in Granite Springs?' He drew a hand through his hair. 'Sorry, Mum, I didn't mean that the way it sounded. There's nothing wrong with Granite Springs.'

'It's all right. I know what you mean. It's not exactly up to your sister's standards. I have to believe she's just biding her time till Eric – as she puts it – comes to his senses. But I think that this time, she may have tried him too far. Though...' Kay tapped on her glass, '...I'm surprised Eric hasn't demanded she take Noah home.'

'I know what I'd do if she was *my* wife.'

'You chose well. Jess is delightful. You have two lovely boys and maybe this next one will be a little girl?'

'I don't mind but Jess would like a girl. It would help even things up a bit. I sometimes think she gets swamped by the three of us, even if Luke's only little.'

'A little girl would be lovely.' Kay thought of Jo with her three granddaughters, all living close by.

Adam yawned. 'I think the flight's beginning to get to me too. Sorry, Mum.'

'Not at all, it's been lovely having this time with you. I'm really looking forward to the next two weeks. It'll all go far too quickly.'

'Then it'll be your turn to visit us – for the new baby.'

'That would be lovely, darling.'

Kay picked up the two empty glasses, and Adam helped her up, giving her a tight hug in the process. His beard tickled her cheek, reminding her of another beard which had tickled her in much the same way.

'Goodnight, son,' she said, as he disappeared through the doorway.

'Well, Milly,' she said to the cat, who was prowling around looking for geckos to catch, 'We have a full house tonight. I just hope Zoe can behave herself. Come on, puss.' Kay led the way into the laundry and checked the cat flap before giving Milly a kiss and a cuddle. The cat leapt up onto the top of the washing machine and settled on the old towel Kay kept there for her. 'Just till we're on our own again,' she said, turning off the light and closing the door behind her. Zoe had made her view on wandering cats very clear, and Kay wasn't sure how Jess felt about them. Better to be safe than sorry, and Milly didn't mind being confined there overnight.

But, as she prepared for bed and examined her face in the mirror, it wasn't *her* family in Kay's thoughts.

She knew that across town there was another family settling down for the night. Kay wondered how Nick was getting on with his two. She didn't think he'd seen her, but she'd caught a glimpse of him at the airport just as they were leaving. His daughter had been with him, but he'd have his son home now, too. Two teenagers – he'd have his hands full!

And in two weeks, they were going to have dinner again. She couldn't suppress the anticipation that flooded her at the prospect, even though, deep down, she knew there could be no future in any relationship with Nick Kerr.

Twenty-five

Adam's visit was almost over. The two weeks had passed in a flash and now there were only a few days left. Today was Good Friday and on Monday they'd be going back to England. And Zoe would still be here.

At least she'd managed to curb some of her more outrageous remarks during their visit. After that first night when she'd shocked Adam and Jess with her veiled reference to Jess's pregnancy, she kept a low profile. But Kay had been delighted to see how well Noah and Luke played together. She'd even hoped Zoe would reconsider having another child, seeing Noah so happy with his cousin. It was a faint hope.

'All set, Mum?' Adam walked into the kitchen, rubbing his hands together. 'I don't know when I was last at a picnic race meeting. I'm looking forward to showing Jess a slice of Australian country life. Young Adam's looking forward to it too. His first race meeting. He's planning to brag to his friends when he goes back to school.'

Kay turned from where she'd been packing the picnic hamper with rolls, ham, tomatoes, cheese and a few other delicacies. 'Almost there. Can you fetch a bottle of chardonnay and a couple of beers from the fridge – and some juice for the kids. Then we can be off.'

It was sheer luck that the Granite Springs Turf Club had decided to revive the old Easter Picnics this year. It had been a popular event when she and David were growing up but had fallen into disfavour with the increasing popularity of the July races. Fortunately, the weather promised to be on their side, though there was an ominous bank of clouds in the distance.

'Mum!' Looking exhausted already, Jess walked in to give Kay a kiss on the cheek. 'Adam's told me so much about these country race meetings. I can't wait to experience one for myself. You're sure it's all right for Lukey to come?'

'My goodness, yes. It's more like a family day out than a race meeting. The horses are almost an afterthought. Some people never get beyond the car park.'

'Really?'

'I want to see the horses race,' young Adam said, walking in. 'We will, Grandma, won't we?'

'Of course we will.' Kay smiled at the boy. He was so like his dad had been at that age; her heart filled with pleasure just looking at him.

'Do we have to go?' Zoe wandered in with a sullen expression on her face, Noah following at her heels.

'Can we go to see the horses, Grandma?' the little boy asked. 'Mum says...'

'Yes to both of you.' Sometimes – often – Zoe infuriated Kay and this was one of those times. 'It's a family day out. It's not often we are all together. It'll be fun.' She crouched down to Noah's height. 'First, we'll have a picnic by the car. We're packing food and drinks and chairs. We'll need your car to fit everyone in,' she said to Zoe, rising to speak to her, 'and we'll be leaving soon. Are you intending to go like that?' She looked pointedly at Zoe's outfit which was more suited to a day lounging around at home than a country race meeting. 'Everyone will be dressed up, it's quite an occasion. Don't you remember?'

Zoe walked out muttering something that sounded like, 'I'm trying not to.'

'What's bugging my dear sister now?' Adam asked, staring after her.

Unexpectedly, the answer came from Noah.

'I talked to my daddy this morning,' he said. 'He has an Easter egg for me and says he's coming to see me.'

You could have heard a pin drop.

Kay was first to recover. 'That's nice, Noah. Did he say when?'

Noah shook his head and ran off to try to catch Milly who was lying in a pool of sunlight.

'That should be interesting,' Adam commented.

'Not for you. I don't expect him to arrive this weekend. But that could explain Zoe's mood this morning.'

'Zoe doesn't need an explanation for her moods. My sister's always been like this when she doesn't get her own way, Mum. She's not being fair to Eric. He's a nice guy. I know how I'd feel if Jess bolted with one or both of the boys. He has my vote.'

'Jess would never do that.'

'But Zoe did. And it would serve her right if Eric sued for divorce and got custody.'

'Oh, no!' Kay put a hand to her heart. 'I hope it won't come to that. Noah needs both his parents. I just wish Zoe would see reason. It would be lovely for Noah to have a little brother or sister. He's so enjoyed having Luke to play with and he loves Emily Rose. She's the little sister of his friends Lottie and Livvy.'

'The twins?' Adam chuckled. 'He's been telling Luke about them. Having him wonder if there could be two babies in his mummy's tummy. Thankfully not!'

Fifteen minutes later, Zoe reappeared, this time she was wearing a smart summer dress and jacket with high-heeled white sandals and carrying a cartwheel straw hat. 'Will this do?' she asked, pirouetting in front of Kay.

'You look lovely, dear. Now, can we get moving? We want to find a good spot to set up in the car park.'

All except Zoe were laughing as they piled into the two cars, now bursting at the seams with adults, children, canvas chairs and picnic baskets – Kay had managed to fill two of these.

"Bye, 'bye, Milly,' Noah called to the cat, who was sitting on the front doorstep watching them leave, and they all set off.

*

'I didn't think it would be this crowded,' Zoe grumbled, when they finally found a spot to park the two cars together.

'It's Easter and school holidays. There will be a lot of visitors here. Oh, there's Jo and Col.' She waved furiously as she caught sight of her old friend several car spaces away.

'Twins!' Noah yelled, and grabbed Luke's hand to drag him away. Their older brother followed more slowly. He'd heard a lot about these identical twins too.

'Where are you going?' Adam called after the pair.

'It's okay,' Kay said. 'The twins and their parents are with Jo and Col just over there. They're not going far away. Do you remember Eve Slater?'

Adam looked across, squinting. 'I don't think so. Should I?'

'Maybe not. She was in Zoe's year – too young for you to notice, I expect.'

'Not one of your old girlfriends?' Jess nudged him with a grin. 'I was teasing him about reconnecting with his exes on this trip.'

Adam turned red. 'Nothing of the sort.'

Kay felt good. This was the way it should be, the family together, a little friendly teasing.

'Can I help?' It was Jess, always ready to give a hand.

'You just sit down and rest,' Kay said. 'I'll unpack the baskets if you can put out the chairs, Adam. But Adam had already begun to unfold four chairs and also the old camping table Kay had thought to pack at the last minute. 'We didn't bring seats for the children, but I suspect they won't be still long enough to sit down.'

'Where's Zoe?' Adam asked, gazing around. His sister was nowhere to be seen.

'Who knows?' Kay replied.

'There she is,' Jess pointed to where Zoe was picking her way across the clumps of grass and making her way between the parked cars. She was leaning on the arm of a tall man who looked vaguely familiar to Kay.

'Guess who I found wandering around?' Zoe asked gaily, the man with her appearing faintly embarrassed.

'Hello, Adam, Mrs Jackson,' he said.

Kay peered at him, the sun in her eyes distorting her vision. The tanned skin and close-cropped bleached blond hair confused her for a few moments, then she recognised the face, now fifteen years older, but quite unmistakable.

Adam beat her to it. 'Miles Younger. What are you doing back here? Last I heard you were living it up in some tropical clime – Thailand, wasn't it?'

Miles Younger gave a self-conscious smile and shook free of Zoe's grasp. 'That's right. There's money to be made in South-East Asia with the right contacts.'

'And you'd have those.' Adam didn't sound impressed.

Miles tapped his nose.

Kay remembered him now. Miles had been in Adam's year at school, though not a friend. Popular with the girls, Zoe had a huge crush on him and had been thrilled when he invited her to his Year Twelve dance. She'd thought it was going to be the beginning of something special, but he'd left town at the end of the school year. Kay didn't think he'd been back since.

'Ah… Mum passed away a few weeks ago. I'm just back to finalise things. I should go, Zoe. Call you.' He backed away. Clearly, he didn't want to stay around to be interrogated by Zoe's family.

'You weren't very nice to him.' Zoe rounded on her brother. 'I asked him to join us for a drink.'

'A drink? Him? Do you even know what he does in Thailand?'

'What does it matter? He's good company, always has been.'

'Rumour has it he runs a nightclub – otherwise known as a go-go bar. And you know what happens in those places?'

'You never did like him. I think you were jealous.'

'Jealous of that?'

Kay and Jess looked on with amusement as the two sparred, just like they had as teenagers, Kay thought. Some things never changed.

'Just remember you're a married woman,' Kay said.

'I'm not likely to forget it, with Eric on the phone demanding to talk to his son, and Noah whining to see his dad again. I need a drink.'

'Coming up.' Adam unscrewed the wine and poured two glasses. 'Juice for you, Jess? I'll stick to beer. Should we eat now, Mum?'

'Good idea. I'll fetch the boys.' Kay knew she had to get away from Zoe before she said something she'd regret. *How could she have raised such an unfeeling child?*

By the time Kay herded the three boys back – she'd discovered young Adam making friends with Jo's two grandsons – Zoe had calmed down and was helping herself to some food.

'Mummy!' Luke raced up to Jess and flung himself on her lap, causing her to caution him to take care, 'It's what Noah says. They look just the same as each other.'

'And what about you, Adam?' his father asked him.

Adam shrugged. 'They're just two girls. I saw the horses first. They look amazing. I've never been so close to one before.'

'You didn't...?' Jess asked in a worried tone.

'He'd have been quite safe,' Kay said. 'No one's going to let him near the animals. How did you end up with my friend, Jo?'

'Is Mrs Slater your friend? I met Tim and Liam looking at the horses. They were with their dad. Tim's the same age as me. I walked back with them, and Luke was there with Noah.'

'Yes, she's my friend, and she's Mrs Ford now. I should have thought of introducing you to her grandsons earlier, but...' She hesitated. She couldn't tell Adam that the boys' mother was so difficult to communicate with. 'Well, I'm glad you've met them now.'

'Mum!' Zoe's warning remark came as they were packing up, ready to watch the races. Kay looked up to see Nick weaving his way across the parking lot, followed by a sulky Sam and an eager young boy who could only be Ryan.

'Oh!'

Adam and Jess looked at her in surprise.

'What is it, Mum?' Adam said, stopping in the middle of loading the chairs into the boot.

'Nothing. It's Professor Kerr, the dean of the faculty. He...'

At that moment, the trio reached Kay and her family.

'Hello, Kay,' Nick said, 'I thought we might see you here. Enjoying the day?' His glance took in the entire group. 'You've already met Sam, and this young man is Ryan. Are you going to introduce me to your family?'

Kay made the introductions, referring to Nick as Professor Kerr.

'Call me Nick,' he said easily, offering a hand to Adam. 'Any good tips? I like the sound of *Brave Heart*.'

Kay blushed. He couldn't mean...? Not in front of everyone. But it seemed he was only talking about a horse.

'I saw that one too,' Adam replied. 'Looks good, but my money's on *Silver Dollar*.'

'Good luck. Good to see you, Kay.'

They walked away, leaving Kay confused.

'That your boss, Mum?' Adam asked.

'He's a bit more than that,' Zoe said, winking at her mother.

'More?' Adam appeared puzzled, then the penny dropped. 'You mean? Oh, Mum, I'm happy for you.'

'Me too,' Jess said, giving Kay a hug. 'You need someone special in your life. It's been three years since David died.'

'But he's not… It's not…'

But even as she spoke, Kay wondered if what they all imagined was possible. Could she really find love again?

Twenty-six

A whole child-free week! As he drove home from the airport, Nick couldn't believe how much the idea excited him. He loved his kids and having Ryan here for two weeks had been fantastic, even though he and Sam were at loggerheads much of the time. But that's what brothers and sisters did. Now they were both with their mother – Sam for the last week of her holidays and Ryan until his next holidays. It was only fair, what he'd agreed with Michelle, and it seemed to be working out.

It had been hard to part with Ryan that morning, the boy clinging to his dad despite his attempts to be a cool teenager. But now Nick was free – free to spend time with Kay. They'd been very circumspect during Ryan's visit, introducing her only as Nick's PA when they met at the races. Sam had sniggered, but Ryan had been too excited about being at a race meeting to notice.

Once home, Nick realised he had some cleaning up to do before the house was ready for entertaining. Having two teenagers rampaging around the place for two weeks had left its mark. He tuned the radio to his favourite station and set to work.

It was late afternoon before Nick felt the house was presentable again. In fact, he thought it looked pretty good. He gazed around the tidy living room with satisfaction. Just time to freshen up and organise dinner.

Having already treated Kay to his prowess on the barbecue, he wanted to impress her with a different meal. His range was limited, but over the past two weeks he'd fished out some old cookbooks of Michelle's and had been trying out various recipes with Sam and Ryan. Most of their responses had been pretty lacklustre to say the least, but there was one stand-out. A simple meal of baked potato served with pork chops cooked in orange juice had won their approval, so Nick had decided to cook that for Kay. He could just about manage that.

He popped a bottle of chardonnay into the fridge and, whistling to himself, headed upstairs to shower and change.

*

It was later – much later. Dinner had been enjoyed, the wine drunk, and Nick and Kay were together on the new sofa, the floor lamp sending a dim glow across the room, a slow melody playing in the background.

'Happy?'

'Mmm.'

Nick stretched an arm around Kay's shoulders, feeling her shudder. 'Cold?'

'No.' She turned her head to smile at him, and he couldn't resist the temptation to kiss her. The kiss was all he'd imagined it would be, and he felt a bolt of desire sweep through him. Discarding his plan to take things slowly, Nick pressed his body against hers, feeling an answering pressure as Kay melted under his touch. They slid down the sofa till he was lying on top of her. Both were breathing heavily.

'I'm too old for this,' he said, propping himself up on one elbow, wary of spoiling the mood. 'Are you...? Shall we retire to somewhere more comfortable, more in keeping with our advanced years?'

Kay's gurgled laughter was her reply as she allowed herself to be led upstairs into the master bedroom. Nick gave thanks he'd had the presence of mind to tidy this room too and change the sheets. It had been a wild hope, something he'd only dreamed about, hadn't really believed could happen.

Their coming together was as wonderful as it was unexpected. Nick felt all his Christmases had come at once. He'd forgotten it could be like this. Had it *ever* been like this for him before now? Their bodies fitted together as if they'd been meant for each other, as if all his life he'd been waiting for this moment, for this woman. Time stood still as he gave himself up to the sheer delight of their intimacy.

Nick and Kay were still lying coiled together when his phone emitted the Star Wars theme that signalled a call from Ryan, extinguishing his desire as surely as if his son had entered the room. 'Sorry,' He withdrew from their embrace. 'I have to take this.'

'Ryan, what's wrong? It's late. You should be in bed.'

'I had to wait till Mum and Terry went to bed. Dad, he doesn't want me here. Sam said I should ring you.'

'What do you mean? Who doesn't want you there? Terry?'

'It was awful. When we arrived, I went straight to my room to put my things there and…' Nick could hear him trying to hold back a sob, '…there was a notice on my door. It said, "*Ryan doesn't live here anymore*".'

'What did your mum say?'

It was Sam who answered. 'Mum doesn't care, Dad. She's completely under Terry's thumb. She said it was just Terry's little joke. But Ryan's really upset. I think…'

'Let me speak with him again.' Nick pulled on his ear and glanced pleadingly at Kay. She rose, collected their glasses, and tactfully disappeared downstairs.

'Ryan, son. What do you want me to do?'

'Can I come home, Dad? I don't want to stay here.'

Without thinking Nick said, 'Of course you can. I'll book you a flight tomorrow and call you then. I suppose I'll need to speak to your mum, too.' He dreaded to think how that conversation would go, but he knew he couldn't have his son staying with a man who did something like that. How could he treat a fourteen-year-old as if he was a used piece of clothing? And how could Michelle allow this to happen?

When he hung up, Nick realised his fists were clenched. He slowly released them and, taking a deep breath, followed Kay downstairs and into the kitchen. He found her standing by the sink rinsing their wine glasses. She turned and must have seen the anguish in his expression.

'Something wrong?'

'Ryan.' Nick shook his head and rubbed his brow as if to ward off a headache. 'Seems his mother's new partner doesn't want him there. I'm bringing him home as soon as I can get a flight booked.'

'Oh!'

'Sorry.' Nick moved to take Kay in his arms, her pliable body moulding to his with the promise of more sensual delights. 'I'd hoped we would have this week, but...' He inhaled the citrus and musk fragrance he now associated with her.

'I'm sorry too,' she murmured. 'But I understand.'

Twenty-seven

Kay dressed hurriedly, wanting to put as much distance between Nick and herself as possible. What a fiasco! The sex had been good – better than good. Then his son had phoned. Of course, Ryan had to come first, family always did. She knew that, but it reinforced all her earlier objections to this relationship. It wouldn't work, couldn't work.

And she had to front up at work tomorrow as if nothing had happened. Kay couldn't stay there. It was an impossible situation. She should have known better. She wasn't a lovesick teenager. Nick already had two of those to contend with at home.

And in the morning, there would be Zoe. Zoe with her knowing looks. How had Kay allowed herself to get into this mess? She'd hand in her resignation tomorrow. Zoe was right about that. She didn't need the money. She had enough to see her through. The only issue would be how to fill her time. Damn the man! She'd been quite happy without this complication.

*

To Kay's surprise, next morning at breakfast Zoe made no reference to Kay's night out. Instead, she appeared to have some secret of her own, smiling to herself from time to time and being more tolerant of Noah's demands than usual. She waited till Noah had left the table and gone outside to play with Milly, before pouring Kay a second cup of tea.

'Mum?' she said in the wheedling voice that told Kay her daughter was about to ask a favour – might even be about to say something she knew her mother wouldn't approve of.

Kay took a sip of tea, then met Zoe's gaze. 'Yes?'

'Tomorrow.' She fiddled with her knife, letting it fall onto the table where it deposited a large smear of marmalade. She tried to wipe it off with her finger with the result it spread across a larger spot.

Kay waited.

'I've been invited out to dinner. Would you look after Noah?' she asked, the words coming out in a rush.

Kay's eyes widened. Zoe had been invited out. She tried to recall the old friends she'd been in contact with since she arrived. There was Eve and Donna. But both of those had children Noah's age and Kay couldn't imagine they'd invite Zoe without her son. 'Who with?'

Zoe gave a nervous smile. 'Remember at the picnics when I ran into Miles Younger? He called last night when you were out. He's invited me to dinner tomorrow night.'

'But you're a married woman!' Kay knew it was the wrong thing to say. It marked her out as one of the older generation, as well as questioning her daughter's morals. And who was she to talk? Nick Kerr was still married too.

'I know that! But don't I deserve some fun? I'm stuck here in Granite Springs with no decent company. Is it too much to want to go out to dinner with an old flame?'

'You admit he's an old flame?'

Zoe blushed and looked away. 'He could have been,' she said dreamily. 'But that's beside the point. He's an interesting man. He's not a country bumpkin. And he's asked me to dinner. I didn't object when you raced off to dinner with your professor.'

It was Kay's turn to blush. 'That was different. Anyway, I doubt I'll be doing that again.'

Zoe glanced up. 'Why? What happened? Did he proposition you?' The way she asked indicated to Kay her daughter imagined that would be the last thing to happen to her mother.

'His son rang and will be back home this week. He's going to have two teenagers to look after. That's enough to keep anyone out of mischief.' *And enough for me to want to keep out of his life.*

'And what about Eric?' Kay tried again.

'What about Eric? He's not here. He's part of the problem. If he hadn't been so stubborn, *I* wouldn't be stuck here in this hick town.'

Kay took a deep breath. 'Granite Springs isn't a hick town. It's the town you grew up in. It's actually quite a large regional centre. We have the university, the wool mill, the fruit processing plant...'

'I know, I know. Uncle Tom Cobbly and all.'

'And it was your choice to come here.'

'Where else could I go with a child in tow?'

Kay was lost for words. She'd known all along she was a last resort for Zoe and Noah, but to have it flung in her face like this was almost too much.

'So, will you?' Zoe asked.

'I suppose so.' Kay knew Zoe was perfectly capable of going out and leaving Noah even if she didn't agree. It wasn't fair to the little boy.

'Thanks, Mum.' Zoe beamed. 'Shouldn't you be getting off? You *are* working today?'

Kay checked the kitchen clock.

'Yes.' She'd need to get a move on if she was to get in before Nick arrived.

*

Kay breathed a sigh of relief. She'd made it! She was holding her resignation letter in her hand ready to place on Nick's desk – she'd printed it out before going to bed last night, before she could change her mind – when Nick appeared behind her.

'What have you there?' he asked, grinning.

'I... My letter of resignation. I thought, after last night, I can't...'

Nick's face fell. 'I don't understand.' He pulled on one ear. 'I thought... Was I mistaken? Didn't you...?'

Kay blushed. 'I did. But with your son here, and your daughter will be back soon, too. There's no place in your life for someone like me. It's best I leave here too. It would be a daily reminder. I understand you won't want me here.'

Nick held up one hand. 'Please don't. There's no need. I *need* you here. We'll work something out. Please, Kay.' He rubbed a hand over his head in the gesture she'd come to recognise meant he was confused. How could she continue as his PA feeling as she did? Kay finally admitted to herself she did have feelings for this man, feelings she'd been at pains to deny, feelings she'd never imagined she'd ever have again for a man. It was better to leave before she became more involved.

Nick put a finger under Kay's chin, lifted it up, and gazed into her eyes. Her heart thumped and she felt weak. The memory of the previous night, of their bodies moving together as one, seemed to hang between them.

There was the sound of footsteps. They sprang apart.

'Professor Kerr,' Ann Baird's voice pulled them both back to the present.

'You'll take care of that – following my instructions?' he asked Kay, before turning to the other woman. 'What can I do for you, Ann?'

Kay watched helplessly as he led Ann into his office and closed the door.

Twenty-eight

The morning dragged for Nick. Every time he tried to have a word with Kay, she was either on the phone, engaged with another member of staff or away from her desk. Was she deliberately avoiding him? What had he done wrong?

He dragged his mind back to Ryan. He'd managed to book the boy on a flight this afternoon and had texted him the details. But he needed to talk it through with Michelle. He picked up the phone.

Half an hour later, having suffered a tongue lashing from Michelle, Nick hung up. His jaw clenched, he strode over to the window and gazed out unseeingly, rubbing the back of his neck. That bitch! She knew exactly what Terry had done and she didn't care. Ryan was her son, too. How could she be so unfeeling, so insensitive to his needs? And how could she imagine Ryan could stay in the same house as the man who so clearly didn't want a bar of him?

It was one thing for him and Michelle to make decisions about their children's futures, but Ryan and Sam were old enough to make decisions about their own lives.

At last he'd finally managed to have her accept that Ryan was coming back home. Sam seemed okay up there for another week. Maybe she could salve her mother's conscience, but he doubted Michelle had one.

Kay was sitting primly at her desk when he left to pick up Ryan, but Phil Little was leaning over her dictating something she was typing up. Damn! He'd hoped to have a private word with her before he left.

'Excuse me,' he said.

Kay looked up, her dark eyes full of something he couldn't identify.

'I won't be in tomorrow. Working at home. I need to settle Ryan in – uniform, enrolment, etcetera.' He waved a hand in the air in an attempt to indicate all the various things that needed to be taken care of.

'The young man returning home?' Phil asked. 'Good news. He was a loss to the school footie team.'

Trust Phil to think of that, when there were so many other important issues at stake.

'Right. I'm off, then.' Nick looked at Kay again, hoping for some indication of what she was thinking, but there was nothing in her eyes to give him any kind of clue. 'Right,' he said again and jammed his briefcase under one arm.

*

Next day was busy, preparing Ryan for school. Re-enrolling him was a simple affair, but he'd grown so much in the months since the end of the previous year, he needed a full school uniform. It took time and patience – which didn't come easily to Nick – before all this was completed to Ryan's satisfaction. Then, just when they'd finished and Nick intended to really get to the bottom of why Terry Wilson was so antagonistic towards his son, Ryan slipped off to catch up with his mates.

Left to his own devices, Nick's first impulse was to drop back to the office to see if he could mend matters with Kay. But, remembering how she'd managed to avoid being alone with him yesterday, he quashed that idea before it had time to take root. No, he had to be more cunning in his approach. He took out his mobile and, after considering carefully, constructed a text message asking her to look out a particular document for him and telling her he'd drop round to her home that evening to pick it up.

He pressed *send* with some trepidation, knowing how easily it could backfire. She could ignore it, refuse, even suggest she drop the necessary document into him. But knowing Kay as well as he thought he did, she'd do none of those.

Once he got to her home, he'd have to contend with her daughter, but he'd face that hurdle when he came to it.

As luck would have it, glad to be back home in Granite Springs, Ryan had wandered off after dinner with a couple of his old mates who were glad to see him back, leaving Nick free to pursue his own agenda.

There was no sign of the daughter when Nick rang Kay's bell at seven o'clock that evening. The door was opened by the small boy he'd seen with Kay before. He was naked and left the door wide-open before running back inside yelling, 'It's a man, Grandma.'

Chuckling, Nick followed him inside, finding himself in a wide hall with doors on either side. A frazzled-looking Kay emerged from one of them carrying a towel, beads of moisture on her forehead. She was wearing jeans and a plain white tee shirt, her face devoid of makeup, her hair tied back in a band. She looked younger and more vulnerable. Nick wanted to pick her up and hug her.

'Oh, it's you!'

Not the best of welcomes, but at least she didn't toss the document at him and tell him to leave.

'You'd better come in while I put this one to bed. His mother's gone out to dinner.' The way her lips tightened as she spoke told Nick Kay didn't approve.

Nick followed her in, and she gestured to a door at the far end of the hall. It led into a large living room overlooking what appeared to be a well-maintained garden, though it was difficult to see properly in the sliver of moonlight.

At first, he stood awkwardly in the middle of the room. Unsure of his welcome, he felt disinclined to sit down. From the other end of the house, he could hear sounds of Kay putting her grandson to bed, then her voice beginning to read a story. She wasn't going to be back in a hurry.

Nick gazed around the room. He hadn't been to Kay's home before and was curious what it might tell him about her.

It was a warm room – lived in. As unlike his as could be. Even the new furniture and the cushions hadn't managed to transform his house back into a home. This room was lit by several floor and table lamps providing the sort of atmosphere he'd tried – perhaps unsuccessfully – to create when he invited Kay to dinner.

It emanated a sense of peace and – he sniffed – there was the faint aroma of Kay's perfume, or was it from the bowl of potpourri sitting on the coffee table? It epitomised a woman's touch.

On a sideboard was a picture showing a much younger Kay with a handsome tall man and two children. Feeling brave, Nick picked it up. It was a happy family photo, obviously taken before any scandal hit. It showed four people who must have believed life would continue to be good for them – before everything went sour for Kay and her husband.

He and Michelle probably had similar photos, he reflected. One never knew what the future had in store. It was a sign you should grab happiness while you could, before it was snatched away by a cruel fate. He gave a grim chuckle. Is that what Terry Wilson was – a cruel fate?

'There you are.'

Nick guiltily replaced the photograph. 'Your husband?' he asked.

'Yes.' Kay picked up the photo and stroked it. 'One of the good memories I have.' She seemed lost in thought for a moment.

'He looks like a kind man.'

'Thank you. He was.' She replaced the photo, repositioning it slightly. 'I have that document you want.'

Nick cleared his throat, moved from one foot to the other, and offered a smile that didn't meet his eyes.

'But that's not why you're here, is it?'

Sprung!

'I needed to talk with you. About Monday night. About your resignation.'

'I haven't changed my mind.'

Nick's heart sank. What could he say to persuade her? He'd known it wouldn't be easy, but had thought she'd at least be prepared to listen to him. Her blunt retort came as a surprise.

His disappointment must have shown on his face.

'Well, now you're here, would you like a drink? I could do with one after dealing with Noah. It's a long time since I had to put a four-year-old to bed. I'd forgotten how exhausting they can be.'

'Love one.'

'Take a seat. I'll fetch the wine.'

'Can I help?'

'No. Won't be a moment.'

While she was gone, Nick heard a small voice call, 'Grandma', followed by Kay's footsteps, her voice saying something so low he couldn't catch it, then a door closing.

'Here we are.' Kay appeared carrying a bottle of red wine and two glasses which she set down on the coffee table. The scent he remembered became stronger as she joined him on the sofa.

A couple of glasses later, Nick dared to again raise the subject close to his heart. 'The other night was good for me. It wasn't just the sex, it was more, much more.' He risked an arm around her shoulders. She didn't pull away.

'For me too,' she said.

Was there a note of regret in her voice?

'But,' he said daringly, 'if you don't want to continue, I can accept it. What I don't understand is why you think you need to leave your position in my office.'

Kay laid down her glass and twisted her hands in her lap. Nick wanted to hold them, to comfort her, but stopped himself. This wasn't the time.

'It's all part of the same thing.' Kay turned to face him. 'I like you, Nick – a lot. But your life is complicated. You have two teenagers to care for. It's not an easy age. I know you don't have time to engage in anything serious. And you're still married.'

Nick opened his mouth to reply, but she held up her hand. 'Let me finish. I don't think it's fair to either of us to spend every day together if we can't… Oh, I'm not saying this properly.'

'My turn. First, we both have children, that's a given. They're not going to go away, but that's no reason to put our lives on hold. I'm sure you'll agree with that. And as for still being married. As you're well aware, my marriage ended some time ago. Michelle and I are arranging the divorce. These things take time and, in the meantime, we're working out the division of assets – not an easy process.' Nick pulled on his beard. He needed to spend time on that. 'But that doesn't have anything to do with us in the office. I need you there, Kay. You keep everything moving along smoothly. And…' he gave her what he considered to be his most winning smile, '…the sight of your pretty face there every morning brightens my day.'

'Zoe's married too, and she's gone out to dinner with an old flame.'

Nick dropped his arm from around Kay's shoulders and gazed at her in surprise. Maybe this wasn't about them after all.

'What's that got to do with us?'

'Nothing. Everything. Oh, I don't know. People don't seem to take marriage so seriously these days. With David and I…'

'You had a good marriage,' Nick said. 'Some of us weren't so lucky.' He paused. 'But to come back to your daughter. I thought she was only staying with you for a short time.'

'So did I. I was sure she and Eric would patch things up. This Miles Younger thing came out of the blue.'

'Miles Younger – that's his name?'

'Yes. They knew each other at school. He was older, in Adam's year. It seems he owns a night club in Thailand.'

Nick took a sharp intake of breath between clenched teeth and gave an audible hiss. 'Thailand? Sounds a bit suss.'

Kay sighed. 'That's more or less what Adam said. But Zoe's no teenager. She's a grown woman and can make up her own mind about people and choose her own friends – as she's quick to remind me.'

'But I suppose you never stop worrying about them?'

'No. You'll find that out before long.'

'And I thought the teenage years were the worst!' Nick pretended to groan.

'They probably are,' Kay laughed. 'Perhaps because we think we still have some control over their behaviour. But, believe me, it's a fallacy. And I suspect it's even worse now than it was when Adam and Zoe were teenagers.'

'How did you get to be so wise?'

Kay just laughed.

'Getting back to us,' Nick said. 'Can we at least give it a try? You agree we're good together, and we're neither of us getting any younger. It would be a pity to forego the opportunity to find a second chance.' He almost said "a second chance at love" but thought that might be going too far. *Was it love he was beginning to feel for Kay? He'd almost forgotten what it was like to be in love.*

Kay cocked her head to one side and narrowed her eyes, concentrating. 'Maybe,' she said at last. 'But can we take things slowly? It's been a long time… I'm not sure…' She shook her head slightly.

'As slow as you like.' Nick breathed a sigh of relief. This was a sign that all was not over. She was willing to give them – give him – another chance. 'And you will reconsider your resignation?'

Kay nodded.

Nick squeezed her shoulder and dropped a gentle kiss on her hair. 'Thanks,' he murmured.

They sat silently for several minutes.

Then, with another sigh, Nick moved away and said, 'I should go. I have a teenager back home.'

'Yes.' Kay smiled.

At the door, Nick placed a chaste kiss on her lips. Then, drawn in by the now familiar sensation of her body so close to his, the unique and heady fragrance of citrus and musk, with just a touch of something more flowery, he was unable to stop himself. He leant closer. For just a moment, he felt her mould herself to him, then she placed a hand on his chest.

'No. We said we'd take this slowly.'

Sadly, he drew away.

Twenty-nine

Kay groaned and turned over, willing herself back to sleep. But it was no good. The sunlight streaming through the window was a sign it was time to get up – to get up and face Nick in the office. Part of her regretted having given in to his urgings to remain in the position, while another part was filled with a sense of anticipation.

'A second chance'. That's what he called it. Could she really have a second chance at life – at love? Because that's what he meant, even if he hadn't uttered the word.

After a refreshing cool shower, Kay felt more prepared to face the day. In the kitchen she opened the laundry door to let Milly out and filled her food and water bowls. But the cat wasn't interested. She leapt up onto her favourite chair and curled up, ready to spend the day there.

'Enjoy it while you can,' Kay told the cat. 'Zoe will have you off that in a minute when she appears.' It was sad how her daughter seemed to dislike Milly so much. Was it because she was a cat, or a general dislike of animals inside the house? Kay wasn't sure. But it was such a pity. Noah loved the cat and would benefit from having a pet of his own.

At that very moment, Zoe appeared, yawning, a bright-eyed Noah scampering behind her.

'Did he settle okay last night, Mum?' she asked.

Kay nodded, but before she could speak, Noah said, 'There was a man at the door.'

'A man?' Zoe eyed her mother in surprise.

'Professor Kerr called for a document he needed. He texted me earlier.'

But Kay knew she wasn't going to be let off that easily.

'A document? Was that all?'

'And he stayed till after I had my story,' Noah added.

Zoe raised her eyebrows. 'When the cat's away...'

Kay could feel herself redden. 'Nothing of the sort.' She mentally crossed her fingers. 'He arrived just as Noah came out the bath. I couldn't just hand the man the document and turn him away.' As she spoke, Kay caught sight of the offending document sitting on the kitchen bench where she'd placed it when she arrived home the day before. She and Nick had become so caught up in discussing other things, the document had been forgotten. In hindsight, she wondered if it had been an excuse. If so, it had worked very well.

'How was *your* evening?' Kay asked to distract Zoe. 'I didn't hear you come in.'

Zoe yawned again, bearing a striking resemblance to the cat she disliked so much. 'I had a lovely time. We went to The Riverside – that restaurant you took us to for lunch. It's much livelier in the evening. Then we went for a drive. It must have been after midnight when I got back. Miles is an interesting man. He's done so much with his life.'

I'll bet, thought Kay, but kept her thoughts to herself. 'He said he's here to finalise his mother's estate. Then he'll be off – back to Thailand?'

'I suppose so.' Zoe's pretty mouth turned down.

Kay thought how her daughter would avoid that expression if she knew how ugly it was.

'So, he'll be gone soon?'

'In a week or so, I expect. He hasn't actually said.'

Kay poured out the tea she'd been making. 'Toast?'

'Not for me. I ate so much last night.' Zoe took a few sips of tea before giving her mother a cautious look. 'Miles has invited me out again on Saturday. Some dinner dance or other. You'll mind Noah again, Mum?'

Kay wasn't sure whether it was a question or a demand. She nodded, but couldn't help worrying about her daughter. Zoe had always been flighty, never one to take advice readily, but this was going too far. She opened her mouth to offer her opinion.

Zoe held up a hand. 'I know what you're going to say, Mum. You're going to remind me again that I'm married, that Miles is only in town for a short time, that I should be more responsible. Well, I'm tired of being responsible, of being tied to a four-year-old, of my boring, routine life. Why shouldn't I take a bit of excitement when it's offered? I know it's not going to last. And, anyway, *you* can't talk. Your professor is married too.' She slammed her cup down and left the room, almost sending Milly – who'd chosen that moment to jump off the chair – flying in the process.

'Is Mummy angry with me?' Noah asked.

'No, darling. I think it was your grandma who upset her. She'll be fine once she's had her shower.' Kay hoped she was right. Zoe was difficult enough at the best of times. With a chip on her shoulder, she was unbearable.

*

Once in the familiar atmosphere of the university, Kay felt better. She'd forgotten Nick was still working at home, and was relieved there was no threat of his appearing to send her off balance. She'd brought the document back, and now placed it on his desk – a message to him that she fully understood why he'd called on her last night – smiling to herself as she did so.

The morning passed quickly, Nick's absence making no difference to the demands on Kay's time beyond her routine tasks. A call from Jo, suggesting lunch instead of their usual Saturday morning coffee, was a welcome interruption. It would be good to catch up mid-week, and Jo intimated she had something she wanted to tell Kay. What couldn't wait till their usual Saturday coffee? Well, Kay had something to discuss with Jo too. Her old friend was a good sounding board and Kay valued her advice – even if she might not always take it.

When one o'clock came around, Kay tidied her desk, closed her computer and, with a last glance around, left for lunch. She was glad Nick had persuaded her to stay. In the few months she'd been here, she'd come to regard the office as her own fiefdom. She wasn't sure how she'd cope when Fran returned to claim her territory. But that was a worry for another day.

The first to arrive, Kay chose a table by the window where she could watch for Jo. Banjo's, as the students called it, was beginning to empty of students heading back to classes and would provide a quiet spot for their lunch.

Before long, she spotted her friend walking up the path. Jo was elegant as always in jeans and denim jacket open to show a white tee-shirt printed with some sort of emblem, her fading blonde hair caught up in its usual twist which didn't quite deserve to be called a bun. Kay wondered how she appeared to Jo. Her own dark hair was greying, but a good hairdresser helped its natural colour. Kay looked down at her own outfit, the beige pants and matching jacket she'd chosen that morning and paired with a white cotton shirt suddenly feeling dowdy and old-fashioned. What did Nick see in her?

'Kay!' Jo greeted her with a hug, and the pair air-kissed before settling down to peruse the menu, the day's specials being listed on a large blackboard attached to one wall.

'Good to see you, Jo. It's brightened my day,' Kay said, once they'd ordered their meals – smashed avocado with fetta for Kay and a toasted vegetarian pita wrap for Jo – and been served with coffee.

'I thought Professor Kerr did that for you,' Jo chuckled. 'He's not here today?' She glanced around as if expecting Nick to appear.

'He's working from home. His son arrived unexpectedly, and he had a few things to take care of.' Why she felt she needed to explain to Jo, Kay didn't know. 'But you didn't invite me to lunch to talk about him.'

'No.' Jo seemed to be having trouble finding the right words. 'Oh, Kay, all that trouble last year with Carol wanting to have a baby. And now she's pregnant.'

'Yes, you've already told me that. Has Gordon left her again? Is that what's happened?' Kay remembered how, the previous year, Jo's ex had left his new wife and tried to reignite their marriage. That was before she and Col married, of course. There could be no thought of that now.

'Not at all. After a lot of ranting on Gordon's part, his accusing Carol of all sorts of infidelity, he finally took Col's advice to talk with his urologist. The upshot is that evidently there's a one in one thousand chance that the vasectomy will fail in the first year. So, Gordon got Carol to agree to a DNA testing of the foetus.'

'They can do that?'

'Seems so – through amniocentesis. They did the test last week and it's Gordon's baby all right.'

'And? How's he taking it? He doesn't want her to have a termination, does he?' Kay couldn't help but remember how his aversion to the idea of becoming a father again at sixty had caused Gordon and Carol all sorts of problems, not to mention the reaction of his grown-up daughter.

'That's just it!' Jo exclaimed, 'After all his claims to the contrary, he's strutting around like a dog with two tails, telling everyone who'll listen that his sperm are so strong they foiled the knife of the surgeon.'

Kay chuckled. 'Trust Gordon!'

Jo joined her, then sobered up. 'But it's not funny. Eve's devastated.'

'Of course.' Eve, who'd been the favourite – and only – daughter most of her life, only to be ousted from that position a year earlier by a surprise arrival in town. It had taken her some time to get over that shock, now this.

Then it occurred to Kay and she began to laugh again.

'What's so amusing?' Jo sounded insulted. 'There's nothing funny about Eve's distress.'

'Not Eve, Zoe. Here she is, determined to persuade Eric to have a vasectomy so they won't have any more children, and your ex has managed to impregnate his wife after having one. That would serve her right – though would hardly be fair to the child.'

'Maybe she wouldn't tell him,' Jo suggested.

'What a dreadful thought.' But believable. Zoe was just devious enough to have a termination and keep it to herself. Kay was in no doubt about the lengths to which her daughter would go, to get her own way.

'Anyway, enough about that. How are things going with your professor?'

'He's not *my* professor.' Kay loved her friend dearly, but she did wish she'd stop referring to Nick that way. It made her feel uncomfortable, as if there was something to be ashamed of, something secret. And there wasn't, was there?

'Well, how is your *friendship* with Professor Kerr progressing? Does that sound better?'

It did. And, hesitatingly, Kay told Jo about their dinner, the phone call, her plan to resign, and their subsequent decision. 'You see,' she said at last, 'there's not much scope for anything but friendship. He'll have a houseful of teenagers, and I have Zoe and Noah.'

'Where there's a will...' Jo said.

'It's not that simple.'

'I remember thinking exactly that about a year ago. If something's meant to happen, it will, regardless of what obstacles life throws in the way.'

'Hmm.'

'And...' Jo said boldly, '...a man on his own with two teenagers, he'll be needing some help – a wife, even.'

'No, Jo. Not for me. Teenagers! I couldn't contemplate going back to that part of my life again. I had enough to deal with when Adam and Zoe were at that stage. That's enough to put me off, for sure. And after David...' She didn't put it into words. She didn't need to. Jo knew. It was all about trust.

'Well, don't be too hasty to dismiss the idea. That's all I can say. And now, my lips are sealed.' She made a gesture to zip her mouth.

'That'll be the day,' Kay chuckled. She knew Jo so well and was sure she hadn't heard the last of her *advice*.

Thirty

They were having a late breakfast on Saturday morning when they heard the sound of a car pulling up outside. Wondering who could be visiting at this time, and with an inexplicable feeling it might be Nick, Kay rose slowly. Noah was faster. He ran to look out the front window.

'It's Daddy!' he yelled in a delighted voice. 'Mummy, Daddy's here!' He raced to the door, and Kay heard it being flung open.

The two women exchanged glances as they heard Eric's voice.

Then the little boy was pulling his father into the kitchen. 'Look, Mummy!' he shouted again. 'Daddy's come to take us home.'

Kay saw Zoe's initial horrified expression change to something more welcoming. 'What are you doing here?' she asked.

'I told you I'd come, that I wanted to see my son. I miss him.'

'Daddy!' Noah clung to his knees. Eric picked him up, hugged him tightly, then ruffled his hair. 'I'm a big boy now. I can read,' Noah said. 'Let me show you.' He slid down.

Eric's eyes met Kay's over her grandson's head. 'Noah, I need to talk with Mummy for a bit. Can you go with Grandma?'

'Come on, Noah. How about we go to the park?'

Reluctant to be parted so quickly from his dad, Noah agreed, but only after Kay suggested Lottie and Livvy might be there too. She seemed to recall Jo saying something about it when they'd had lunch.

'They're twins, Daddy,' Noah said incredulously, 'and they always match.'

Eric appeared suitably impressed as he waved them off.

Both Jo and Col were at the park with the twins, and Jo seemed surprised when Kay arrived with Noah. Her expression of surprise changed to one of disbelief when Noah announced to the girls, 'My daddy's here. He's come to take us back home.'

'Not exactly,' Kay said, when the children were out of earshot. 'Eric turned up this morning out of the blue. I'm not sure what his plans are, but I don't imagine Zoe's ready to go back to Brisbane just yet, more's the pity.'

'And Miles Younger?'

'She's planning to see him again tonight – or was.' Kay had an idea Eric's arrival might put paid to Zoe's plans for the evening. 'Eric may have arrived in the nick of time.'

'Miles Younger? Would that be Julia Younger's son?' Col asked.

Kay turned to face him. 'It would. Seems he's here to finalise her estate. You know about that?'

'That's the matter Gordon wanted to consult with me about,' Col said to Jo, before turning back to Kay. 'I may be speaking out of turn, but it'll be public knowledge soon. We were the old woman's solicitors. I was the one who dealt with her, mostly. Miles isn't in her will. She was quite adamant about that. Called him a wastrel, a criminal, and other names I won't be repeating. She left all her money – and the house – to a local charity for domestic violence. I don't know if it says anything about her marriage, but she was quite clear as regards her son's attitude to women – and his activities in Thailand.'

'Looks like Zoe's had a narrow escape,' Jo said.

'Maybe.' Kay wasn't convinced that even Eric's arrival would put a dent in her daughter's desire to "have some fun", but she hoped so.

'I have an idea,' Jo said. 'Why don't you bring them all out to Yarran this afternoon? I'll ask Eve and Brad to bring the twins over too. It's a bit too cool to swim but they can have fun running around. It will do Scout good to have children to play with. The dam's low but maybe the men can take the kids yabbying, and Col can put on a barbecue. What do you say?'

'What a good idea. Noah has already told Eric about the twins. He can't seem to get over how alike they are.'

'He's not the only one,' Col laughed. 'They regularly fool me.'

That settled, they watched the children spend time on the swings, before moving to the slippery dip, then the jumping net, till they judged it was time to leave.

Kay worried all the way home, hoping Zoe and Eric might have resolved their differences, but it was a faint hope. She found them seated almost exactly where they had been when she left. Zoe had a stubborn expression on her face, while Eric's held a pinched look.

'We saw the twins, Daddy. You should have been with us.' Noah was first to speak, rushing over to wrap his arms round his dad's neck.

This was something she'd never seen him do to Zoe, Kay realised with a pang.

Zoe looked up with something like relief. 'You're back, Mum. Did you have a good time, Noah?'

'Yes, and this afternoon we're going to... What's it called, Grandma?'

'Yarran. Jo's invited us all out. Eve and Brad will be there too, with the twins and Emily Rose.' Seeing Zoe look doubtful, she added, 'It'll do you both good to be with other people for a bit.'

'You can see the twins, Daddy,' Noah put in.

'Well, in that case, how can I possibly refuse,' Eric said. 'Zoe?'

'I guess.' But Zoe seemed uncomfortable.

Kay assumed she was thinking about her arrangement with Miles and wondering how she could manage to leave Yarran in time to honour it.

'Who's Jo?' Eric asked. 'A friend?'

'An old friend of mine, possibly my best friend, the one who stood by me when David died. She's Eve's mother and the twins' grandmother. Eve and Zoe were at school together,' she added.

'And you mentioned an Emily Rose?'

'Eve's youngest. She's around six months now.'

Eric gave Zoe an eloquent look.

'I'll organise lunch,' Kay said. 'Toasted sandwiches okay?'

'Fine by me,' Eric replied.

'I need to shower and change.' Zoe disappeared.

'Where's Milly, Grandma? I want to show Daddy.'

'I don't know, sweetheart. Why don't you check the garden?'

Noah wandered off, leaving Kay and Eric alone.

'I'm glad to have the chance to talk with you alone,' Eric said. 'I take it you and Zoe haven't come to any agreement?'

'No.' He rubbed his forehead. 'She's being so pigheaded about this. I thought if I came down here, saw her again, I could talk some sense into her. But…' He shook his head. 'You know what she's like.'

'I do. None better. When she has a bee in her bonnet…' Kay sighed. 'How long are you able to stay?'

'Only till Monday. I need to get back to work. It's great to see Noah. He's grown in the time he's been down here. I miss my boy.' His voice broke.

'He misses you too. He talks about you all the time. *He's* ready to go home. Eric, I hope…' Kay put a hand on his shoulder. 'I hope you two can work things out. You're good for Zoe. I'm afraid she's been able to get her own way for too long. She was a bit of a tearaway in her teens. Her dad spoiled her. Then she left home as soon as she could. When she told us she'd met you, we thought she'd met her match, that you'd be able to tame her.'

'No chance of that! But I love her, Kay. I love her the way she is with all her faults. Problem is, I'd like more children, and I think it would be good for Noah to have a sibling – at least one. It that too much to ask?'

'I don't think so, but Zoe seems to. Did she tell you Jess and Adam were here for Easter? Jess is pregnant again with number three, and Zoe was quite unkind about it.'

'She didn't say. How is Adam? I'm sorry I missed him. If I'd known…'

'My fault. I could have told you. He asked about you. I did know Zoe was avoiding talking with you when you rang to speak with Noah. You should be proud of him. He's a bright little boy. He's adjusted to school so well.'

'We had him enrolled up in Brisbane, you know. I had to explain to the school.' He rubbed his forehead again. 'Hell, Kay, how long can she keep this up?'

'When she arrived,' Kay said carefully, 'she told me she'd taken six months long service leave. That'll run out…'

'In three months' time. Do you think she'll last out that long?'

'More to the point, do you? Or will you give in first?'

'I don't know.'

Kay could see he was torn between wanting his wife and son back, and having to back down for that to happen. Was the thought of having a vasectomy, of Noah being an only child, such an anathema to him he'd risk his marriage for it? Kay caught herself up short. She was beginning to think like Zoe.

'I'd better get on with lunch.'

'I'll go out and see where Noah's got to.'

Once Eric had left, Kay took out the ham, cheese, tomatoes and bread she needed for lunch, at the last minute adding a bowl of leftover pasta.

By the time Zoe reappeared dressed in a pair of what looked like designer jeans and a long-sleeved blue and white striped tee shirt, a navy sweater around her shoulders, the meal was almost ready.

'Where are Eric and Noah?' she asked.

'In the garden with Milly.'

Zoe made a face.

'You didn't come to any agreement?'

'He's so stubborn.'

Not the only one.

'What you need is some time together. Why don't I pack you a picnic tomorrow and you go off for a drive? I can look after Noah.'

'Do you think that would work?'

'It depends on you. Both of you. For Noah's sake you need to resolve this, Zoe.'

Zoe didn't reply. Her face still held the stubborn expression with which Kay was so familiar. She sighed. She seemed to be doing that a lot lately.

'Mummy, I told Daddy how much I love Milly, and he says...' Noah ran back in.

'I hope you didn't promise him an animal,' Zoe said, with a moue of distaste.

'I said that when he comes back home, we'd think about a pet. Maybe not a cat or a dog if you're so against them, but there *are* other kinds of pets.'

'Mmm.'

'Let's have lunch,' Kay interrupted before it turned into a full-on argument. 'Noah, if you've been petting Milly, you know you have to wash your hands.'

'We'll do it together, son,' Eric said.

'See what I have to put up with?' Zoe asked Kay when the two had gone to wash up.

'It's only natural for Noah to want a pet of his own. You don't want to give him a brother or sister. Now you want to stand in the way of his having a pet?'

'Whose side are you on?' Zoe asked bitterly.

'It's not a question of sides. I love both of you, and I only want what's best for Noah.'

'And you think I don't? I'm his mother.'

'No arguing with that.' Eric walked back in carrying a giggling Noah.

Kay was glad to see the little boy so happy. He'd been missing his dad, missing having a man in his life. Kay couldn't bear to think what it would do to him if Zoe and Eric couldn't reach an agreement, if the unthinkable happened and they decided to separate, divorce even.

Thinking of divorce automatically brought Kay's mind back to Nick, and what his children must be going through. They were older, but that didn't make it any easier for them. The fact their mother had moved on with another man probably didn't help either. Which brought Kay to her own situation. Would her presence in Nick's life only complicate matters further?

*

It had been a good idea of Jo's to invite them to Yarran. The presence of Eve and her family helped calm Zoe, Brad and Eric got on well, and Noah was in his element with the company of the twins.

When the men, after much commotion and delay, had taken the children off to the dam with buckets and yabby nets, Jo produced a bottle of white wine.

'I thought we might enjoy a quiet drink,' she said.

Zoe looked relieved. Kay knew she hadn't been keen on this visit. She was checking her phone so often Kay wanted to snatch it away. It was so rude the way some of the younger generation didn't seem to be able to survive without social media. Or was that just a sign she was getting older?

After chatting about Kay's work at the university, Jo and Col's plans for their acreage, and Zoe's interviews with Granite Springs' older residents, Kay said, 'You're very quiet today, Eve. Is everything all right?'

'No. It's Dad. Dad and Carol. You do know she's pregnant?'

Kay saw Zoe roll her eyes.

'He told me it wasn't going to happen, that he didn't want another child. He promised. He even had a vasectomy. It's not fair to this little one. Can you imagine her having an aunt who's younger than her and the twins?' Eve gestured to Emily Rose who was happily playing with blocks at their feet. 'No wonder Carol's been going around like the cat that's got the cream,' she said, a hard edge to her voice.

Zoe's eyes which had been closing, snapped open. 'But how could she be pregnant if her husband had a vasectomy?' she asked, her eyes widening.

'Seems there's a one in a thousand chance in the first year. The risk becomes less as time goes on. But it's not the failsafe solution everyone thinks it is,' Jo said.

Kay could see Zoe processing this information.

'I think I'll go for a walk,' she said, and disappeared out the door.

Jo and Eve stared after her and Kay chuckled.

'What's up with her?' Eve asked.

'Zoe is adamant she doesn't want another child and has been demanding Eric have a vasectomy. I think you've just made her reassess her position. I wonder what she'll do now?'

It wasn't long before the fishing group came back. Much to Kay's surprise, their bucket held three small yabbies.

'Look, Grandma!' Noah yelled. 'We caught some of the little bugs and the twins' grandpa says we can eat them for dinner!'

'I'll fire up the barbecue,' Col said. 'Just as soon as I get cleaned up.' He glanced down at his muddy jeans and sandals. 'Should have known better than to go in after the net when Lottie let it go. You're staying to eat, of course?'

'I don't think wild horses would drag Noah away from the chance to eat his very own yabby, though there won't be much meat on it,' Eric laughed. 'Thanks, Col. That was a great experience for us.'

By the time Zoe returned, picking her way daintily through the long dry grass, Col, Brad and Eric were busy cooking steak, sausages and the yabbies. The women were putting out salads Jo had made earlier, and the three children were playing with Scout who was beginning to tire of their lively company.

'Isn't it time to leave?' Zoe asked, frowning, and sending a glance at the group standing around the barbecue with their cans of beer.

'Didn't I say we were staying to eat?' Kay asked, knowing full well what was bothering her daughter, but there was no way Zoe could skive off to meet Miles Younger now that Eric had arrived. 'Get Noah to show you what he caught.'

Hearing his grandmother's words Noah rushed up to grab Zoe's hand. 'Come and see what I caught, Mummy,' he said, 'The twins' grandpa is going to cook it and I'm going to eat it.' He dragged her across to the barbecue, and Kay saw her shudder.

Everyone except Zoe had sat down. Kay looked around to see where she'd gone and saw her in the far side of the yard, talking on her phone and gesticulating madly, no doubt cancelling her arrangement. At least she'd had the sense to do that. Poor Eric! He was sitting with the others enjoying his steak, with no idea of his wife's deceit.

'Sorry!' Zoe gave an apologetic smile as she joined them, taking her place by Eric's side and giving him a peck on the cheek.

Noah, who was sitting with the twins at a smaller table set just for them, called out, 'It's good, Mummy. Do you want to taste?'

'No thanks.' Zoe frowned. 'Are they safe to eat?'

'Perfectly safe,' Jo replied. 'My three never got sick on yabbies from our dam, and they must have eaten lots as they were growing up.'

'You didn't?' asked Eve.

'No!' Zoe shuddered again.

'We lived in town, so didn't have your opportunities,' Kay explained.

'So,' Col said, 'Eric tells me you two are off on a drive tomorrow. Where are you heading?'

Zoe looked down at her plate which now contained a small piece of steak and a portion of salad, then she looked at Eric with an expression Kay couldn't identify. 'We haven't decided,' she said.

This provoked a discussion on local beauty spots, picnics past, and lots of recommendations which lasted for the rest of the meal.

Zoe seemed troubled on the way home, unwilling to join in any conversation either Kay or Eric tried to begin. By the time they reached home, Kay had had enough. 'I'm off to bed,' she said. 'I want an early night. I'll leave you to sort out Noah and do what you want. I'll get up early to prepare a hamper for you both.'

She left them coaxing an overexcited Noah into the bath. But, once in bed, sleep refused to come. Kay switched on the bedside lamp again and, before picking up her book, checked her mobile phone which she'd left sitting on the bedside table while they'd been gone. There was one message.

Missing you. Can we meet tomorrow? Nick x

Thirty-one

Nick pressed *send* before he lost courage.

He wasn't a fan of texting, felt it was more for the younger generation. Certainly, both Sam and Ryan seemed to spend most of their time texting one friend or another. It was their sole means of communication. He doubted they'd know what to do with the phone in the kitchen. They probably thought it was there for decoration.

Sam had arrived back today and was out with her friends already, catching up on what she'd missed in the week she'd been gone. It was strange having both her and Ryan together again. The week Nick had spent with Ryan on his own had been restful. He'd managed to work at home for most of the time and he and his son had got along well. Neither much for conversation, they'd kept to themselves, meeting only at mealtimes. It worked.

But now Sam was back, the dynamics had changed. She moved around the house like a whirlwind, leaving chaos in her wake, and managed to stir Ryan up as she went. Nick longed for time to think. And he longed for time with Kay. He knew she'd be busy with her own family. Her son had left but her daughter was still there. He was aware how much she worried about Zoe and hoped she'd find a way to reconcile with her husband. But he guessed it was going to be difficult with one of them down here and the other in Brisbane.

And, hadn't she said the daughter was out with an old flame? That didn't augur well.

Nick knew both Sam and Ryan had made plans for the next day –

their last hurrah before school started again – and he'd dearly like to spend some of it with Kay. They hadn't had any time together since the night he'd gone around to see her, the night he'd agreed to *take things slowly*. But how much more slowly could they go?

On the few times he'd dropped into the office this week – sometimes accompanied by a silent and morose Ryan – she'd been totally professional with no hint there was anything between them other than a working relationship. Well, that was as it should be. What else did he expect? But there was still that niggle that maybe he was putting more importance on what was between them than was warranted.

He had to find out.

Nick felt he was being as bad as the kids as he kept checking his phone for Kay's reply. He knew it was stupid, but it was as if the phone was lying there like a tiger waiting to pounce.

Watching the damned thing wasn't going to make a text magically appear, and sitting on his desk was the latest set of demands from Michelle. It seemed that, every time he thought they'd come to an agreement, yet another missive appeared from the harridan she'd chosen to represent her. At this rate anything she managed to screw out of him would go on her legal costs. Maybe that was what it was all about.

Sighing heavily, he settled down to read the letter which had arrived yesterday. Solicitors must be the only species remaining who used actual paper to communicate. They were probably keeping the postal service in business. He scratched his head, reading the letter from Ms Somerville, picturing a hard-faced woman with a mannish grey-haired bob. Though knowing Michelle, she was more likely to be a smart fortyish businesswoman, but hard as nails regardless of her appearance and determined to screw the last possible cent from him. Surely the fact he was now responsible for both children counted for something? Nick put the letter into the file with all the others, deciding they were best taken care of by his own solicitor. He'd make an appointment with Gordon Slater tomorrow and let him deal with the bitch.

Stretching, Nick checked the time. Time for a beer? Maybe. And Sam and Ryan should be home soon. He'd warned them not to be late. As if what he said held any sway. He often felt he was ill-equipped to deal with two teenagers, despite loving them dearly.

The house was still silent, an empty shell, and it had turned dark. He walked through, turning on the lights as he went, poured himself a beer, then picked up his phone to check it once again. A relaxed smile crossed his face. She'd replied!

Quickly scanning Kay's reply, he saw she was going to be tied up caring for her grandson all the next day and had suggested they meet at the playground in the botanic gardens where she was planning to spend the morning. Nick grimaced. Not quite what he had in mind. But beggars couldn't be choosers, and right now he felt he was begging for her attention. He quickly agreed. Maybe they could have lunch. He thought the café there was open on Sundays and it would give them the opportunity to talk. He wanted to do more than just talk, but it was a start, and better than nothing.

*

It was a cool day, autumn beginning to make its presence felt. A pair of king parrots and several currawongs were feasting on the berries and fruits still clinging to some of the trees and shrubs, and the ground was awash with fallen leaves from the Japanese maples and crepe myrtles that lined the pathways.

Nick saw them as soon as he entered the playground. The tall, slim, dark-haired woman wearing a brown jacket, a cream and green scarf thrown carelessly around her neck, and the excited little boy, his dark hair – so like that of his grandmother's – falling over one eye. For a moment he stood motionless unwilling to disturb the picture they made, totally engrossed in each other. Then the little boy caught sight of him.

'It's that man again, Grandma,' his voice rang out across the playground, causing several others to turn in his direction in amusement. Kay turned to look towards him too, her face breaking into a welcoming smile.

Nick moved forward arms outstretched only to have her move away. 'Not here,' she muttered, but suffered him to give her a peck on the cheek. Looking around, Nick realised the playground was a popular spot at this time on a Sunday morning, and that, perhaps as a result of Noah's shout, they were the focus of attention.

'Good to see you,' he said. 'Even if we're surrounded by this mob.' He gestured to the other parents and children who had now lost interest in the trio.

'Good to see you too,' she said. 'I can explain. Why don't you join those other little boys on the swings, Noah?' she asked the little boy who ran off eagerly.

'Can we sit down?' Nick asked, and led Kay to a bench overlooking the swings where she could keep an eye on Noah.

Once seated, Nick took Kay's hand in his. He felt her fingers tighten.

'Thanks for coming here,' she said. 'I know it's probably not what you had in mind, but it's a bit difficult at the moment. Noah's dad arrived yesterday and…' Kay proceeded to give Nick a blow-by-blow account of the happenings since Eric came to town. 'So I've sent them off for the day,' she finished, 'in the hope they'll see sense for Noah's sake, if not their own. The news of Gordon and Carol's pregnancy was a shock for Zoe. I'm not sure if that'll make any difference for them.'

'Mmm.' It was of little importance to Nick what Zoe and her husband decided, but it would help him get to know Kay better if she didn't have her daughter living with her. As soon as the thought entered his head, he dismissed it as unworthy.

'I'll be back in the office again tomorrow,' he said at last. 'I hope you've managed okay without me.'

Kay grinned and the sun caught a glint of silver in her hair. Neither of them was getting any younger. They should grab life when they had the chance. 'It's been very quiet,' she said. 'It'll be good to get back to normal.'

They were interrupted by Noah running up to them. 'I'm hungry, Grandma,' he said. 'Can we go home for some of that cake you made?'

Kay threw Nick an apologetic glance. 'Sorry, I baked a banana loaf earlier and I did promise Noah he could have a slice when we got home.' She paused, seemingly unsure of herself. 'Would you like to come with us? Tea and banana bread?'

Overhearing, Noah put in, 'My grandma's banana cake is very good.'

'I'm sure it is, Noah,' Nick laughed. 'I'd be delighted.'

*

Nick followed Kay home to find her standing in the driveway talking with a tall, tanned and muscled balding man who must belong to the silver Porsche Cayenne parked by the roadside. They seemed to be having some sort of altercation.

Noah rushed out to meet Nick when he stepped out of his car. 'The man's angry with Grandma,' he said. 'Come!' He took Nick's hand to pull him towards the pair whose voices had now become loud.

'Just tell me where she is,' the man, who Nick now took to be Miles Younger, yelled. 'She put me off last night, now she's not answering her phone. No one treats me like that. Who does she think she's dealing with? I'm not some small-town hick she can pick up and drop when the notion takes her.'

'Zoe's with her husband, and I have no idea where they are.' Nick heard Kay say in very measured tones. 'She had no business being with you in the first place. And, correct me if I'm wrong, but I believe it was you who did the picking up, not her.'

Kay appeared to be managing quite well without his help, but Nick had seen situations like this go bad very quickly. 'Something wrong?' he asked calmly, walking up to the pair after sending Noah round to the back of the house in search of Milly.

'Who the hell are you?' Miles turned to face Nick, a sneer on his face. Kay's daughter could certainly pick them. For Noah's sake, he hoped her husband was a different sort of person.

'A friend of Mrs Jackson. It seems to me you're not welcome here. I suggest you be on your way.' Nick stood, legs apart, arms folded, lips pressed together tightly, attempting to look menacing.

Miles' eyes raked him up and down, then clearly making the decision he was outmanoeuvred, said, 'I was just going, anyway.' He turned away, waved a finger at Kay and said, 'Tell your daughter to call me. I don't like being messed around.' Then he walked off, got into his car, and drove off with a squeal of tyres.

'Are you all right?' Nick took Kay by the shoulders and stared into her eyes, seeing the beginning of tears.

'I will be.' But she was shaking. 'Where's Noah?' she asked, looking around.

'I sent him to look for Milly.'

Just them Noah appeared carrying a protesting Milly. 'I found her, Grandma. She was hiding under a bush, but I found her.'

'Bless you!'

Nick wasn't sure whether she was talking to him or Noah. It didn't matter. He was glad he'd been here when she needed him. She wasn't a woman who accepted help easily.

Thirty-two

'I'm glad you were here.'

Kay and Nick were sitting together on the veranda with cups of sweet tea, Kay having refused Nick's suggestion of something stronger. Noah was on the lawn teasing Milly with a piece of string, but she knew the cat would scamper off when she'd had enough.

'I'm glad too. What on earth did he hope to achieve, badgering you like that?'

'I suppose he hoped I'd tell him where he could find Zoe – and badger her too.' She gave a weak laugh. 'I always thought he'd come to a bad end, back when Zoe was so delighted to go to the dance with him. I was actually glad when he left town almost immediately afterwards. I hope we've seen the last of him now.'

'I wouldn't be too sure. But I'd imagine her husband would see him off if he tries anything more.'

'He would. Though,' she said, with a worried look, 'Eric is going back home tomorrow.'

'Did Zoe make a better choice with him?'

'Yes, thank goodness. Once she'd flown the nest and become independent, Zoe seemed to find herself. Eric's a good man. I sometimes think he's too good for her. Zoe may be my daughter, but I know all her weaknesses. He's a saint to put up with her. I just hope…'

She felt Nick's hand on her thigh – warm, comforting. Nick was another good man. She wondered what had happened to end his marriage. He'd been vague about it, mentioned the other man. But there had to be something radically wrong in a marriage for a woman to look elsewhere. Kay hadn't asked for more information. It was really none of her business. She knew Nick in his role as professor, was gradually coming to know Nick as a man, and had a brief encounter with him as a lover. She remembered the unadulterated bliss of those moments in his bed, in his arms, moments she never wanted to end. But they had ended, and she'd been the one to slow things down.

His hand tightened on her thigh as if reading her mind. Kay's breath quickened, and her legs parted slightly as if in anticipation. It was ridiculous to feel like this in broad daylight with her grandson playing only metres away.

'You feel it too.'

It wasn't a question, but Kay nodded, her tongue darting out to lick her lips.

'More tea?' She rose quickly. 'Noah, I think Milly's had enough. It may be time to find something else to play with.'

She heard Nick's sigh of disappointment as he said, 'Another cup would be good. You make good banana bread,' the hidden meaning in his words obvious only to her.

Noah headed inside ahead of Kay, and Nick followed more slowly. 'What are we going to do?' he asked, as she filled the electric jug and cut two more slices of the bread. He covered her hand with his. 'We can't go on like this, only meeting when our children are out of the house. I don't want to feel our relationship is something sinful, something to be hidden away. We're free, consenting adults.'

'You're not.' Kay couldn't help herself.

Nick moved his hand away as if stung. 'Is that what's holding you back? Because…' He threaded his fingers through his beard.

'No! No,' she repeated in a gentler voice. 'I don't know what made me say that. It's just…' Kay tried to find the words to explain herself, to explain feelings she didn't understand herself. 'When I met David,' she began, 'I was only eighteen. Everything seemed simple, was simple. We met, fell in love, married, had two children and should have lived happily ever after. But it didn't happen that way. Maybe I wasn't enough for him, maybe he'd always…' She shook her head. 'Anyway, I was left alone. Now you've appeared in my life, and I feel drawn to you, but am I imagining it because I'm lonely? Am I flattered to be the object of attention of a younger, handsome man?

'No!' Kay held up a hand as Nick opened his mouth as if ready to deny it. 'You are. And I know I'm not in the first flush of youth. It never bothered me before. You have children – teenagers, a stage I left long ago. There are so many obstacles. It doesn't seem right.' She ran out of steam.

'Have you finished?' Nick had a wicked gleam in his eye.

Was he laughing at her?

'I think so.' She placed the slices of banana bread on a plate and poured two cups of tea. 'We'd better sit down.' She had to have a seat. Her legs were feeling weak. What had possessed her to invite Nick back here? She should have known something like this would happen. But what had happened? He had only asked a reasonable question, wanted to find out where he stood. What was so wrong about that?

'Me too?' Noah appeared and pointed to the slices of cake.

'Of course, honey.' Cutting another slice for him, putting it on a plate, and pouring a glass of milk seemed to steady her.

'Can I take it in to watch television?' Noah asked.

'Yes. I'll…'

'I know how to turn it on myself, and I'll be very careful,' he said, pre-empting her next comment.

'He's a good boy. Your daughter got that one right,' Nick said when Noah had left. 'Now, let's have that seat you mentioned.'

Kay sank into one of the kitchen chairs. She'd have preferred the comfort of one of the armchairs in the living room, but now Noah was in there. She could hear the theme tune of his favourite program coming through the walls. The little devil must have known it was time for it to begin. Zoe didn't permit him to watch during the day, saying he needed to be outside involved in more active pursuits, but Kay didn't see the harm in the odd television program. And right now it was a good way to keep him occupied.

'Now,' Nick said, taking a bite of the loaf. 'Mmm, this is good.' He brushed some crumbs from his lips. 'Firstly, you have to decide if what we seem to have going is worth pursuing. Hmm?' He cocked his head to one side.

Kay felt a flush creep across her cheeks. She swallowed hard. *Did he really need to ask?*

It seemed he didn't. 'I'll take that as a "yes". So, the next thing is to decide how we can make it happen. Yes?'

'Yes,' Kay said in a small voice. She knew what he was talking about. He was talking about sex. And she had no idea how that could happen again with two lots of children to contend with. She couldn't imagine Zoe's reaction if she and Nick were to go to bed in this house. Although she might think it okay for her mother to have a male *friend* – encourage her even – Kay was sure it would be a different matter for them to engage in an act of sexual intercourse in the same house as her and Noah. Kay's lips curled up in a mischievous grin at the thought.

'Something funny?'

'No, go on.'

Nick took a deep breath. 'Well, it seems to me I'm in a better position than you to make this happen.'

Kay was puzzled, her amusement forgotten. This seemed all too cold-blooded. Surely sex between two consenting adults should be spontaneous, fun, not something to be planned like a campaign. But then she was new to this type of scenario. A dreadful thought struck her. She was new to this, but was Nick? Or was he an old hand in the act of subterfuge? He seemed to read her mind again.

'And no, before you ask, I haven't done this before. It feels as odd to me as it must to you. But...' he took a deep breath, '...my kids have had the experience of seeing their mother with a new partner, living with him even. It might not be such a shock for them to discover their dad is a sexual being too – with needs.'

Kay liked that – *a sexual being with needs*. It conjured up all sorts of images. Images that made her... She pressed her knees tightly together under the table.

*

Nick had gone, leaving Kay in a whirl of excitement and apprehension. Before he left, he'd persuaded her to have dinner with him on Friday – a family dinner. Although she'd met both Sam and Ryan briefly already, this was big. To meet them in their home, to meet them as their father's...what? She could no longer classify herself as only a friend and employee. Was she a friend with benefits – though there hadn't been many of them – a lover, a significant other? There were so many terms these days. It was so much simpler when you were merely a girlfriend – or mistress. The term that would have shocked her mother slipped into her head. It was after dinner time when there was the sound of a car stopping and the chatter of voices. Noah ran out of the corner of the kitchen where he'd been trying to get Milly involved in a complicated game with an old cardboard box and some Lego.

'It's Mummy and Daddy,' he yelled running towards the door, Kay following at a more leisurely pace and hoping the day out had worked some magic. That pair certainly needed it.

'Hello, Mum.' Zoe was first out of the car and, to Kay's assessing gaze, she appeared more relaxed than she had since she arrived in Granite Springs.

'Hi there, little man.' Eric hoisted Noah up in his arms, a smile on his face.

Maybe they'd sorted things out.

'Noah's been waiting for you to get back,' Kay said. 'He's had his dinner but wanted to wait for his mummy to bath him. Our dinner is in the oven.'

'I'll do it.' Zoe took Noah from Eric, giving him what Kay construed as a tender smile, and headed to the bathroom.

Kay watched her go, then looked at Eric. 'You look as if you could do with a drink. Beer? Wine?'

'A beer would be good,' he said, taking a seat at the kitchen table. 'It's been a long day. I should get the picnic things out of the car. Thanks for preparing that for us, Kay. It was a real treat.'

'Where did you get to?' she asked, as she poured him a beer, though what she really wanted to know was if they'd patched things up between them.

'We drove towards the mountains, stopped at Talbingo and found a peaceful spot by the river.' His eyes took on a faraway look. 'I can't remember when Zoe and I last spent time together like that – just the two of us with no deadlines, no work issues, no demanding youngster to worry about.' He gave a rueful grin. 'Not that Noah's a worry, far from it.'

'I know what you mean. So, it was a productive day?' Kay couldn't help herself.

'Very.' Eric took a gulp of beer. 'Zoe'll probably tell you herself, but we did come to an agreement. And she's gone off the idea of a vasectomy.' He grinned.

Kay was curious but realised Eric wasn't going to give anything else away. She'd have to wait till Zoe had bathed Noah and put him to bed.

'I'll do the story tonight,' Eric said, clearly seeing her frustration,

'Right, I'll just check dinner.' Kay busied herself checking the oven where the chicken and chorizo casserole she'd prepared was cooking away slowly. It would be ready when they were.

A dishevelled Zoe appeared in the doorway. 'Your turn, I think,' she said to Eric. 'I'd die for a glass of wine, Mum.'

Just in time, Kay stopped herself from telling her daughter she knew where it was and could get it herself. Zoe did sometimes act as if this house was a hotel. 'White or red?'

'White, I think. Did I see a bottle of chardonnay in the fridge?'
You know very well you did.

'Coming up.' Kay fetched the bottle and two glasses. There was no sense in antagonising her now.

'Good day?' she asked when they were both sitting down.

'I think so.' Zoe twirled her glass. 'I've made a decision.'

That was so typical of Zoe, Kay thought. *It was always about her.* I've *made a decision not* we've *made a decision. As if Eric had no say in the matter.*

'And?'

'I'm going back to Brisbane.'

Kay let out a sigh of relief. It was what she was hoping for.

'After what Eve said about her dad, I've realised a vasectomy isn't the answer. I still don't want another child, but…' she took another sip of wine, this time running her fingers around the rim of the glass afterwards, '…I can keep taking the pill for a bit longer, then we'll see.'

Kay didn't say that the pill wasn't failsafe either. She knew a few people who'd been caught out that way. But if Zoe did become pregnant against her better judgement, Kay just hoped she'd go through with it. The good news was she was returning home.

'Eric's going back up tomorrow…' She left the question unasked.

'I can't possibly leave just yet. I've made a commitment to Donna and I'm still on long service leave. What would I do with myself if I went back now?'

Spend time with your husband and son?

Kay said nothing.

'I feel I can make a difference with this project,' she said, as if recognising her mother's disapproval.

Kay took a deep breath. 'I hope you're not staying with the idea of seeing that Miles Younger again. He came around here today looking for you and was most unpleasant. If Nick hadn't been here, I have the feeling he might have resorted to violence.'

'Violence, Mum? That's ridiculous. Miles isn't violent. He may get a bit worked up sometimes, that's just the way he is, but he's not violent.'

'How would you know what he is now, Zoe? You haven't seen him since he was eighteen. People change, and Adam said...'

'Adam!' There was a wealth of contempt in the way she said her brother's name, reminiscent of their teenage squabbles.

'But you will promise not to see him again?'

'I don't promise anything.' Zoe's habitual pout was back.

'Zoe told you the good news?' Eric asked, coming back in. 'Noah was sound asleep before I finished the first story.'

Zoe seemed to brighten up with Eric's arrival, no doubt glad to put an end to the conversation about Miles Younger, Kay thought.

'Noah will be able to finish off second term here and we'll be back in Brisbane ready for him to start school there at the beginning of third term. It'll all work out,' Zoe said to Kay, the expression in her eyes daring her mother to say anything.

Kay winced. No mention of Zoe's own agenda. She was treating this as if it was all for Noah's benefit. Though Kay couldn't deny it would be less disruptive for him to move schools between terms rather than be taken from one school and thrust into another in the middle of a term. 'That sounds like a good plan,' she said weakly.

No more was said about the arrangement during dinner. Both Eric and Zoe seemed happy with it. But Kay knew her daughter and couldn't help wondering if Miles Younger did figure in Zoe's plans to stay in Granite Springs, and if it would all end in disaster.

Thirty-three

'Can we have a family conference?' Nick asked when they'd finished dinner. He'd waited till the middle of the week before broaching this with Sam and Ryan but knew he couldn't leave it any longer.

'I suppose,' Sam shrugged, as she helped clear the table and stack the dishwasher. Nick's decision to allocate the children household chores seemed to be working, despite their initial reluctance. 'But I do have homework to do and you're always saying it must come first.'

'This won't take long. Living room?'

Once they were settled, Nick haltingly began. 'You've both met my PA, Mrs Jackson – Kay.'

They nodded, and Nick detected a smirk on Sam's face as if she'd guessed what was coming next.

'Well, she's become a friend – more than a friend. I've invited her to dinner on Friday and I hope you'll both make her feel welcome.' He paused, trying to judge their reaction.

'I hope that doesn't mean we have to stay in. Friday's one of the only nights I get to go out with all the homework we have this year,' Sam said.

Ryan nodded. 'It's just dinner, Dad?'

'Yes, I'll only expect you to stay for dinner. But...' he drew a breath, '...Kay will stay longer. She might even...' He mentally crossed his fingers, 'What would you say if she stayed the night?' Nick wasn't sure if he'd manage to entice Kay into his bed again, never mind stay the night, but he wanted to be open and honest with his children.

Ryan didn't say anything, but the tips of his ears turned red, doubtless at the thought of his father having sex.

'I hope you don't make the same sort of noise Mum and Terry do,' Sam said. It's gross!'

'Just put your ear pods in,' Ryan said, 'That's what I do.'

'Is that all?' Sam asked.

Too stunned to say more, Nick nodded. He couldn't wait to tell Kay, though that might not be such a good idea. She was worried enough already. The thought of making love while his two teenagers had their ear pods in to block out the sounds of their pleasure might be too much for her. He decided to say nothing.

*

Nick had decided on a lasagne, pleased Sam had offered to help him with the recipe though she'd drawn the line at actually helping to cook it. It wouldn't be very romantic, but it wasn't meant to be. It was a family dinner, an opportunity for Kay to get to know his children and vice versa. He hummed to himself as he layered the pasta, mince and bechamel sauce, hoping he'd got it right. The glass of red wine he'd poured to accompany his efforts was doing little to boost his confidence.

'Smells good, Dad,' Ryan said, wandering into the kitchen.

'Better than the usual Friday night pizza?'

'Mmm. I like pizza too.'

Ryan was easy to please. Even before Michelle left, they'd eaten takeaway pizza every Friday without fail. But Michelle hadn't always been there to eat it with them, Nick remembered. She'd always considered Fridays to be her night off and had tended to go out with friends, then the friends became one friend, who became Terry.

'When's dinner?' Ryan asked, revealing the real reason for his being in the kitchen. 'The guys are meeting at Jake's place tonight. He has new music that's fire.'

'I invited Kay for seven. That suit you?'

'It's a bit late,' Ryan grumbled and drifted off, eyes on his iPhone.

By quarter to seven, Nick was ready. The lasagne was almost cooked, the table was set in the dining room, a bowl of green salad resting in the middle, and there was wine for him and Kay. Nick took a moment to relax. He sat down at the table, trying to imagine how it would look to Kay's eyes. *Not too bad*, he thought, smoothing down the jeans he'd rescued from the laundry basket and ironed before wearing with an open-necked blue and white striped shirt.

The bell rang. He opened the door. Kay was standing there, holding a bottle of wine and looking as if she was about to flee. Wearing a loose outfit in her customary cream shades, she looked good enough to eat, though eating her wasn't exactly what Nick had in mind. For a millisecond he wondered what she'd look like in brighter colours. Then, 'Kay, you're looking wonderful as usual,' he said, giving her a peck on the cheek, with a suggestion of more to come.

Dinner went well. The lasagne was perfect, the kids polite. Sam even asked Kay about her children, seemingly interested to know they were quite grown up and Kay was a grandmother.

'That makes me sound old, doesn't it,' Kay asked, chuckling.

'No...oo,' Sam replied, but she clearly thought it did, and Ryan raised his eyes to the ceiling. Did they think their dad was dating an older woman? Well, he supposed he was, but what were a few years at their age?

'Kay married young. Your mum and I did too, and if we'd had you earlier in our marriage we could be grandparents by now, too.'

'No way!' Sam said, the idea of being a parent completely unthinkable.

Dessert – a cheesecake courtesy of The Cheesecake Shop – was barely out of the way when Ryan slid his chair back. 'Can I go now, Dad?'

'Okay.'

He left, Sam quickly following suit, though she did take time to say goodbye to Kay adding awkwardly, 'I'm glad Dad has someone, too,' before disappearing.

A few minutes later, she appeared at the door again. She'd changed and was wearing an off-the-shoulder sweater with a skirt so short, Nick thought it wouldn't take much for her underwear to be on display. Long tasselled earrings hung from her ears.

'Can I have the car, Dad?'

'You're not going out like that?' he asked without thinking.

'What's wrong?' Sam's voice held a belligerent quality.

'I think you look very nice, Sam,' Kay said, and Nick felt her nudge him gently under the table. 'Very fashionable. You won't be too cold like that?'

Sam sent a grateful look in Kay's direction while glaring at her dad. 'I'm fine, Kay. We'll be inside. A local band's playing at the club. The car, Dad?' she asked Nick again, placing her hands on her hips and scowling.

With a grimace to Kay, Nick fished the car keys out of his pocket and threw them to his daughter. 'Drive carefully. Don't be too late, and, remember, no alcohol.'

'Yeah, yeah. I'm not eighteen yet – remember?' And she was off, the front door banging behind her.

Nick covered his face with his hands. 'I don't know why I'm like this,' he said, 'I know she's a careful driver, she almost always makes curfew and – as far as I know – she doesn't touch alcohol – or drugs. Are all parents like this? Were you like this with your two?'

'I think all of us feel that way at one time or another. We want to protect them from the big, bad world out there – the world they're so anxious to explore and be part of. I must confess to be glad I don't have to deal with teenagers anymore. But Sam's just trying things out, flexing her wings, testing her independence. She seems a good kid, polite, friendly. And,' she chuckled, 'her outfit is pretty standard for these days. It could be worse.'

'Hmm.' Nick couldn't imagine much worse, but Kay was a woman and a mother. He guessed she knew what she was talking about. He'd seen students around campus dressed like that too, but they weren't his daughter. He refilled her glass. 'Now we're alone, let's forget about children for the rest of the evening. What do you say we find the sofa and some restful music to enjoy the rest of the wine with?'

In the living room, Nick dimmed the lights and turned on a favourite playlist. As he reached an arm around Kay's shoulders, he felt the tensions of the day ease away. This was what he'd yearned for – a romantic atmosphere, a beautiful woman, and a peaceful house. He put his own glass down, and removed Kay's half-full one, placing it beside his on the coffee table.

Tipping up her chin, he breathed in her familiar fragrance, then their lips met, and he was lost in a swirl of desire, two bodies moving in tune.

He surfaced with just enough breath to murmur, 'Bedroom?', stunned when Kay drew back.

'I don't think... I'm sorry.'

What the hell!

Kay gently caressed his cheek with one finger. 'It's not that I don't want it, want you. I do. Surely you can feel that?' Her finger reached up to stroke his eyebrow sending tremors through his body.

He couldn't take much more of this.

'It's just,' she continued, 'not tonight. Not this time. Your children have only just met me properly. What would they think if we were in bed when they got home? And I have Zoe and Noah at *my* house.'

Nick recognised the regret in her eyes, he knew she was vulnerable, still suffering from the humiliation of her husband's suicide, but he wanted to hit out at something, and she was nearest.

'How long are you going to use them as an excuse? If you don't want me, just tell me. Don't lead me on like this, then draw away. He moved to the other end of the sofa and rubbed the top of his head. 'You're not being fair to me. I'm only human.'

'I should go.' Kay gazed around the room as if fixing it in her mind, picked up her bag and left, the door closing so quietly behind her it barely made a sound.

Nick sat in stunned silence.

What had he done? He'd been a fool!

He dropped his head into his hands.

Thirty-four

'You're back early?' Zoe said.

'He has children, Zoe. Did you expect me to stay the night?'

'Why not? It's about time.'

'For just that reason. What would they think?' Kay remembered Nick's reasoning – the reasoning that had flown out of her head when he suggested they move to the bedroom. She forgot she'd all but promised to stay. All she could think of was the embarrassment of being found in bed with their father.

'For God's sake, Mum. They're not young kids. They know what's what. The daughter's probably sexually active herself. Didn't you say their mum was living with a younger man? Bet the kids are used to them being at it all the time.'

Kay gasped. This from the daughter who'd been shocked at the idea of her mother having a sex life only a short time ago.

'You've changed your tune.'

'Living here with you has made me realise you still have a lot of life in you. You're not over the hill yet.' She laughed. 'Anyway, how did it go?'

'The dinner was lovely. It was good to meet Sam and Ryan properly. They're nice kids. Though, as you say, not really kids. Sam looked quite grown up when she went out.' Kay frowned. 'Do you really think….?' She couldn't imagine how Nick would react to news that his beloved – and seemingly innocent – daughter might not be a virgin.

'Most kids are, these days. It's not like it was when we were teenagers, though even then…' Zoe gave a sly smile.

Kay didn't ask. She didn't want to know what Zoe had got up to in her teens. It was difficult enough keeping up with her now, and she was supposed to be a respectable married woman. She just hoped the Miles business was over and done with.

'So, you just upped and left? Or did you make some other arrangement?' Zoe asked.

'I left. He got angry, and I left.' Saying like that made her sound so... 'I didn't handle it very well, did I?'

'I'd say not. What happens now?'

'I don't know.' Kay felt like weeping. She'd really stuffed things up this time. First, she'd demanded they take things slowly then, after agreeing to dinner – knowing full well there was to be more than dinner on offer – she'd piked out at the last moment. What must Nick be thinking? It would serve her right if he never wanted to see her again.

She dropped her face into her hands. 'I've really messed up, haven't I?'

What a quandary she was in – inviting help from her daughter, the daughter she'd recently been at odds with. But family was family and, right now, Zoe was all she had.

'Well,' Zoe seemed as taken aback with the situation as Kay, 'It seems to me, Mum, that the ball's in your court. I'd say your professor has every right to feel hard done by and it's up to you to make things right. Go around. See him. Talk to him. Maybe it's not too late.'

'Now?' Kay's eyes widened as she looked at the clock. It was almost midnight.

'Maybe not right now. Though it would show your remorse. Tomorrow will probably do.' She yawned. 'I'm off to bed now. See you in the morning.'

*

Kay didn't sleep. She tossed and turned, castigating herself for being such a fool, for behaving in such a stupid way. She didn't blame Nick for getting angry with her. He was right. They had had an unspoken agreement. She *had* wanted him. And then she'd behaved like a silly young girl, leaving like that. Would he forgive her? It would serve her right if he didn't.

She must have dozed, because suddenly, the room was filled with sunlight, the resident kookaburras were providing their morning chorus, and there was the aroma of coffee wafting through the house.

'Sleep well?' Zoe was cooking pancakes while Noah watched.

'Not really.' Kay yawned and pushed a hand through her already dishevelled hair. She had still to shower and her mouth felt like the bottom of a birdcage. 'Coffee would be good.'

'Mummy's making a special breakfast, Grandma,' Noah said, wrapping his arms around her knees.

'I can see that, sweetie. What's the occasion, Zoe?' It was so unlike Zoe to take the initiative like this.

'I just felt like it.' Zoe shrugged.

Kay felt a chill. *Zoe was up to something. Was she going to ask Kay to look after Noah today again? How would she be able to see Nick if that was the case? Maybe it was just as well. Going around to apologise was a stupid idea.*

'Coffee coming up,' Zoe said, filling a mug and handing it to Kay.

Kay took a sip, the shot of caffeine coursing through her succeeding in wakening her up. 'What do you have planned for today?'

'We're spending the day with Eve and the twins, aren't we, Noah?'

'Twins!' Noah agreed.

Kay let out a huge breath. 'That'll be nice.'

'So, you'll be free to see the professor.'

'Yes.' Kay took another sip of coffee. She did want to see him, didn't she? She did. But the thought of walking back into that house where she'd made such a fool of herself, begging his forgiveness, filled her with apprehension.

'Pancakes, Mum?'

Kay looked at what was normally one of her favourite breakfast dishes. Her stomach recoiled. 'Not this morning, love. It's a nice thought, but I think I'll stick to toast and vegemite. I may have a shower first.'

'Suit yourself.' Zoe's tone was pleasant enough, but Kay could tell she was disappointed. She'd made this special breakfast – maybe to cheer her mother up – and Kay had refused it.

'I'm sorry, Zoe,' she said. 'My stomach's just not up to anything sweet this morning. I appreciate all your effort, and I'm sure Noah's enjoying them.'

'It's okay, Mum.'

Why was she being so amenable? This wasn't the Zoe she was used to.

Milly appeared from nowhere and began to curl herself around Kay's ankles. 'Oh, Milly!' Zoe hadn't changed that much. The poor cat still needed to be fed. Kay filled her bowls, then headed for the shower.

Half an hour later, dressed in a pair of smart cream pants topped with a white cotton sweater and her favourite cream and brown scarf, Kay was feeling much better and ready to take on the world. But was she ready to take on Nick Kerr?

Zoe and Noah left. Kay tidied the kitchen. She checked her emails and sent a text to Jo to call off coffee. Finally, she knew she couldn't put it off any longer. With a tightness in her chest, she slipped into her car and headed towards Nick's home.

The streets were busy this Saturday morning, students jostling with each other, eyes focussed on their iPhones, country women from surrounding properties loading their cars with huge bags of shopping, and joggers weaving in and out of the crowd. As she passed the entrance to the botanic gardens, Kay thought she caught sight of Eve with the twins and Noah. There was no sign of Zoe, but Kay drove past so quickly, she could easily have missed her. Why did she have a niggle of doubt that something wasn't quite right? She dismissed it as being part of her paranoia. Her head was all over the place this morning. She wasn't thinking straight.

Kay arrived at Nick's house before she was ready to face him. It looked uninhabited. Maybe there was no one home? She sat in the car trying to summon up the courage to confront him, then, chewing the inside of her cheek and biting her lips, she opened the car door.

Standing outside Nick's front door, the door of the house she'd left in such haste the night before, Kay swallowed hard before ringing the bell. She hoped there *was* no one home, that she could leave without…

The door opened. Nick stood there, a look of astonishment on his face.

'Can I come in?' she asked in a small voice.

Without speaking, he opened the door wider.

Kay walked in and hesitated.

Nick pushed past her and went through into the kitchen, still without speaking.

Kay followed. This was going to be more difficult than she'd imagined.

Once in the kitchen, Nick took up a position, his back to the sink, arms folded, legs splayed, his face closed.

Kay had never seen him like this. At least there was no sign of the children. Unless they were still asleep.

'What can I say?'

Nick didn't speak, his face emotionless.

'I'm sorry. Can you ever forgive me? I don't know why I acted the way I did. Can you give me another chance?'

Still nothing. She was about to turn tail and leave again when Nick spoke. 'Give me one reason why I should.'

Kay blinked away the tears that threatened to spill down her cheeks. One reason? She had a lifetime of reasons, but would Nick be swayed by any of them?

She opened her mouth to speak, but there was a lump in her throat, and nothing came out. She cleared her throat to try again, this time the tears did come, the tracks raining down her cheeks. 'I'm so sorry,' she blubbered, past caring how she looked, how she sounded. Her ears were filled with the sound of her sobs.

Suddenly, Kay felt a pair of warm arms enfold her, and her knees turned to water.

'Don't cry,' Nick murmured into her hair, so softly she could only just make out the words. 'Please don't cry.'

Kay raised her eyes to see Nick's were filled with concern. She hiccupped. 'Sorry,' she said again. 'I can go now.'

'Not again!' But there was amusement in his voice. 'I don't think I'm going to let you go this time.'

Kay weakened to the sensation of his lips in her hair, on her neck, on her lips. Then his body was pressing against hers. In a distant part of her mind, she thought of the children, then all thought was gone in a sea of desire, the heat of their need for each other.

*

Sometime later, Kay heard a door bang shut somewhere at the other end of the house. They'd progressed from the kitchen to the bedroom with scarcely any distance between them. Now they were lying naked on Nick's queen-sized bed in the middle of the day. The sound made her start.

'What's that?'

'It'll be one of the kids coming home.' Nick traced the outline of Kay's face with one finger. 'Have I told you how beautiful you are?'

Kay glowed with pleasure, but she was torn between this feeling and concern that at least one of his children was home, downstairs. Sam or Ryan might come upstairs at any moment and discover them. She struggled to rise.

'It's okay. I told you. They're okay with it. They're used to Michelle and Terry. Come back here, I'm not finished with you.'

But for Kay, the pleasure of the morning had died away with the sound of the door, and no amount of reassurance was going to change that.

'My car's outside,' she whispered. 'Won't they wonder where we are?'

'Sam – or Ryan – whichever – is probably too busy with their own concerns to worry about your car, if they even noticed it.'

Kay didn't speak.

'I can see you're not going to be persuaded,' Nick said. 'Pity. But there's always next time. There will be a next time.'

'Yes.' Kay knew there was no going back. And maybe, in time, she'd even get used to the idea of Sam and Ryan knowing she was sleeping with their dad.

'Okay.' Nick leapt out of bed. 'Shower first, then we can check out who's home.'

It was a long time since Kay had shared a shower, not since the early days of her marriage to David. After the children came along, they were both too busy, then when Adam and Zoe had grown up and left home the pattern had been set. Kay always rose first, organised breakfast, then did the household chores while David either went for a run or went into the office early.

Standing in the shower so close to a man with whom she'd recently made love was something she'd forgotten. Kay had thought – if she'd thought about it at all – that she'd never again experience this feeling of intimacy, of being at one with someone as his hands lathered her body and the water coursed over both of them, the steam rising around them.

It was almost a relief to leave the shower and feel the cool air on her body, Nick's deft hands towelling her dry, then his lips on hers. She slipped out of his grasp and went into the bedroom to dress.

'Spoilsport,' he said, but this time it was amusement, not anger, in his voice.

They walked out of the bedroom together to meet Sam coming up the stairs. Kay froze. She drew in a sharp breath.

Nick didn't appear fazed. 'Kay dropped around. I was just showing her something,' he said.

'Oh yeah?' Sam rolled her eyes but didn't seem bothered. Maybe Nick and Zoe were right. Maybe it was no big deal. Maybe Kay had worried too much and it was all in her mind.

'Dad, can I go to the Winter Solstice Music Fest this year? I'll be eighteen by then. Jackie and Ruby are getting tickets. We can all go together. It's gonna be lit.'

Nick frowned. 'Let's talk about that another time,' he said. 'You know how I feel about those music festivals. They're a haven for drugs and alcohol and goodness knows what else.'

'Da…ad!' Sam stomped up the rest of the stairs, into her room and slammed the door.

Nick grimaced. 'Teenagers. How did you cope?'

'I don't remember music festivals back then, but I suppose there were some. Maybe I just have selective recall.' She laughed. 'Are they really as bad as that?'

'There are always items in the news about drug busts, and now there's a movement afoot to allow for drug testing at the festivals. The fact they're readily available seems to have gone unchallenged. I don't want to spend a few hundred dollars to have Sam in an environment like that.'

'Wow! How could I have missed that. I guess I'm not on that planet. Are those festivals really so expensive?'

'They sure are. And now she'll be sulking for days after I refuse to pay for it.'

Kay couldn't believe it. She was doubly glad her two were way past the teenage stage. The worries when they'd been teenagers were mild in comparison, the dangers of underage drinking, the odd rumour of marijuana being passed around at school and parties. And then, of course there was the prospect of underage sex and an unwanted pregnancy. She supposed that never changed, remembering Zoe's comments about Sam. Was she sexually active? Had Nick considered it? Was that why she was so blasé about Kay and her dad?

Kay didn't think she could cope with this generation of teenagers. She admired Nick for his calm approach to what must be an enormous worry.

'How about something to eat? You must be hungry.'

Kay checked the time. It was almost two o'clock and Nick was right. She was ravenous. 'Sounds good. Then I suppose I should be getting back.'

'Only when you promise we'll do this again soon.' Nick grabbed Kay by the waist and, to her surprise, swung her up in the air. 'You're as light as a feather,' he said, 'and, see, I can span your waist with my hands.'

Kay looked down, but she didn't need to. She could feel his big hands around her waist. Those hands were one of the first things she'd noticed about him, when they'd met. Big hands, strong hands, the hands of someone with whom she'd be safe. Had she really thought that or was she imagining it now? It didn't matter. It was how Nick made her feel – safe, as if in his hands nothing bad could ever happen to her again.

Thirty-five

Pleased she'd reached home before Zoe, Kay ensured Milly was okay, feeling slightly guilty leaving her for so long on a weekend. But Milly didn't seem to mind, purring loudly as usual when Kay scratched her ears, then padding off to find a sunny spot, as if to demonstrate she didn't need company and only suffered Kay's attention to be polite.

She was making herself a cup of tea when there was a knock at the door. Opening it, Kay was stunned to see Eve Tait and Noah.

'I'm so glad you're home,' Eve said. 'I'd expected Zoe to have picked up Noah by now. I have to take the twins to dance class and...' She looked flustered. 'I have them in the car with Emily Rose, but I thought it would be boring for Noah to watch a group of small girls bending, stretching and pirouetting.' She gave Kay a pleading look.

Kay gulped. 'She's not with you? Zoe?'

Eve seemed surprised. 'No. She said she had an appointment, somewhere she couldn't take Noah. I did originally invite both of them, but... Is something wrong?'

Something's very wrong, Kay thought. *Zoe's lied to me.* But all she said was, 'No, nothing. Thanks for bringing Noah back.'

'No problem. Sorry, I must dash.'

Kay could see two little girls in the car waving madly at Noah, who stood beside her yelling, 'Bye, twinnies!'

Kay closed the door and walked inside, drawing in slow, steady breaths, a pinched expression on her face. She didn't want Noah to see how annoyed she was. It wasn't his fault his mother was behaving like a tramp, because Kay was sure she knew what Zoe was up to. She'd be willing to bet she'd arranged to see Miles Younger again, despite promising not to. But had she? Kay thought back. She'd asked Zoe to promise not to see him again. What had she replied? Then it struck her. Zoe had replied that she promised nothing. Damn her!

What was Zoe playing at? She had a loving husband in Brisbane and her son here in Granite Springs. She'd made the decision to return home in two months' time. Was she willing to jeopardise all that for a quick roll in the hay with this waster from her past, for a bit of temporary fun? Or was she just impressed by the way he seemed to be splashing money around? Kay shook her head.

'Hungry, Noah?' she asked, seeing Noah head for the kitchen.

'Yes please, Grandma. Where's Milly?'

At least Noah didn't seem to be affected by his mother's negligence. He was his usual bright, bubbly self.

'Did you have fun with the twins today?' she asked, filling a beaker with milk and putting a couple of Tim Tams on a plate. She felt he needed a treat after his mother abandoned him.

'Lots of fun,' he said. 'Livvy and Lottie's mum took us to the park, then we went to the library, then we went home and had lunch and... and I ate a whole pizza.'

'A whole pizza? And you're hungry again?'

'It was a small one,' he admitted. 'Oh, there's Milly.' He dashed off to try to pick up the cat who, seeing him coming, slipped away and slid behind the dresser. 'Milly!' he called, running after her and getting down on his knees to peer into the narrow opening.

'I don't think Milly wants to play right now,' Kay said with a smile. 'Let's wash your hands and you can sit up here and have your milk and biscuits. She may feel more like it later.'

*

Kay checked her watch for what must have been the tenth time. Six o'clock and Zoe still wasn't home. Noah had eaten dinner, been bathed and was ready for bed. The poor little mite wanted to know where his mother was, why she wasn't here to read him his story. Kay would dearly like to know that too, though she was pretty sure she knew where Zoe was.

But this was inexcusable. To leave Noah with a friend for all this time – Zoe wouldn't know Eve had brought him home. Didn't she care? Had she so lost sense of right and wrong she thought it was okay to make use of people like that? What had happened to the Zoe who'd been so understanding the night before, who'd counselled Kay to go to see Nick, to apologise?

Without her urging, Kay doubted she'd have done it, and look what she'd have missed. Her face softened, remembering how she'd spent her own afternoon, and the promise it held. She didn't know where it would lead, but she didn't need to think about that. It was enough to know the lovely Nick – the very correct Professor Kerr to others – thought she was okay – more than okay. Kay glowed at the memory of his body on hers, the surprising softness of his lips, the way his eyes crinkled when he was amused, the…

'Stop!' she told herself. 'You're getting carried away.'

'Where's Mummy?' Noah asked again in a grumpy voice, walking up to her, the soft toy figure of Winnie the Pooh hanging from one hand. 'I want Mummy to put me to bed. She promised to read me *The Wild Things* book tonight.'

Kay could see he was close to tears. *Your mother promised a lot of things*, she thought bitterly. 'She'll be back soon,' she said in what she hoped was a cheerful voice. 'Why don't I read your book for you tonight instead? It was a favourite with your mummy and your Uncle Adam when they were your age, and I often read it to them.'

Reluctantly, Noah agreed and allowed himself to be carried into his bedroom and tucked up in bed. When Kay finally read, 'and it was still hot.', his eyes slowly closed, a smile on his lips. Kay gave a sigh of relief, closed the book and sat there for a few moments, marvelling at how innocent he looked. *How could Zoe have left him for so long?*

Eventually she pushed herself up. She should have her own dinner. There was enough for two, so if Zoe did come back in time… For a brief moment, Kay wondered if she was maligning her daughter unfairly. What if there had been an accident? But surely she'd have heard if there had been.

The phone rang.

Kay rushed to pick it up, her heart in her mouth.

It was Jo. 'I wanted to know how it went with Nick this morning. In the message you left to call off our coffee, you said you planned to see him to make amends. I've been curious all day, waiting to hear from you. Amends for what? And did you? What's been happening?'

'Oh, Jo!' Kay was relieved to hear her friend's voice. She immediately poured out her news, telling Jo everything that had happened, ending with, 'I'm really worried now, Jo. What do you think I should do?'

'Firstly, I'm so happy you and your professor seem to have worked things out at last. This has been a long time coming. But as regards Zoe… Are you sure she's with this Miles guy?'

Kay exhaled. 'I can't think where else she could be. I have to admit it's not like her to leave Noah for any length of time, and she told Eve she'd be back early afternoon. It sounds as if she was planning to lunch somewhere. But look at the time now!' Kay ran a hand through her hair.

'Calm down. Would you like me to come into town?'

'No, but thanks.' While the idea of her friend's company was comforting, there was nothing Jo could do to help. 'I'll just have to wait.'

'Well, keep me in the loop.'

'Hold on!' Kay heard a car pulling up, the sound of what seemed to be angry words, then the slam of a door. 'I think that's her now. I'd better go.'

A moment later, Zoe came barging through the door. 'Where's Noah? Is he all right?'

'He's asleep. No thanks to you. What were you thinking of leaving him with Eve? She brought him around here when she had to go out.'

'Oh, Mum!' Zoe sank into a chair and leant her arms on the table. 'I meant to get back for him I really did. But…'

'You lied to me. You were with Miles Younger again, weren't you?'

'Yes,' Zoe said in a subdued voice. 'I know what you said, but he was so persistent, and I thought it would be okay to go to lunch.'

While Kay's tension eased a little at the word lunch, she knew that wasn't the whole story. 'That was a pretty long lunch.'

'I know. I didn't expect… Oh, Mum, I did think we were just going to have lunch in town. But Miles drove out to the airport. He'd arranged to hire a small plane. Can you imagine? It was so exotic. We flew to Canberra – for lunch! It was glorious. I've never flown in such a small aircraft before. It was amazing! Then we took a taxi and had lunch in a restaurant on the edge of Lake Burley Griffin. It was so special. But it took so much time. I knew I should get back, but Miles wouldn't listen. He became quite angry when I tried to insist. I know he planned it as a special treat, but I hated the way he seemed to change. He barely spoke to me all the way back. Noah *is* all right?'

'No thanks to you. He was fretful and rightly so. I was beginning to get worried myself as the time went on. You've been gone all day.'

'I know. I should have called, but...'

Kay thought she knew her daughter, but this lack of consideration was beyond belief. 'It's as well I was here when Eve brought him back. I'd just got back from Nick's.'

'Nick's? Oh, how did that go? Did he accept your humble apology? Did you make up?'

It was clear to Kay Zoe had completely forgotten about her mother's upset, and her own advice. 'Yes,' she said. 'You were right about that.'

'See? I get some things right.'

'But Miles. Is it finished now?'

'Definitely. I saw a different side of him today. I discovered he doesn't like being thwarted. You might have been right when you said he could be violent. Maybe not, but I don't intend to give him the opportunity. I told him this was the last time. I expect he'll be leaving town soon anyway, once he has his mother's estate all settled. He's just waiting for the money to come through.'

'Mmm.' Kay remembered Col's comments about Julia Younger's will. There would be no money coming to Miles. How would he react to that news? Should she mention it? Kay took a sideways glance towards her daughter. Probably not. If she really meant it when she said she wasn't going to see him again it was none of her business.

'Is there any dinner left?'

'I was about to have some, and there's plenty for both of us.'

They had almost finished eating and the bottle of chardonnay Kay had opened – they were both in need of some – was empty, when Zoe smiled across the table at her mother.

'So, you and the professor, huh?'

Yes, Kay thought, inwardly rejoicing, *me and the professor.*

Thirty-six

Kay was already seated at her desk when Nick opened the office door with that familiar smile on his face and a spring in his step. The very sight of him had her smiling right back. It was Monday morning, one of the many Monday mornings since she and Nick had been seeing each other on a regular basis. Over the past few weeks, they had fallen into the habit of meeting a couple of evenings a week and spending most of their weekends together – apart from the Saturday mornings she met with Jo. Things were going well. Kay had overcome her initial concern about Sam and Ryan who barely seemed to notice she was there.

'Morning, Kay. What a glorious day!'

'Good morning to you, too.'

'Did you have a good day yesterday?'

'Eventually. There were a few issues with Zoe, but it's all fixed now.'

'Good.'

Kay could see Nick was wondering if he should enquire further and was glad he didn't pursue it.

'You?'

Nick sighed. 'Not so good. I told Sam there was no way I would pay for her to go to the music festival, which resulted in the anticipated sulks and a call to her mother no doubt to complain how mean I'm being. She and Michelle are always at loggerheads when they're together, but apart, Sam views her as her saviour and the recipient of all her grievances.'

'Not good.' Kay had folded her arms on her desk while they were speaking. Now she unfolded them again and placed her hands on the keyboard. 'Sorry, I have a pile of emails to get through before I can start on the day's tasks.'

'And I'm holding you back. Sorry!' Nick held up one hand.

'Oh, before I forget. The vice chancellor wants to meet with you immediately after the faculty heads meeting – in his office.'

Nick stopped in his tracks. 'What have I done wrong now? Did he say what it was about?'

'It was Sheila who contacted me. Just the time and place. Sorry.'

'Okay.' He sounded worried.

Kay knew it wasn't like Aaron Peters to summon him to a meeting at short notice. The vice chancellor normally had his diary dates set in place well in advance. And Mondays were reserved for meetings with faculty heads and other senior staff. One-on-one or disciplinary meetings were usually held later in the week.

'Looks as if I'm going to be tied up till lunchtime, then. Join me for a bite in Banjo's?' Nick asked.

'Is that wise?' Kay's face paled.

Nick laughed. 'We've nothing to be ashamed of. And it's best we make a clean breast of things. It'll get out soon enough. I wouldn't be surprised if Sheila Allan was feeding the gossip mill already. She lives not far from me and she'd have seen your car...'

Kay covered her mouth with her hand. 'But it hasn't been there overnight. Oh!' she said as Nick grinned, and she realised he was joking.

'I'm off.' He blew her a kiss, grinning again when she blushed.

*

The morning dragged slowly by. Kay wondered how long the meeting had lasted and what the vice chancellor wanted with Nick, as she checked her watch for the umpteenth time.

Finally, just as she was about to give up on him, Nick rushed into the office, out of breath from hurrying across campus.

'I was about to have lunch by myself,' Kay greeted him.

'Sorry. The meeting went on forever, then...'

She grinned at his impatience.

'I'm here now. Let's go.'

Once they were seated in the café and he'd taken his first long gulp of coffee, Nick sighed. 'That's better, I don't know what they put in that stuff in the executive centre.'

'I suspect it's instant. Cheaper.'

'Right. What'll you have?'

When Kay had chosen tomato soup and Nick had ordered a BLT, he leaned back in his chair. 'You'll never guess?'

'You received a warning for being too familiar with the staff?'

Nick laughed. 'I don't think sleeping with my PA contravenes any employment guidelines. The powers that be probably haven't even considered it. No, Aaron wants me to represent him at an international conference on university leadership. Me!'

Kay leant forward. 'He obviously values you.'

'Mmm. Maybe. Anyway, it's in late June and to be held in Chicago.' He rubbed a hand over his hair. 'You'll make the travel bookings for me, won't you?'

Kay felt a flicker of disappointment. Just as they were getting on so well, he was being sent off to this conference. 'Sure, I can do that. Just give me the dates.'

'I don't have all the details yet. Can you check with Sheila?'

Kay nodded.

'Now,' he said, 'when are we going to get together again? I'm going to be tied up a bit this week. Ryan has a couple of school events I should go to. I'm sorry,' he added, clearly seeing her disappointment.

'No, don't worry, I understand.' But the fact she understood his family must come first did nothing to avert her disappointment.

After a bit of toing and froing they settled on Friday with the possibility of spending most of the weekend together again. That decided, they were able to enjoy their lunch.

'What about your children when you're gone?' Kay asked 'They're probably old enough to take care of themselves but...'

Nick drew a hand through his hair.

Kay realised he probably hadn't given a thought to Sam and Ryan when Aaron asked him to attend the conference. She knew he must have been surprised and thrilled to be chosen. It was an honour to represent the university. She also knew Sam and Ryan were old enough to take care of themselves, but were they responsible enough to be left alone for however many days he'd be gone?

'Oh, hell, that hadn't occurred to me. I got so caught up with the excitement of Aaron wanting me to represent the university – and Michelle texted me just as I was about to leave.'

Kay saw him grimace and wondered whether to ask what his wife wanted. She looked at the set expression on his face and decided not to.

'She was responding to Sam's call complaining how unfair I was being about the music festival.' He dragged a hand through his hair. 'Sam always does that – plays one of us against the other. Michelle should try having her full-time. No, wait, she had, when Sam spent her holiday week with her. That didn't go well either,' he said bitterly.

Kay didn't speak. She had no intention of badmouthing the woman who was still his wife. But she could well imagine how it irked him to have Sam ignore her father's decision, go behind his back to her mother for support. This was yet another reason why she was wary of becoming too involved. But was their relationship already past the point of no return?

Thirty-seven

'Mum,' Zoe's voice was shaking, 'can I talk with you for a minute?'

'Sure thing.' Kay finished filling Milly's bowl and stood up. 'But I have to leave soon to have coffee with Jo. Is something the matter?' She took one look at her daughter who was trembling all over, her face as white as a sheet. All thought of her meeting with Jo disappeared.

'Oh, my darling, what's wrong?' She wrapped her arms around Zoe, feeling her shudder.

'Oh, Mum. I've been stupid. And now...' she hiccupped and began to sob.

'Whatever it is, we can fix it,' Kay said, but a dreadful suspicion occurred to her. *Zoe hadn't continued to see Miles Younger, had she?*

'I know what you said, and what I said last time,' she sobbed, 'but when he kept calling and texting, I thought... I said he could come around.'

'Around? Here? You said that bounder could come to my house? When Noah was here?'

Kay couldn't believe her ears. After what happened last time, when he'd taken her off to Canberra, when she'd left Noah with Eve...

'Only a few times... when you were out – and when Noah was asleep.'

'When I was out?'

The ashamed look on Zoe's face told her everything.

'Yes, Mum. When you were at Nick's place. I'm sorry.'

Kay gasped. She'd assumed Zoe was happy to be at home with Noah on her own, yet she'd been sneaking around behind her back.

'He's been here?' Kay asked again, unable to believe her ears. She gazed around the room as if she could see vestiges of him still present. 'Last night, too?'

'That's what I'm trying to tell you. It was all okay till then. We talked, had a few glasses of wine, the odd cuddle.' She glanced at Kay out of the side of her eyes. 'I know I'm married, but I wasn't doing anything to hurt Eric.'

That's a matter of opinion.

'But last night he was different. He said he'd had some bad news, that the thing with his mother's estate wasn't going to plan. I've never seen him so angry. He ranted and raved and… I thought he was going to hurt me.' Zoe wrapped her arms around her body as if to fend off an assailant.

'I told you I thought he could be violent.' Kay couldn't help herself.

'You were right. He didn't hurt me, but he broke the vase in the hall – the tall green one.'

The vase Kay had always hated. But it had been a wedding gift from a favourite aunt.

'Never mind about the vase. He didn't hurt *you*? You're sure?'

'No, he didn't. But he scared me. You were right,' she repeated. 'I shouldn't have seen him. I don't want to risk it again, but…'

'You didn't? You didn't say you would?'

'He's not easy to say no to.'

Kay thought quickly. There was only one thing for it. 'You have to go back home.'

'To Brisbane? But…'

'No excuses this time. Donna will have to do without you and Noah can go to school in Brisbane, just as he would have if you hadn't taken it into your head to run away.'

Kay was so angry she didn't mince her words. She didn't care what Zoe thought. Her concern was for her grandson, the little boy who'd been asleep at the other end of the house while this was going on, the little boy who could easily have woken up when his mother was drinking wine and 'having a cuddle' with a man who wasn't his dad, a man who had violent tendencies.

'When did you intend to see him?'

'T…tonight,' Zoe stuttered. 'When you are with your professor. But…'

'You can't!' Kay yelled, then lowered her voice. 'You can't see him again, Zoe. I know about his mother's estate. Col told me. Miles gets nothing. His anger isn't going to go away. And a man like him will lash out at anyone in his way. You can't risk it. He's probably on drugs, too,' she added almost to herself, then, 'What? You knew?' she asked, seeing the expression on Zoe's face.

'Well... he did mention... asked me if... But I refused, Mum! I wouldn't...'

'I should hope not.'

How could all this have been going on in her house while she was enjoying herself with Nick?

'First thing,' Kay said, thinking out loud, 'we need to get you and Noah booked on a flight to Brisbane. Then,' she pointed to Zoe, 'you need to call Eric, tell him when you'll be arriving, and...'

'But...'

'I don't care how you explain your change of heart to Eric,' Kay said reading her daughter's mind. 'Use whatever reason you like – apart from the real one.'

'Alright,' Zoe said, I'll get dressed and see about flights.'

Left alone in the kitchen, Kay exhaled loudly. What a disaster. And how was she to handle Miles Younger tonight when he arrived? She had to be here and maybe...? Picking up the phone she pressed speed dial to connect with Nick.

'Kay! How are you this morning? What a lovely surprise. Don't tell me you've decided to have coffee with me instead of your friend,' he said, chuckling.

'No.'

There must have been something in her voice which told him all was not well.

'What's wrong?'

'It's Zoe.' Kay proceeded to fill Nick in on Zoe's transgressions, concluding with, 'So I think maybe we need a man to be here tonight.'

'I agree. I'm your man – always.'

Kay let out a sigh of relief. 'Oh, thanks, Nick. I hoped you'd see it that way. I don't know when he's due to arrive. I didn't ask. I was too stunned.'

'Five o'clock do?'

'That'd be good. I'll make dinner.'

'Will Zoe be there?'

'It depends. I'm not sure if she'll be able to get flights today. It's pretty short notice. But if she is, I'll make sure she keeps out of the way. At least she's seen the light where he's concerned. Just a pity she didn't see it earlier.'

'Five o'clock, then. And Kay… I love you.'

Kay looked at the phone. Nick had said he loved her. It was a first. She hugged his words to herself. At least some good might have come out of Zoe's mess.

'Grandma!' Noah came running into the kitchen. 'Mummy says we're going home. I'll be back in my own house and my own bed tonight. And I'll see my daddy!'

Kay shot a glance at Zoe who was following him, phone in her hand.

'Six o'clock, then. See you. Love you,' she said, before finishing the call.

'You managed to get flights today?'

'We leave at one-thirty. So we need to pack after breakfast. You go ahead with your coffee. I'll contact Donna – and the garage to have them sell the car, and… oh, the school.'

'I can see them on Monday and explain there was a family emergency and you and Noah had to go back to Brisbane. I expect they'll be able to forward any records.'

'Thanks, Mum. And thanks for all your support.'

Kay gave her a hug. 'That's what mums are for. Remember that.'

'How will you cope with Miles?' Zoe asked in a low voice when Noah was busily scooping up his cereal, Milly waiting patiently below his chair for the milk she knew would splash down to her.

'Nick,' Kay said. 'We'll both be here tonight. Nick managed to frighten him off once before. I don't think he'll try anything.'

'Thanks,' Zoe said again. 'Now hadn't you better be leaving if you still intend to have coffee with Jo?'

Jo! Kay checked the time. She'd all but forgotten her friend. 'You'll be all right?'

'I'm not a child!' The sharpness in Zoe's voice told Kay the old Zoe was back. Now everything had been arranged to her satisfaction, she was once again in charge of matters and wanted to be rid of Kay's interference.

'Okay. I'll be back to make an early lunch. See you soon, Noah.' Kay kissed the little boy and ruffled his hair. She'd miss him, but it was right he go back to Brisbane. That's where his dad was, where his home was.

*

'So that's where it stands,' Kay finished recounting Zoe's latest exploits to Jo.

'How could she be so stupid? No, don't answer. I know your Zoe, and from what you've told me about her in the past few months, I shouldn't be surprised. You didn't suspect she was still seeing him?'

Kay glared at her.

'No, obviously not. Well, at least, it's finished now – or will be. I wonder…'

'What?' Kay took a sip of her coffee, the caffeine helping her regain her composure.

'I seem to remember Col saying he was Julie Younger's lawyer. Would you like us to be there, too, when you have to face him? Two men would be better than one. And Col is familiar with the situation – the legal situation.'

'That's a thought.'

'If you don't mind us intruding into your evening with your professor.'

'I wish you'd stop calling him *my professor*,' Kay said. 'His name's Nick. But, no, of course I don't mind. In fact, now that I think of it, it's a damn good idea. I've been meaning to organise an evening with the two of you to introduce you properly. Let's do it. Col won't mind the short notice?'

'I'm sure he'll be delighted to get a look at how Miles Younger has turned out. I believe his mother spoke about him a lot – not in a positive way.'

'Good.' Kay was glad to have this settled. 'Nick's coming at five, so any time after that. I have no idea when Miles is due to show his face.'

'Okay, we'll plan to come early. And don't worry about dessert. I can bring a pavlova or something.'

'Thanks.'

*

Kay waved Zoe and Noah off at the airport, glad to see her safely on her way, and headed home to have a tidy up and change the beds before starting on dinner. This would be the first time Nick had spent the night here, and, despite the impending appearance of Miles Younger, she couldn't subdue a frisson of anticipation.

It was good to have the house to herself again. Kay was sure Milly was pleased too – to be able to wander around unconstrained by Zoe's disapproval. And she thought the cat also appreciated being free from Noah's excited attention. Kay did hope Zoe would agree to him having a pet of his own. She was sure Eric would see to that.

By four-thirty, the casserole was in the slow cooker, the salad in the fridge, and Kay was completing her makeup. On an impulse, perhaps in an attempt to impress, she'd made an effort to do something different with her hair, pulling it into a knot on the back of her head. Not as elegant as Jo's creations, she decided, checking the back view in the mirror, but it would do, and it made her feel more confident, more in control.

She might need that if she had to face Miles Younger, though perhaps the men would take care of him.

Nick arrived first.

'How're you coping?' he asked. 'Did your daughter and grandson get off safely?'

'They should almost be in Brisbane by now, thank goodness. And, though I hate to say it, it's good to have the place to myself again.'

'I think I know how you feel. I sometimes feel I'm overrun with my two about the place.'

'But you wouldn't be without them.'

'Not now. No. Something smells good,' he added, following Kay into the kitchen.

'Just a casserole,' she said. 'And Jo and Col are coming to dinner, too. I've been wanting you to meet them properly and...'

There was a ring at the door. 'That'll be them now. Excuse me.'

'Love the hair, by the way,' Nick called after her as she went to answer the door. Kay self-consciously put her hand up to the knot which felt unfamiliar and smiled.

'You've met Jo and this is…'

'Nick!'

'Col!'

The two men shook hands.

'Of course, you know each other. I forgot,' Kay said, as Jo beamed at her.

'Col took care of all my legal stuff until he decided to retire and marry this lady,' Nick said. 'Now I have to make do with his former partner.'

'I hope he's treating you well,' Col said.

'Can't complain. He seems to be handling the bitch Michelle has instructed pretty well. But we're not here to talk about me.'

'Drinks?' Kay asked, pleased when Nick offered to take charge and soon all four were seated in the courtyard, the women with glasses of white wine and the men with beer.

'Now, we just have to wait,' Nick said. 'What do we know about this guy? I've already crossed swords with him when he bailed Kay up about her daughter some time back. I thought I'd cruelled his pitch then. Seems not.'

'I've never met him as an adult but have a vague recollection of him as a teenager. He was pretty wild then,' Col said.

'And all the girls thought he was sex on a stick,' Kay put in. 'Zoe included. I'm sure I wasn't the only mother who was glad when he left town.'

'I second that,' Jo said. 'Eve didn't succumb to his charms, or maybe she wasn't his type. But I certainly didn't shed any tears when he left. Col, you know a bit more about him and what he's involved in in Thailand.'

'Only what his mother told me.' Col put his glass down on the table. 'She hated what he'd become. Julie was a staunch Christian – attended church every Sunday – and she despaired of his lifestyle, the girls, the alcohol, the drugs. Didn't want him to get one cent of her money. I guess he's discovered that now. Your Zoe had a lucky escape.'

'Yes.' Kay knew how close Zoe had come to falling foul of one of Miles' rages.

At seven-thirty, when they were half-way through dinner, and Col was in the middle of an amusing anecdote, they heard a car draw up. Kay felt herself tense, waiting for the sound of the doorbell.

'We'll get it,' Col said as he and Nick stood up.

Kay glanced at Jo, who nodded. 'Let them handle it, Kay. Men's business.'

Taking a long gulp of wine, Kay tried to listen to the men's voices, then she heard the front door close again. 'I think they've gone outside,' she whispered. 'They wouldn't...'

Seeming to understand Kay's concern, Jo shook her head. 'Col may have retired, but he's still on the right side of the law,' she said. 'And I can't imagine Nick taking the law into his own hands, either. He strikes me as a man who uses words, not fists.'

'You're right,' Kay said, but she couldn't relax till there was the sound of the front door opening and closing again, then the two men appeared in the doorway.

'You should be right, now,' Col said. 'I don't think he'll be bothering you again. In fact, it wouldn't surprise me if he's off back to Thailand before you can wink.'

'What?' Kay asked.

'Col was amazing,' Nick said. 'He didn't need me at all. After reminding the bastard he'd been his mother's solicitor and privy to all she knew about his dealings in South East Asia, the reason she'd written her will the way she had, he began to crumble. Sad to see a grown man turn to jelly. It was good you were there, mate. I couldn't have done it on my own.'

'I think that deserves a celebration,' Jo said. 'Do you have any bubbly, Kay?'

Kay went through and reached into the fridge where she'd put a bottle to cool, thinking she and Nick might enjoy it later. But they deserved it now.

Later, when Jo and Col had left, Nick took Kay in his arms. 'A lovely evening. I like your friends. Although Col was my solicitor for years, we never met socially. He's a great guy, and Jo's a lovely lady. Thanks for this evening.'

'Thank *you*. I couldn't have coped with that man on my own. My damned daughter, leaving her mess for us to clear up.'

'Well, I think we may have done Granite Springs a favour. The town won't be seeing him again. That's for sure.'

Kay's phone buzzed as they were on their way to the bedroom.

A quick glance showed her son-in-law's number. She pressed to see the message.

Don't know how you did it, but thanks for giving me back my family. Eric.

Thirty-eight

'It's my birthday in two weeks, Dad. Can I have a party?'

Nick had been expecting this. Turning eighteen didn't happen every day, and he knew Sam deserved to celebrate it. But he'd hoped they could perhaps make do with a family dinner. He should have known better.

'A party? How big?'

'Not big. Just a few friends. Can I have it here?'

'Here?'

At the mention of a party, Nick had envisaged having to hire a hall somewhere, organising catering and all the associated costs. But to have one here? He'd read so many horrendous tales of parties being advertised on social media attracting crowds of gatecrashers, of houses wrecked, neighbours complaining, police being called.

'Just a few friends, Dad. Nothing outrageous. Honest. Please?' Sam said in the wheedling tone he'd always found difficult to refuse since she was little.

'We…ell.'

'Oh, Dad You're a star!' She flung her arms around his neck.

But, left on his own again, Nick wondered what he'd let himself in for. Did Sam think, now he'd spent one Saturday night at Kay's, that was going to be their pattern? That Sam and Ryan were to be left to their own devices every weekend? While the idea had some appeal, he dreaded to think what the two of them might get up to if he wasn't there to supervise their comings and goings. They were good kids, but even good kids could get into trouble. Look what had happened with Kay's daughter when she'd been left alone – and she was no teenager.

He and Kay planned to spend the day together. Now she no longer had Zoe and Noah to consider, she was a free agent, and before he'd left her at some ungodly hour this morning, he'd promised to be back for lunch.

Sam and Ryan were no problem. They both regarded Sundays as a day when they could do pretty much as they pleased, within reason, as long as they were home for dinner and in time to ensure all their homework was completed.

As Nick cleared up after breakfast, he reflected how his apparently well-designed schedule of tasks seemed to have broken down. Both Sam and Ryan had disappeared after eating leaving him to clear the table and stack the dishwasher, not to mention tidying up the kitchen. But perhaps it was worth it to have two happy children. He wasn't sure.

The thought of the party he'd agreed to was in the forefront of his mind when he arrived at Kay's house. He didn't mention it but, after a leisurely lunch consisting of leftovers from the previous evening washed down with a light beer, Kay asked, 'Something bothering you?'

'Not really.' Nick pushed his fingers through his beard to scratch his chin. 'It's Sam's birthday on the ninth,' he said. 'Her eighteenth. I've agreed she can have a party at home, but…'

'Eighteenth's a big one. You're worried it might get out of hand?'

'It's not that I don't trust her, but her friends… I don't know any of the boys she goes around with and…' Nick suddenly recalled Sam's revelation about Brett Cooper months ago, 'What if she's mixing with a bad crowd?'

'You mean like Zoe?' Kay chuckled. 'She only turns eighteen once. It should be special. Could you set limits – on numbers, noise, etcetera?'

'I suppose. And I'd need to be there.'

'She's turning eighteen, Nick, not eight. I don't think your presence would be very welcome.'

'Hmm.' He thought for a moment, then asked, 'What about if we were both there? Not at the party as such, but in the house – in my bedroom? She'd feel independent and we'd be there to handle any trouble. I keep thinking of all those reports of teenage parties going wrong. Are you up for it?'

'If Sam's okay with it. But you may be expecting too much. I'm not sure…'

'Good.'

*

The next two weeks flew by. With Kay's help, Nick had organised Melody and Jason from Mouthfuls to provide catering, and Sam had agreed to restrict the numbers to thirty. Even thirty sounded a lot to Nick, but Kay persuaded him it would be fine. He hoped so and had agreed – with some reluctance – to also provide what he considered to be a reasonable amount of alcohol, given that Sam – and most of her friends – were of drinking age. He did have a few concerns about the fact Ryan would also be at the party with his two best friends, but just had to hope he'd act sensibly.

Sam had made a solemn promise not to mention the party on social media and he trusted her. He hoped her friends had honoured her request to keep it off social media, too. At breakfast that morning, they'd sung Happy Birthday, and Sam had opened her presents – a new iPad from Nick and a pewter goblet with her name and birthdate inscribed on the side, plus a pair of silver earrings from Kay, which elicited an, 'I love them, Kay. Thanks!'

Then Sam let out a yell of delight when she opened the card from her mother and out fell a ticket to the Winter Solstice Music Fest. 'Wow! She did it! I didn't really think she would,' Sam said, gleefully.

Nick's lips tightened into a thin line. Michelle knew he'd refused Sam's demands to attend the festival. *Was this a form of revenge?*

'See? I have to go now, Dad,' she said, grinning.

*

'All set?'

'As I ever will be.' Nick thrust a hand through his hair. 'Do you think we should be there to greet everyone when they arrive?'

Sam, appearing behind them, heard his final words. 'No, Dad! Don't embarrass me in front of my friends. I'd never live it down if they saw you treating me like a small child. It's bad enough you'll be upstairs.'

But Nick had the strong suspicion she was glad to know they'd be there if anything did go wrong.

'You look lovely, Sam,' Kay said, and Sam twirled to show off her mid-thigh length dress with the deep V-neckline.

'Thanks, Kay,' Sam smiled, then pouted at Nick who was looking worried.

'You don't think it's a bit...' he began.

'No!' Sam and Kay said together, then Kay laughed. 'Sorry, Nick, but it's what all the girls are wearing these days, and the style suits Sam.'

Sam poked her tongue out at Nick, who held his hands up defensively. 'I can't argue with you both.'

'Now, Dad. Will you please disappear before everyone arrives?'

Nick grabbed a bottle of wine and two glasses, looked around the immaculate and peaceful house, shuddered to think what it might look like next morning and, taking Kay by the hand, led her upstairs.

Nick poured two glasses of wine and tried to relax, but he jumped each time the doorbell rang. Finally, as the party got going and the music became louder, Kay put a hand on his arm. 'You'll go mad if you carry on like this all night. She'll be right. They'll be right. We're not going to get to sleep anytime soon. Why don't we watch a movie on your iPad?'

'I don't think I could concentrate.' But Nick fired up the iPad and they chose to watch, not a movie, but the latest episodes of a Scandi thriller on SBS On Demand.

They were lost in the dark world of politics and crime, when there was the sound of footsteps running up the stairs, followed by giggling, and voices outside the family bathroom. Nick sighed. He'd hoped to keep upstairs out-of-bounds, but guessed the downstairs toilet was occupied. The iPad emitted a chord of dramatic music then there was a pregnant pause. In the pause a loud female voice yelled, 'These are *my* tits. Don't touch *my* tits!'

Nick and Kay broke into a peal of supressed laughter.

'That's Sam's friend, Ruby,' he said, when they'd calmed down. 'Glad she's not taking any nonsense from whoever she's with. She does have a good pair.'

Kay aimed a punch at him.

'Sorry!'

'If that's the worst that happens, there's no need for you to worry,' she said, snuggling down to enjoy the rest of their program.

The music eventually died down to a manageable level, and Nick and Kay were drifting off to sleep when there was a loud drunken yell from outside.

'Sam! Sammy! We heard it's your birthday!'

The yell was followed by the noise of the engines of what seemed like an unruly mob of motor-bikes revving and doing donuts on the road outside. There was more yelling, then the sound of the doorbell being rung continuously, accompanied by Sam's name being called again and again.

'What the hell?' Nick sat up and began to pull on his shirt and trousers. There was a gentle knock at the door.

'Dad?' Sam asked. 'Are you awake?'

'As if anyone could sleep through that racket,' Nick grumbled. 'You stay here,' he instructed Kay, who was rising, too. 'I'll handle it.'

He opened the door to discover a dishevelled Sam, eyes wild, her face pale. 'It's them, Dad. Declan's friends. The one that had the Harley out at his place when Ruby got hurt. He's brought his mates. I don't know what to do.'

'Is Declan at the party?' Nick asked as they went downstairs to where those of the party guests who were still there were standing wide-eyed. Sam nodded and bit her lip. There was no sign of Ryan or his friends. Nick hoped they were already in bed asleep, though he couldn't imagine anyone sleeping through this commotion.

He threw open the door. A couple of long-haired youths in leather jackets stood there, a couple more sitting on bikes in the roadway, engines still revving. They appeared stunned when they saw Nick.

'What do you want?' he asked, standing with his legs spread, his arms folded.

'We came to wish Sammy a happy birthday.'

'I think you've already done that. In fact, I think the entire street heard you.' Nick gestured to the neighbouring houses where lights were being switched on. *Exactly what he'd been trying to avoid.* 'Now, I think you should be on your way.'

'But we just wanted to…'

Nick could sense Sam trembling behind him. He partially closed the door, screening her with his body. 'Now!' he said with more confidence than he felt. 'Or I'll have to call the police.'

'But…' The youth who'd been doing all the talking tried to jam the door open with his foot. But one of his friends on the bikes yelled, 'Give up, Ray. We don't want the cops.'

The one called Ray turned to reply, his foot slipping out of the doorway, and Nick closed the door and locked it. He stood just inside till he heard the bikes leave, then turned to Sam.

'Thanks, Dad. It's been good till now.'

'Goodnight. It must be about time to finish up. See you in the morning.' He made his way slowly upstairs, glad he'd managed to chase the youths away, unsure what he'd have done if they'd decided to challenge him *en masse*.

When he reached the bedroom, he found Kay had fallen asleep.

*

Next morning, he awoke and drew Kay into his arms, inhaling her familiar fragrance and enjoying the feel of her soft skin against his.

'Good morning, sweetheart,' he murmured.

'Mmm.' Kay returned his embrace, the touch of her fingers on his body releasing all sorts of wonderful sensations.

It was some time before they surfaced again.

'Did you manage to get rid of those hooligans last night?' Kay asked, as they drew apart. 'I must have fallen asleep. I didn't hear you come back to bed.'

'You were dead to the world,' he said fondly, stroking a strand of hair out of her eyes. 'And, yes, I did send them on their way. Thank goodness. I don't think it was Sam's fault. It seems they were friends of Declan.'

Kay sat up. 'Isn't that the guy who…'

'Was responsible for the earlier Harley incident. Yes.'

'I suppose we should get up.'

'We should. I dread to think how we're going to find the place after last night.'

'Never mind, I can help clear up. It can't be too bad.'

'I wouldn't be too sure.'

Downstairs, they found the expected pile of dirty dishes, half-eaten food, empty bottles and glasses and a number of crushed cans. The garbage bin was overflowing, a sign someone had made an attempt at cleaning up, and there were dried puddles of a sticky substance coating the kitchen floor. The place stank of stale alcohol with a whiff of what was either cigarettes or marijuana.

'Yuck!' Kay said, wrinkling her nose.

Working together, it didn't take them long to tidy up the debris. Then Kay mopped the kitchen floor while Nick went around to open all the windows, discovering several bodies lying asleep on the living room floor.

'Some of the guests didn't make it home,' he said, drawing Kay in to have a look. 'Do you think we should provide them with some wake-up music?'

'That would be unkind,' she said giggling. 'But I'll get breakfast going. How about I fix a batch of pancakes?'

'Sounds just the shot. I'll check on Ryan.'

But at that moment, a sleepy and tousled Ryan appeared in the kitchen doorway. He blinked when he saw the activity going on there. 'What time is it?' he muttered.

'Close to nine o'clock,' Nick said. 'Kay's making pancakes.'

'Ugh!' Ryan said, and disappeared again.

'What's the matter with him? He loves pancakes. We haven't had them for breakfast since Michelle left.'

'You don't think…?' Kay asked, nodding towards the empty bottles and cans now filling the recycle bin.

'Ryan? He's only fourteen.'

'How old were you when you had your first taste of alcohol?'

'I don't remember. But I'm sure I was older.' Nick didn't want to believe Ryan could have been sampling any of the drinks provided for the eighteen-year-olds.

'Morning, Dad, Kay.' Sam bounced into the room, looking much brighter than her brother. 'Oh, is that pancakes you're making, Kay? Yum!'

At least she wasn't suffering from a surfeit of alcohol.

'You might want to waken your friends,' Nick said, inclining his head toward the living room. 'Kay's making enough for everyone.'

'Sorry, Dad. I said they could stay the night. It got late and…'

'That's okay. Better they spend the night here rather than drive with too much to drink,' Nick said.

'Can we have it outside? I'll set up the table. And thanks again for getting rid of those guys last night. I told Declan what I thought of him, but he just shrugged it off.' She gave Nick a hug. 'Have you seen Ryan this morning?' she asked, before she left, 'He and Jake got sick last night after drinking a bottle of cider Jake brought along.'

Nick and Kay exchanged a grin. That explained Ryan's brief appearance and his unfocussed eyes.

When she'd gone, Kay kissed Nick on the cheek. 'See, not too bad,' she said.

'No, but I can't leave them on their own when I'm in Chicago.' He took Kay by the shoulders and met her amused eyes. 'I know it's a lot to ask, but could you… would you be willing to stay with them while I'm gone?'

Thirty-nine

Kay waved Nick off and returned to her car with a heavy heart. Why did he have to go to this conference just as things between them were so good? She knew it was an honour for the vice chancellor to have chosen him to represent the university, but why Nick, when there were so many others to choose from?

She supposed the week would go quickly, and he'd promised to be in touch every day. But Kay knew the time difference would make that difficult.

She didn't regret agreeing to stand *in loco parentis* for Sam and Ryan while Nick was gone, but it would feel strange to be in his house without him. Fortunately, the two children didn't appear fazed by Nick's decision that they needed her supervision. Apart from Sam's initial, 'What do you think we're going to get up to, Dad?' she hadn't made any further protests.

Kay suspected this was due to her role in calming Nick down about the aftermath of the music festival. Unable to prevent Sam attending after Michelle had provided the ticket, Nick spent the whole weekend on tenterhooks waiting for a phone call from a hospital or the police. When none came, and Sam arrived home apparently unscathed, he'd breathed a sigh of relief.

Then, only a few days ago, Sam was removing her sweater and her school shirt rode up to display a small tattoo at her waist which she admitted she'd had done at the festival. Kay thought Nick was going to burst a blood vessel until she managed to calm him, persuaded him it wasn't a big deal, was quite common these days, and gained Sam's gratitude.

When she and Nick left that morning, both the children had still been asleep, having said their goodbyes the previous evening, making an exception to their busy life to spend the Friday evening at home with Kay and Nick. Both had told her they planned to be out all day Saturday to make up for it, so she would be left to her own devices.

Milly had arrived with Kay yesterday and, to her surprise, had settled in well to her new surroundings. The two teenagers had welcomed her arrival, particularly Sam who immediately made a big fuss of the cat.

Now Kay was free to meet with Jo for her usual Saturday morning coffee.

Knowing she'd have more free time in the coming week, Kay took her time choosing her library books before venturing to the café.

'That's a bigger bundle than usual,' Jo said, when Kay walked in carrying books by Lin Anderson, Caro Ramsay, Karen Shaw, and Jo Thomas. 'Do you plan to read all of those this week?'

'Probably. I'll be at a loose end with Nick gone, and I don't expect Sam and Ryan will want to spend much time with me.'

'You'll miss him.' It wasn't a question. Her next words were, 'When are you two going to stop dilly-dallying around each other? You're practically living there now. Why don't you make it more permanent?'

'Oh, I don't think so, Jo. It's one thing to spend time there, even to take care of the place while he's gone, but… anything more permanent.' She hesitated, considering the very matter that had been exercising her mind for some time now. 'There are Sam and Ryan for one thing.'

'That's two.'

Kay continued as if her friend hadn't spoken. 'Then there's my own house. I can't just leave it empty.'

'I thought you were planning to sell it anyway before Zoe landed on you.'

Kay thought back to the beginning of the year. It seemed so long ago. Six months. That was all. Yet so much had happened. 'I did,' she said, reflectively, 'but I intended to buy something else, something smaller. If I sell and move in with Nick… what if things don't work out? I'll be left homeless.'

'You can always stay with us for a bit.'

'Anyway, he hasn't asked me.'

'But you think he might?' Jo wasn't going to let it go.

'Who knows?' Kay shrugged. This conversation was making her feel uncomfortable. What she and Nick had was private, not something to be bandied about over coffee with Jo, even though she was a good friend. And Kay still found the thought of taking on two teenagers on a permanent basis to be daunting.

'If you could choose, what would it be – to live on your own or with Nick?' Jo persisted.

Their coffees arrived at that point, and Kay was able to use the interruption to change the subject, but Jo's words stayed with her.

If offered the choice, which would she decide?

*

As the week progressed, Kay was surprised how easy Sam and Ryan were to be with. Teenagers these days were different. They weren't like they'd been when Adam and Zoe were that age. As soon as they arrived home from school, they'd disappear to their rooms, ostensibly to do homework. It was difficult to police these days. All homework seemed to be done on their laptops, so schoolwork blended into recreational activities, which took the form of computer games for Ryan and movies for Sam.

By the time Monday came along, Kay was glad to have the distraction of work to fill her mind, though thoughts of Nick were never far away, his empty office sitting next to hers like a yawning chasm.

She spent most of the morning trying to work out the time difference to calculate when she might hear from him. Kay knew the time he was due to arrive in Chicago if the plane was on time – his timetable was imprinted on her brain. But that had been the middle of the night here. As the morning progressed, she kept checking to see if there was a text, disappointed when none appeared.

Halfway through the bank of emails that always accumulated over the weekend, Kay faltered at one with an unfamiliar address. She hesitated, wondering if she should assign it to the spam folder, then decided to take the risk and open it. She was glad she did. It was from Fran Reilly, the woman whose place she'd taken as Nick's PA. It was addressed to her.

Kay skimmed the contents, then settled to read it more carefully. It appeared Ann Baird had been in touch with Fran who knew Kay had stepped into her role.

Hello Kay,

I was pleased to hear from Ann Baird that you'd stepped up to be Professor Kerr's PA in my absence. I felt bad leaving him at such short notice but, as I think you know, my mother became very ill. I hope you haven't found him too trying to work with. I know he's very set in his ways and can be difficult at times.

Kay smiled. *Was this the Nick she knew?* She continued reading.

I had intended to write before to ask if there was anything with which you needed help, but it's been a difficult time here and, sadly, it's over now. Mum passed away a week ago and I'm still trying to come to terms with my loss.

Having lived in Australia for many years, we weren't as close as I'd have liked, but it was good to be able to spend these final months with her. I know you understand loss.

As I've just written to Ann, I need to be here for another month at least, while I sort out her estate, sell the house etc. I look forward to seeing you when I return and to re-joining the choir.

Kind regards,

Fran Reilly

Another month at least. Kay read that line again. It meant Fran would most likely be back some time in July or August. What would she do then? Go back to the general office? She didn't think she could bear the gossip and backbiting that went on there after the independence and responsibility she'd had as Nick's PA. Maybe she could find a similar role in one of the other faculties? She'd discuss it with Nick when he got back.

At that moment her phone rang.

Forty

Nick gazed around as he checked into the Blackstone Hotel. It was years since he'd been here, and it appeared to have undergone a substantial restoration. He recalled reading somewhere that it had been closed for several years for safety reasons, and was glad it still retained its age-old atmosphere as the stately old lady which had hosted many celebrities and boasted the title *Hotel of Presidents*.

Located as it was in downtown Chicago, it was a good choice. It was only a ten-minute walk to the conference venue in the Hyatt Regency, and he could also walk to anywhere else he wanted to go. Nick was pleased he wasn't staying in the conference venue itself. He knew he'd want to get some respite from the rarefied atmosphere of the conference to relax.

Accepting his room key, Nick headed to the elevator. Seconds later he exited to find his room had a view over Lake Michigan, and, when he investigated the ensuite, that there was even a marble bath. The luxury room had originally been booked for Aaron by Sheila and it fitted Nick's needs perfectly. Exhausted from the long trip, without undressing, he dropped onto the king-sized bed and was soon lost to the world.

Nick awoke with a start to find himself in darkness. Where was he? Then he remembered. He was in Chicago and it was almost nine o'clock at night. He sat up feeling hungry.

After a quick wash, Nick removed his jacket and tie, opened the top button of his shirt, and rolled up the sleeves. There would be time enough tomorrow to present the professional image required at the conference. Once downstairs, Nick once again admired the vast ceilings and the ornate staircase. It was a trip down memory lane, but back then, he'd stayed in one of the cheaper rooms.

His requirement for food was pressing, and he stepped outside, the blast of humidity coming as a shock after the air-conditioning inside the building. Nearby was a Spanish restaurant. It seemed to be attached to the hotel and was advertising tapas. He walked in, hearing the unfamiliar yet well-remembered accents. It reminded him of his student days. He was back in the United States.

After ordering a selection of meat and vegetarian tapas and a bottle of mineral water – his internal timeclock couldn't face the alcohol being noisily swilled by the other patrons – Nick took out his phone. Nine o'clock on a Sunday evening in Chicago would be Monday morning in Granite Springs. He could catch Kay at work.

'Hello?' Kay's voice was guarded. He guessed she wasn't in the habit of answering her mobile at work.

'Hi, Kay. I wanted to let you know I'm here in Chicago. I got in a few hours ago and conked out. I'm just having a bite to eat – that's the noise you hear in the background,' he added, conscious of the hubbub of chatter and laughter around him. 'I had an urge to hear your voice.'

'Nick! I hoped it might be you. I don't usually answer my mobile in the office. I normally keep it turned off. But you did say you'd be in touch and... Sorry, I'm babbling. How was your trip?'

'Exhausting. We should have gone for business class. The seats in economy aren't made for legs the length of mine.'

He heard her chuckle. They'd had a minor dispute about that very thing. Kay had been right. He now regretted not taking her advice. And he had the return trip to look forward to.

'I can change your return flight,' she offered as if reading his mind.

'No, don't bother. I'll survive. How are you coping? Are Sam and Ryan behaving themselves?'

'Everything's fine here. Maybe too fine. I'm just waiting for the storm to break.' He heard her chuckle.

'You know how grateful I am you agreed to help out. They'd likely have been okay, but...'

'I understand. The horrors of returning home to find the house has been turned into a drugs den, to find odd pieces of clothing hanging from the lampshades, the place reeking of cigarette smoke, empty bottles lying around the floor, not to mention comatose bodies… But, believe me – I speak from experience – it would all have been put back to normal before you returned.'

'That's what I was afraid of – that I'd never know.'

'Oh, you'd know all right. I remember when Jo and her then husband left their three for a weekend. They live on an acreage and returned to an immaculate house with all the windows wide open – in the middle of winter!'

'You've relieved me.' It was Nick's turn to chuckle. 'So, nothing dire has happened at home or work since I left?' Nick suddenly felt isolated from his life – as if he was on another planet. It was strange to think of everything carrying on as usual without him.

He heard Kay chuckle again, the sound was music to his ears. It was almost as if she was right there with him. 'You've only been gone since Saturday. We had a quiet couple of days. They saw friends, caught up on homework, and got off to school this morning.'

'Sorry. It seems like forever. My internal timeclock is shot to pieces. I miss you.'

'I miss you too.' There was a yearning in Kay's voice he hadn't heard before.

Nick wanted to touch her, to feel her in his arms, to smell her unique fragrance.

'Coffee, sir?' The waiter was leaning towards him with a large jug of black coffee. How could he have forgotten Americans lived on the stuff? Nick shook his head. If he had coffee now, he'd never get back to sleep. Maybe he should have tried to remain awake. Wasn't that what you were supposed to do to avoid the dreaded jetlag?

Kay was speaking. 'I almost forgot. Sam wants to know if she can go skiing the weekend after next. I said I'd check with you when you called.'

'I suppose she said everyone else is going?'

'Pretty much.' He could hear the smile in her voice.

'I don't see why not, as long as there are proper arrangements made. I'll be back before then so…'

They were both silent, imagining what it would be like for him to be home again. Nick had just arrived in Chicago and already was wishing himself back home.

*

To his surprise, Nick did manage to get a good night's sleep, awakening refreshed and ready to face the raft of conference sessions Aaron had earmarked for him. Arriving at the venue in plenty of time, he had just registered and received his conference materials when he heard a vaguely familiar voice behind him.

'Nick Kerr! It is you, isn't it? What are you doing here?'

Nick turned quickly to see a face he'd thought never to see again. Nadia Porter had dated his roommate when he was studying for his doctorate. They'd seen each other a couple of times, then Nick had told her he couldn't see her again, couldn't do that to his friend. As far as Nick had been concerned, it had been a brief interval, ending with no recriminations on either side. They'd gone their separate ways and he later heard she'd married another student and moved to Hawaii.

She was the last person he'd expected to encounter in Chicago.

She'd worn well. The slight dark-haired pixie-like girl he remembered, had filled out somewhat and the dark hair was now streaked – or highlighted – with grey. But the eyes were the same and now held a mischievous gleam, and her reddened lips were turned up in her old attractive grin.

'Nadia! What the...? I'm representing our vice chancellor. I head up the Faculty of Education in a regional university in Australia.'

'I heard you'd gone back to the other end of the earth – and married.' She shook her head in either disapproval or disbelief.

'Not anymore,' the words slipped out without any thought. 'But you? I heard you married and were living in Hawaii.'

'Old news. I'm living here in Chicago now and I'm part of the organising body for this affair.'

As she spoke, Nick noticed she was wearing a lanyard with a tag which indicated she was some sort of co-ordinator.

'Must dash, but you are coming to the cocktail party tonight? You mustn't miss it. See you there.' She winked.

Before Nick had time to consider what had just happened, he was buttonholed by a fellow Australian. Rod Barron came from Sydney and he and Nick had met at previous conferences over the years. 'Your boss managed to get out of it, too?' he asked. 'I've heard it's going to be boring as shit apart from the session on…' He prattled on, but Nick had ceased to listen. What were the chances of coming halfway across the world and bumping into Nadia Porter, and why did he feel guilty about it?

He decided he would give the cocktail party a miss. It would probably be full of old fogies. Grabbing a coffee from a passing coffee-cart, Nick identified the room for the first session he was due to attend and, with a, 'See you later, mate,' to his companion, he headed in that direction.

*

The day passed more quickly than Nick had expected. Some of the sessions were interesting, some not so much, but he felt very virtuous as he dutifully took notes for Aaron as requested. To his relief, there had been no sign of Nadia all day, but as the time for the cocktail party drew closer, he was dismayed to sense an irrational annoyance at her apparent expectation he'd be willing to rekindle a relationship which had barely existed all those years ago.

About to head back to the Blackthorn, Nick found himself shoulder-to-shoulder with Rod Barron.

'Heading to the cocktail party, mate?'

'Not tonight, Rod. Still a bit jetlagged. Planning an early night.'

'Don't be a party-pooper. We Aussies need to stick together, and I've heard there'll be some good sorts turning up.' He gave a smirk which made Nick more determined than ever to avoid the event.

'Sorry.' Nick loosened Rod's hand which had firmly attached itself to his elbow. 'It's not for me, Rod. You enjoy it.'

But Rod wasn't to be brushed off so easily. 'Just for a few minutes, Nick. You can't leave me alone with all those old blokes who don't even speak proper English.'

Nick had to laugh. He weakened. 'Okay. But I'll only stay for one drink. Then you're on your own. Right?'

'If you say so.'

As Nick had anticipated, the room where the cocktail party was being held was already filled to capacity with aged academics, intent on getting their hands on as many free cocktails as they could in the allotted time. The sound of their conversations was deafening, and Nick regretted giving in to Rod's demands even before he walked in.

Immediately they entered, the two men were offered a selection of drinks from a tray, then became separated in the crush. So much for Aussies sticking together, Nick thought. He took a slug of the unidentified liquid, grimaced at the strength of the alcohol, then looked around for an escape route.

He was about to make his getaway, weaving his way between groups of chatting conference participants, when he came face-to-face with Nadia Porter.

Tonight, she was dressed in a slinky number which left little to the imagination and clearly demonstrated the curves she hadn't had when Nick first knew her.

'I've been looking for you,' she said, swaying closer, her glass tipping over to spill most of its contents over Nick's shirt. 'Oops,' she said with a grin. 'Have you been hiding from me? Naughty, naughty!' She pointed the now empty glass into his face.

The woman was drunk! How long had she been here, and how many of these lethal mixes had she consumed?

There was no way he could avoid her or leave without causing a disturbance. 'I think you may have had enough of those,' he said, relieving her of her glass and depositing it, along with his own, on a nearby table.

Nick could feel people turning to look at them, could hear their tut-tutting. The tips of his ears turned red. He just wanted to get out of there, but there was no way he could leave Nadia in this state.

He knew he shouldn't have come!

There was no sign of Rod. He was on his own – on his own with an intoxicated woman who thought he… what *did* she think?

'Let's get you out of here,' he muttered, taking the still swaying Nadia by the arm and manhandling her through the crowd which now parted – with murmured comments – to allow them through.

Once at the door, he stopped, unsure what to do now, but Nadia handed him a set of keys. 'Car's underneath,' she slurred.

Nick looked at the keys and the silver keyring with the familiar VW logo. At least he knew which model of car to look for. But Nadia was too far gone to drive.

As if realising that at the same time he did, she said, her voice still slurred, 'You'll need to drive me home, Nicky.'

Nick grimaced. No one had called him Nicky for years. He wasn't that person any longer. Now he was Professor Nick Kerr, respected member of the community, father to two teenagers, undergoing a divorce from his first wife and trying to make a fresh start.

How had he managed to get himself into this situation?

Once in the car with the windows down, Nadia recovered sufficiently to give directions to her condo in a modern apartment block on the north side of the city. As he drove into the underground parking, it occurred to Nick she must be earning a good whack to be able to afford this.

'Will you be right now?' he asked, turning to his companion, ready to leave and find a cab. But Nadia seemed to have fallen asleep, her head lolling against the window frame. Nick cursed.

Picking up her bag from her lap, Nick hesitated for a moment, then searched for her wallet. He detested handling women's handbags, always having avoided Michelle's like the plague. He found her wallet and, inside that, her driving license. He read the address and, on discovering she lived in apartment 1203, which he assumed was on the twelfth floor, managed to half-carry Nadia to the elevator, where he propped her against the wall while he pressed the button.

At level twelve, Nick was pleased to see number three immediately opposite. He managed to open the door and make their way into the bedroom where he dropped Nadia's now inert body on the bed, before going to the kitchen to help himself to a glass of water.

Intrigued to see more of the apartment, Nick took his drink into the living room, impressed by the expensive-looking furniture and the city views from the floor-to-ceiling windows. But it was time to go, time to find a cab in the street below, time to get back to his own life, time to call Kay.

Before he left, Nick decided to check on Nadia to ensure she hadn't been sick. Maybe he should place a bowl beside the bed in case that happened? She was lying where he'd left her, one arm across her body, the other stretched above her head. She was very still.

Nick leant over her to make sure she was still breathing, only to find her eyes fly open and her arms wind round his neck enveloping him in a tight embrace.

'Nicky! Stay with me! Please don't go!'

Nick recoiled, as much as he could, given the tight grip of her arms. He reached to release himself. 'No, Nadia!'

'But we're both lonely. You told me your marriage was over. Two lonely souls in a lonely city.' She tried to tighten her grip.

How had she made such a fast recovery? Or had she been pretending? Had it all been a ploy to get him here?

'I'm not lonely, Nadia,' he said gently, trying to remove her hands again, 'I'm sorry if you are. You're a lovely woman. There is someone out there for you, but it's not me. I do have someone back home and she will be expecting my call. Now, I must go.'

Suddenly Nadia released her grip. 'Go then, but you'll be sorry! No one rejects what I have to offer.' Her lips curled up making Nick wonder how he could ever have thought her attractive and wishing he'd never set eyes on her again, never come to this damned conference. And he had still to make it through the next five days of it before he could go back home.

Forty-one

Kay looked at the empty desk in the next-door office. Nick had been gone five days and she missed him so much. She missed his reassuring presence in the neighbouring office, his voice calling through the doorway and, let's face it, she told herself, she missed him in her bed. Only one day to go.

The mail lay where she'd dropped it after her morning tea break and now she picked it up and flicked through the bundle, putting aside anything deemed as personal for Nick's return, the more official ones in a pile for her to deal with, and dropping the junk mail in the bin. It was very much an automatic process, one she did every day, and required very little thought.

But, this morning, her hand hesitated over one envelope. Bearing a United States stamp and a Chicago postmark, it was addressed to *Professor Kerr's Office*. Was this some joke of Nick's? It had been sent the day after the conference started and it was amazing it had travelled so quickly.

Kay slit the envelope with the letter opener she'd had no use for till she started here. It was a neat little gadget she'd found on a market stall on one of her visits to Brisbane and had immediately fallen in love with the tiny silver object with the rose-patterned handle.

Phil Little came in just as she was opening the letter and scanning its contents. Her eyes dulled, her mouth falling open as she read the first sentence.

'Is everything all right, Kay?'

His question brought Kay back to the present. She tore her eyes from the sheet of paper and tried to focus on him. 'Sorry, Phil. What did you want?'

'Do you have the list of the New Zealand schools that have agreed to provide placements for our students? You've gone very pale. Are you sure you're all right? Do you want me to come back later?'

'No. Yes. Sorry, Phil. I've just had a shock. Later would be good, or I can email you the list.'

'Fine.' He gave her another worried look and left, closing the door quietly behind him.

Kay picked up the letter from where it had fallen, and re-read,

My Darling Nicky,

It was so wonderful to meet you again last night, to discover we still had the same magic as all those years ago. It felt so right to be in your arms again. We…

Kay couldn't read any more. Nick! Her Nick! The Nick who rang her every day, who claimed to love and miss her was… cavorting with some woman from his past in Chicago. How could he?

She carefully folded the letter and replaced it in the envelope, but not before catching sight of the sender's name – Nadia. It evoked the image of an exotic blonde beauty – someone who was her complete opposite. Taking the envelope into Nick's office, she placed it centrally on his desk, where he'd be sure to see it as soon as he walked in. Then she went to the ladies and washed her hands, wishing she could wash away the memory of those words as easily.

The rest of the day passed in a blur and by the time Kay left for home – Nick's home – she was exhausted. She didn't want to go there today to face his two children. All she wanted to do was to return to her own home, go to bed, and hide under the covers for a long, long time. But she couldn't do that. She'd made a commitment to Nick to take care of Sam and Ryan while he was gone and, although he might have defaulted on his commitment to her, his children didn't deserve to be abandoned.

Nick was due home next day and she'd been planning a special welcome home meal. Now, she was dreading his return.

Remembering Ryan had soccer practice after school, and Sam was planning to spend the evening studying with her friend, Jackie, Kay decided to take a detour on the way back. Jo lived on the same side of town as Nick, albeit further out, and she desperately needed a shoulder to cry on.

Kay felt her mood change as her car bumped across the cattle grid at the entrance to Yarran, the acreage where Jo and Col lived. It was impossible to feel the ambiance of this peaceful spot and not be affected by it.

'Kay, what's happened?' Jo greeted her at the door, her dog, Scout, padding behind her.

'Do I look that bad?' Kay tried to joke, but her voice broke. 'Oh, Jo! It's Nick.'

'Has there been an accident? Isn't he still at that conference of his?'

'No accident and yes, he's still in Chicago. That's…' She began to sob.

'Sounds like you need a drink. Col's playing golf today and won't be home for ages. It's one of the few times he and Gordon get together these days and they tend to make the most of it. I expect my ex will be bending his ear about his forthcoming foray into fatherhood – for the fifth time. He's behaving as if no one ever had a child at his age before!'

Kay was grateful for her friend's inconsequential chatter. She knew it was designed to give her time to gain control of her emotions. 'Wine would be good thanks.'

Once the two were settled in Jo's large family kitchen with their wine, Jo asked, 'Now, what's this all about?'

Wiping her nose and eyes with a tissue, Kay began to speak and haltingly told Jo about the letter, reciting what she had read, the words imprinted on her memory.

'Oh, my dear!' Jo put a hand on Kay's arm. 'But that doesn't sound like your Nick. What was in the rest of the letter?'

'I don't know. I couldn't bear to read any further.' Kay took a gulp of the wine, then put the glass down remembering she had to drive back into town and face Nick's two children. 'What should I do? I don't think I could continue to work there if…' She felt the tears begin again and used the now damp tissue to scrub her eyes.

Jo handed her a fresh tissue.

'Thanks.' Kay rubbed her eyes again, then scrunched the tissue in her hand.

'Well, you can't do anything right now. There are those two children of his who'd do goodness knows what if you weren't there to keep an eye on them. We both know what teenagers can get up to – even the ones that appear most responsible. And you can't leave the university in the lurch either. I think you'll need to tough it out till he gets back and take it from there. Maybe he'll have some explanation.'

'Unlikely. Oh, Jo! How could I have got it so wrong? To have been lied to by one man, then this. Is there something wrong with *me*?'

'Not last time I looked. And it's hardly the same. There may well be some simple explanation.'

'How can there be? Why would any woman write to a man like that if there hadn't been something…?'

'Neither you nor I would, but there are some women who think nothing of making up to a man like that.'

'But what she said? "In his arms"? They must have…'

'As I said. I think you should wait till he gets back and ask him about it.'

'But it was addressed to him,' Kay wailed. 'I opened his letter. I'd never have known otherwise.'

'You're his personal assistant. Isn't it your job to open his mail?'

'His work-related mail.'

'And was there anything about this one to say it wasn't?'

'No…oo.'

'Well then. You've nothing to worry about.'

Jo sounded so certain, so matter of fact, but Kay knew it wasn't that simple. Nothing about it was simple. How was she going to survive until Nick got back? More importantly, how was she going to survive *when* Nick got back?

Forty-two

The rest of the conference passed in a blur for Nick. It seemed to be one boring speaker or panel after another. He took notes religiously and tried to avoid Nadia between sessions. It proved easier than he thought. Maybe she'd got the message and her parting shot had been one of bravado. He didn't imagine many men refused her predatory advances. He shivered. That's what they had been. She'd resembled one of those man-eating spiders he'd heard about, the ones which mated then ate their partners alive. At least he'd escaped that fate.

Now it was all but over, there was only the conference dinner to get through and he was done. Tomorrow, he'd be on the plane back to Australia and, two days later, back in Granite Springs. He couldn't wait to see Kay again. He thought she'd seemed a little distant on the phone these past couple of days but excused her by reason of the time difference, and regretted they hadn't been able to skype more. Even facetime hadn't proved effective. She had looked tired. Maybe the whole business of looking after Sam and Ryan had been too much for her. After all, she wasn't used to teenagers, hadn't been for a number of years. He thought of what he planned to propose to her on his return. Would taking on two teenagers prove an obstacle?

It would be good to see the kids again, too. Kay had said there were no problems, but would she have told him if there were? Probably not. She wouldn't want to worry him. She was like that – considerate. If it had been Michelle, there would have been a flurry of texts complaining about this and that, wanting decisions about the other.

Nick remembered what it used to be like. He'd have had no peace. It was as if she wanted to punish him for going away each time he'd gone to a conference. Then *she* was the one who'd left *him*.

Now he hummed as he showered, trimmed his beard and dressed for the dinner. He'd made arrangements with Rod to meet him at the pre-dinner drinks session and intended to stick close to him all evening. No way was he going to get caught the way he had been at the cocktail party. Once bitten twice shy where that one was concerned.

Had Nadia always been like that, he wondered, trying to think back to his student days at the University of California, Los Angeles. It was so long ago, his memory was blunted by his desire to finish his degree and get back to Oz and on with his career.

Nadia had been a local girl, a master's student in the School of Business who'd been dating one of his friends. She'd come onto him one night when they were all celebrating something or other – a football game, he seemed to recollect, when the Bruins had roundly defeated their rivals. His mate had been out of it, having quaffed a yard of ale early in the night and gone on from there. Nadia had been pissed off at his drunken state and, looking around for a replacement, had settled on the only unattached male in the group, who happened to be Nick. They'd got together for a brief time but, for Nick, his studies came first. It had never been meant to last.

'Hey, Nick!' Rod greeted him, his glass already close to empty. 'You have some catching up to do. We've been here since... where is she?' His eyes roamed around the room in search of someone, then he turned back to Nick. 'You wouldn't believe my luck,' he said in a confiding tone. 'Met this cracker of a woman – one of the conference organisers – and let me tell you...'

He was interrupted by the arrival of the woman in question wearing a slinky red dress, her face caked with makeup, and a sly smirk on her face. 'So, we meet again, Nick. I was beginning to think you were avoiding me,' Nadia said.

'You know each other?' Rod appeared surprised. 'Nadia?'

'Old friends,' Nadia said coyly. 'Wouldn't you say, Nick? Or somewhat more than friends?'

Nick felt his ears go red. She certainly knew how to embarrass a man. 'We knew each other briefly back when I was studying in LA,

Rod. Long time ago.' He glared at her, daring her to mention the cocktail party.

'That's all right then.' Rod exhaled loudly. 'Now, what say we three make a night of it? Nadia here knows all the live spots in Chicago. We can carry on after the dinner and hit the town. It's bound to be a dull affair.' He gestured towards their fellow conference participants, none of whom looked as if they were going to set the town on fire.

'I don't think,' Nick began, only to be interrupted by Nadia.

'Great idea,' she said, linking arms with both men as everyone moved into the dinner.

Nick was barely conscious of what he ate as he tried to work out how he was going to escape his two companions after the meal. He made sure he drank more water than alcohol, so he was in no danger of getting drunk. It was when the dessert arrived – a rich concoction of chocolate, cream and strawberries – that he made his move.

'I'm sorry,' he said rising and holding his stomach. 'Not feeling too good. I think I'm going to be sick.' Waving away Nadia's offer to accompany him, and Rod's, 'Too bad, mate. We'll wait for you after', he made his way out of the room, leaning against the wall in the hotel foyer before calling a cab.

Once in the cab, he breathed a sigh of relief. That had been a close call. Nick didn't want a repeat of what happened all those years ago. He knew he wasn't flattering himself by imagining that was what Nadia had in mind. Had she even got involved with Rod in the first place to put Nick in her path again? Surely that was beyond even *her* wiles?

Back in his hotel room, Nick made sure everything was ready for his departure in the morning. He sent texts to Sam and Ryan, telling them how much he missed them and warning them of his return, then sat down on the side of the bed and opened his iPad to skype Kay. Almost midday in Granite Springs.

Without much hope, he pressed her number. She'd be busy at this time of day, and unlikely to be available, but he was desperate to see her face. It rang and rang with no reply. Disappointed, he texted her too, then closed the phone and sat looking at it, wondering exactly where she was right now, what she was doing, who she was talking to. He had imagined her sitting at her desk, her dark hair falling over her face, an intent expression as she busily typed away. Maybe she was in a meeting, or in the library, or having an early lunch. Nick wondered if she was missing him as much as he was her.

He remembered everything about her, the feel of her skin, the way her eyes twinkled when she was amused, the delightful fragrance that followed her around. That's it! That's what he'd do. He had no idea what the perfume she wore was called, but he knew he'd recognise it. The scent was stamped on his brain. He'd leave early enough to spend time in the duty-free section of the airport and, if he had to, try every fragrance till he found the right one.

Forty-three

Kay arrived back at the same time as both Sam and Ryan. She couldn't stop thinking about that letter, wondering what this Nadia looked like. Was she the blonde beauty she'd imagined, or was she a sultry dark-haired charmer? She'd be intelligent. If they'd met at the conference, she'd most likely be an academic or in some sort of leadership position. The image behind Kay's eyes reformed as a slick professional woman, smartly dressed, with designer styled hair and simple but expensive, gold jewellery. It made her feel dowdy just imagining it.

She was beset again by the doubts Nick had helped her suppress. What could he see in her? How could he be attracted to an older woman, a widow with more baggage than a busload of tourists?

'Hi, Kay,' Sam called dropping her bag on the hall floor and heading for her room, the door closing behind her.

'Anything to eat?' Ryan followed Kay into the kitchen. 'I'm starved. I made the team for Saturday. Will Dad be back?'

'He'll be back tomorrow. Remember? Early afternoon, I think.' Think? The date and time were tattooed on her brain, or had been till this morning. Now, all she wanted to do was forget him. But how could she do that when she was living in his house, taking care of his children? What a mess!

'Take an apple if you're hungry,' she said. 'I'll make a start on dinner. It won't be long.'

Glad there was plenty left over from the weekend roast, Kay dumped her bag in the bedroom she'd shared with Nick. She grimaced in the mirror at the extra lines around her eyes that seemed to have appeared since morning and set to fixing a meal for the three of them, managing to down a glass of wine while she was cooking to dull the ache around the place her heart used to be.

In her anguish she almost forgot about Milly, only reminded when a loud meow claimed her attention. Poor Milly! The cat had settled into her new temporary home this week without too much fuss, quickly choosing Sam as her new special person. To Kay's surprise, the eighteen-year-old seemed flattered to be the object of Milly's no doubt fleeting attention, allowing the cat to sleep on her bed and feeding her titbits.

'I always wanted a cat,' the girl confided in her, 'but Mum hates them.' Milly's presence in the house helped Kay feel more at home in the strange house and had helped her bond with Nick's older child.

There was no need for a cat to help her bond with Ryan. The boy had accepted her straight away, his experience in Queensland with his mother's partner making him grateful for her more welcoming manner.

'Dinner's ready!' she called through to the study where she could hear Ryan on the computer. He seemed to spend an inordinate amount of time there, either on homework or one of those dreaded computer games she'd read so much about. But it wasn't her role to discipline him when Nick was away, and she wouldn't be around after he got back. 'Can you let Sam know?' she added, knowing her voice wouldn't carry upstairs and through the door of Sam's room.

'You need to go up. She won't hear you,' Kay said, hearing Ryan only repeating her words from where he was sitting. She sighed, feeling frustrated at the lazy behaviour she'd normally ignore, or even be amused by. Teenagers hadn't changed much since her own, she'd discovered. They were still self-centred, careless of the needs of others and unwilling to help around the house unless pushed. But, until today, she'd enjoyed spending time with these two.

Dinner over, Kay felt restless. There was nothing on the television that appealed, and she couldn't concentrate on the book she was reading. Even Milly had abandoned her to join Sam. She decided to take a bath and have an early night.

Kay's phone rang before she made it to bed. Seeing Zoe's face on the screen, she took a deep breath expecting a list of her usual complaints, but she was in for a surprise. Her daughter's voice was so weak Kay could barely hear her.

'What's wrong, darling? You sound dreadful.'

For a moment there was no reply, then a voice Kay scarcely recognised as her daughter's said. 'I'm sick, Eric's sick, we're all sick with an awful gastric bug and I don't know what to do.'

Kay wanted to hug Zoe. This was the excuse she'd been waiting for. 'Would you like me to come up to Brisbane until you get on your feet again?'

'Mum, would you?' Kay could hear the relief in her daughter's voice. 'I didn't like to ask.'

That'd be a first.

'I thought you'd be too busy with your job and… didn't you say you were taking care of your professor's kids?'

'They're old enough to take care of themselves,' Kay said rashly. 'And anyway he'll be back tomorrow. I can check with Ann Baird tonight about work and book a flight. I'll text you when I know more.'

Kay was feeling almost jubilant as she finished the call. Ann wouldn't be pleased, but surely she'd be able to find someone from the office to fill in for a bit. With Nick away, everything was pretty much up-to-date, and Kay could go in to brief her in the morning.

She was right. Ann wasn't pleased, muttering something about families, sick children, and work ethic. Kay didn't care. Ann had agreed to approving her leave. Next, all thought of an early night forgotten, Kay searched the internet for flights, finding to her amusement that she could book a seat for the return flight on the Qantas-link that was bringing Nick home. She didn't stop to think about the wisdom of that, she was so eager to leave town, and Zoe *did* need her. Refusing to consider how she'd have reacted to Zoe's phone call if there had been no letter, if she'd still been looking forward to her reunion with Nick, she made the booking to Sydney and the connecting flight to Brisbane, then texted Zoe before finally going to bed.

*

'Your dad will be home today, and I have to go to Brisbane.' Kay broke the news to Sam and Ryan over breakfast next morning.

The pair looked at her in amazement.

'But I thought you were going to cook a special meal to celebrate his return. You said you would,' Ryan said, shovelling up his cereal as if there was no tomorrow.

'I was. I did. But my daughter and her family are all sick and they need me there to help.' Kay felt bad at leaving them in the lurch, but the relief at having an excuse to leave was too great to refuse.

'What about Milly?' asked Sam.

Milly! In the rush of making bookings and packing, Kay had completely forgotten about her cat. *How could she have?*

As if hearing her name, Milly chose that moment to appear in the kitchen meowing loudly. 'Poor Milly,' Kay said, picking up the cat and giving her a cuddle. 'I'll need to leave her here. Can you take care of her till I get back, Sam? You know where her food is, don't you?'

'I suppose so,' Sam muttered, giving Kay the impression that, while she loved the cat's company, it would be a chore to actually take care of her.

'Thanks.'

Once the children had gone off to school, Kay made sure everything was tidy and there was no evidence left of her stay. Then she filled Milly's bowls, gave her a cuddle, and set off for the university.

Ann Baird's expression mirrored her displeasure, but she introduced Kay to Wendy, the young girl who'd agreed to step in for her, and Kay spent the morning explaining and handing over the routine tasks. 'Professor Kerr will let you know about anything else he needs done tomorrow,' she said at last.

'What's he like to work for?' Wendy asked in a tremulous voice. 'Is he difficult? I've only ever seen him at a distance.'

Kay remembered how she'd felt that first morning when Ann took her up to Nick's office, and how he'd put her at her ease so quickly. An image of him smiling at her appeared in her mind's eye, immediately followed by one of him in a more intimate situation. Trying to dismiss it, she replied, 'I think you'll find him easy to work for. Be sure to ask him about anything you don't understand.'

'When will you be back?'

It was a reasonable question, and one to which Kay didn't have an answer. She didn't want to come back at all, and maybe she wouldn't, but she couldn't tell this poor girl that. 'I'm not sure,' she said. 'It depends on how long it takes my family to recover. But I'll keep in touch with Ann. She'll be able to let you know.' *And that'll save me contacting Nick.*

It was with a feeling of loss that she drove away from the campus in Nick's car and headed towards the airport. Kay knew she'd have to meet Nick there. When they'd arranged this meeting, it was to have been a joyous reunion, now she didn't know how she could bear to see his cheating face, the face of the man she still loved, but who she had to force herself to forget.

Forty-four

Nick couldn't supress the quiver of excitement that gripped him as he saw the rooftops of Granite Springs below him. It had been a long flight, made longer than usual by a delay in Los Angeles, then another in Sydney, but he was almost home now and couldn't wait to see Kay. He couldn't believe how much he'd missed her. It had confirmed what he suspected before he left, but had taken their separation to confirm. He, who had vowed to himself never to fall for a woman again, had fallen hook, line and sinker for his PA.

Of course, Kay was much more than that. It wasn't the clichéd office romance. Far from it. Kay had come into his life when he was at his lowest ebb, and they fitted together like two pieces of a puzzle. He intended to tell her so that very evening, once Sam and Ryan had gone to bed. He knew it was a lot to ask her – to take on two teenagers when her brood were already grown and had flown the nest, but he was hopeful.

Nick smiled to himself anticipating Kay's reaction – surprise followed by delight and acceptance of his proposal. Of course, he couldn't promise marriage until his divorce came through, but surely she would have no objection to moving in with him. She'd been living there while he'd been gone, and things appeared to have gone smoothly.

Or was he fooling himself? Would Kay be loath to give up the independence she'd enjoyed since her husband died? He hoped not.

The aircraft landed with a bump and taxied into place outside the terminal. Nick hauled his hand luggage down from the rack and joined the queue of passengers making their way down the aisle and out of the plane. As soon as he reached the foot of the stairs and started across the tarmac, he could see her familiar figure through the terminal windows.

Nick entered the building and strode towards Kay, dropping his bag, and taking her in his arms. But the warm welcome and kiss he expected was missing. Kay made no attempt to return his embrace. In fact, to his surprise and disappointment, it seemed to him that she stiffened slightly before moving away.

'What's wrong?' Nick searched Kay's face for some explanation. But she refused to meet his eyes.

'I have to take the return flight. Zoe and her family are all sick. I need to go to Brisbane to help out.'

'What? But I've just got back!' Nick felt like a little boy denied the treat he'd been waiting for.

'I know. I'm sorry. It can't be helped. Your car's in the car park. Here are the keys.' Kay fumbled in her bag and handed him the spare set of keys for his car. 'I left Milly with Sam. She promised to look after her. Can you see she does?'

Nick couldn't work out what had happened to Kay. Why had she changed? Where was the warm, affectionate, loving woman he'd left here just over a week ago?

Would all passengers for Sydney please make their way to the gate?

The announcement from the loudspeaker broke into his thoughts. He knew there was a quick turnaround with these local flights, but this was ridiculous. Maybe the delay at the other end meant they were trying to make up time here?

'I need to go.' Kay turned away.

'No! Wait!' But he was too late. Kay had gone through the door and had already joined the line of passengers walking across the tarmac to the aircraft from which he'd recently exited, full of excitement at the prospect of seeing her again.

Shaking his head, Nick collected his luggage and made his way to his car and home. Maybe Sam and Ryan could help him understand Kay's coldness. Maybe something had happened there to make her like this. But Nick couldn't imagine what it could possibly be.

The house felt empty when he arrived home. Both Sam and Ryan were in school. Nick went straight to his bedroom with his case, expecting to see remnants of Kay's belongings still lying there. But there was nothing to remind him of her, no evidence she'd ever been there, apart from a lingering fragrance in the ensuite. He inhaled it greedily, remembering how Kay felt in his arms, aching to hold her again.

Exhausted from the trip, Nick was tempted to collapse onto the bed which he could see had been made up with fresh linen – no remnant of Kay there either. Instead he headed for the kitchen. He needed coffee if he was to survive till the children returned from school.

He was filling the coffee machine when he heard a loud meow and a ball of fur wound itself around his ankles. 'Milly!' he said. 'Kay said she'd left you here. She's abandoned both of us. Do you feel as miserable about it as I do?' How he wished the cat could talk. Maybe she held the clue to Kay's sudden and unexpected departure.

By the time Sam and Ryan came home, Nick had showered and changed and felt like a new man.

'Hi, Dad!' Sam rushed past him upstairs, taking the steps two at a time. Ryan came next, barely greeting Nick, but joining him in the kitchen to grab a packet of biscuits from the pantry and a can of Coke from the fridge before he made his getaway. 'Homework,' he mumbled through a mouthful of crumbs.

It was as if Nick had never been away.

*

Next morning, Nick left before Sam and Ryan. Sam, to his surprise and delight, was ensuring Milly had enough food and water while Ryan was asking who had seen his social studies assignment. No one mentioned Kay, though she was in the forefront of Nick's mind, and he wasn't looking forward to the office without her.

Ann Baird waylaid him as soon as he set foot in the building. 'Professor Kerr. Good to see you back. We've had a little hiccup,' she said.

Hiccup! It was a damn sight more than that where he was concerned.

'Kay Jackson has been called away on a family emergency,' she continued, 'and Wendy here,' she drew forward a young girl who couldn't be more than twenty-five, 'will be filling in for her. Kay was kind enough to spend some time with her before she left, so I'm sure there won't be any problems. But if there are, please let me know.' Ann's mouth tightened in what Nick took to be disapproval – whether at Kay's leaving, her handover, or the idea that he might have problems with her replacement, Nick wasn't sure.

'I'm sure she'll be fine.' He gave the girl, who looked terrified, a disinterested smile. 'Thanks, Ann. I need to get on now. A bit of catching up to do.'

'Professor,' she gave an obsequious smile and disappeared through her office door.

'Well, let's get started, shall we? I assure you I'm not a monster, whatever you might have heard,' Nick said, remembering how he'd said much the same thing to Kay a few months earlier.

Wendy followed him upstairs and Nick entered his office, dropping his briefcase on the desk, before firing up his computer to see a long list of emails. Debating whether to have his new PA take care of them, he scanned down the list choosing to open only those from the vice chancellor's office and from faculty staff. The most urgent was one from Sheila Allen requesting – no, demanding – a meeting with the vice chancellor that morning to report on the conference. That was easy.

He slid his iPad out of his briefcase, asked Wendy to take care of the rest of the emails, and swung out of the office and back down the stairs. If he moved quickly and kept busy, maybe he could stop thinking about Kay, stop speculating what had gone wrong, stop wondering if he was imagining things.

Once out in the fresh air, Nick felt better. In the city noise and the energy-sapping humidity of Chicago, he'd missed the fresh air of Granite Springs. He breathed in the scent of the gums that were dotted around campus, sneezing as a sudden breeze released some blossom from the wattle. He was glad to be home.

'Nick! You're back! I hope you enjoyed the conference. How was Chicago?' Sheila Allen didn't wait for a reply, ushering him into the vice chancellor's office where Aaron greeted him with a firm handshake.

'Good to see you back, Nick. Thanks again for taking that on for me. I hope it wasn't too dull a trip for you. Always liked Chicago. Great place. Sorry I couldn't make it myself, but needs must. Take a seat. Sheila will be in with coffee.'

Nick hadn't been clear on why Aaron couldn't attend himself, and this did nothing to clarify the situation. He took a seat and opened his iPad.

Some thirty minutes and two cups of coffee later, Aaron leant back in his chair. 'Well, that was quite a summary. I almost feel as if I'd been there. Thanks, Nick. I knew you were the right man to send. And how were the social events? The organising committee for that association usually pull out all the stops. I hope you weren't guilty of overindulging?'

Nick coughed. 'I didn't spend much time at them. Met an old colleague from Sydney and we had a few glasses together, but that was all. I'm not much of a social animal.'

Aaron appeared surprised. 'Sorry to hear that. But everyone to his own.'

Back in his office, Wendy had some questions for him, then several of the academic staff called in to welcome him back. It wasn't till early afternoon when Wendy brought in his mail, that he thought to move his briefcase from the desk.

'I didn't open any of them,' she said. 'I wasn't sure what to do.' She looked so woebegone that Nick almost laughed. 'I'll go through them all today,' he said, 'but, in future, feel free to open anything that comes in addressed to the office or to me as Professor. I rarely receive any personal mail here, but if I do, it will be addressed to Nick Kerr. Okay?'

'Oh, thanks, Professor Kerr.'

Nick almost asked her to call him Nick, as he had Kay, but, looking at her young face, her apprehensive expression, decided it would be a mistake. Best to keep this on a more professional footing. She was young enough to be his daughter, and he probably seemed like a father figure to her.

He flicked through the letters, fewer now than there used to be. Most of his correspondents used email, but many of the publishers still liked to do things the old-fashioned way. He missed Kay's capable hand in this and supposed he'd have to instruct Wendy on which to keep and pass on to him and which to dump in the bin.

Making a small stack of those he needed to take care of, he set them aside and began to go through the other documents that had accumulated in his absence and were awaiting his attention. He barely noticed when Wendy tentatively popped her head through the door to ask if it was okay for her to leave. He nodded and waved her away, only thinking to check the time after she'd gone.

Five-thirty already! It was time to go home. Nick leant back, stretched his arms above his head, then placed them on the edge of his desk to push himself away. In the process he managed to dislodge the neat stack of letters. Cursing, he bent to pick them up.

One of the letters caught his eye. It looked different from the others. It was addressed to Professor Kerr's Office and had been opened.

Surely Wendy hadn't opened it? The poor little mouse had been terrified of doing the wrong thing. He turned the envelope over in his hands seeing a Chicago postmark. What the…?

Nick slid out the foolscap sheet and began to read, his eyes widening as he took in the words. How had Nadia found out about Kay? He hadn't mentioned her, only that he had someone back home. He wrinkled his brow. Rod! He'd told Rod. He must have told Nadia – though Nick couldn't imagine how that had come about. And then Nadia… She'd have guessed Kay would open his mail.

He knew she was spiteful, but this was beyond anything he might have imagined.

Forty-five

Glad to be away from Granite Springs and memories of Nick, Kay tried to enjoy her flight. But she couldn't dismiss the expression on Nick's face when she told him she was leaving.

It had been hard not to respond to his hug at the airport, but Kay had steeled herself, knowing that, if she let her guard down for even a moment, she'd be sunk. Now she was in the air, however, and being carried further and further away from him, she wondered if she should have taken Jo's advice. Her friend had suggested she should show Nick the letter, watch for his reaction and ask for an explanation. But she'd taken the coward's way out.

Had he seen the letter yet?

It was lying in the middle of his desk designed to be the first thing he saw when he walked into the office. But perhaps he wouldn't go straight to the university today. He'd be jetlagged and might need to sleep. So, maybe tomorrow?

The plane reached Sydney while Kay was still trying to imagine Nick's reaction. At least now he'll know why I didn't greet him with a kiss or return his hug, she thought, though it gave her no pleasure. The bitter coffee in the airport café did nothing to alter her mood either. But when the connecting flight descended into the balmier Queensland weather, Kay felt her sprits lift somewhat. Despite knowing she was about to enter a house of sickness, to be exasperated by her petulant daughter, she was glad to be there.

A short cab ride later, Kay emerged at the Northern Brisbane house where Zoe lived with Eric and Noah. A typical Queenslander, the single storey timber house with its corrugated iron roof stood on tall stilts, a veranda surrounding it on three sides. The house had been pretty rundown when Zoe and Eric purchased it before Noah was born, and they'd done a good job of renovating it. Situated opposite a park and close to the local primary school, it was ideal for a family. Kay hoped Zoe would change her mind about having another child, but at least she was back home now. That was the first step.

It was so different here from her own home in Granite Springs that Kay always felt she'd come to a different country when she visited. The air was different here, too – softer, moister.

Kay picked up her case and headed up the front steps to ring the bell.

'Mum, thank goodness you're here!' Zoe greeted her. 'We're almost out of food. Not that any of us feel like eating but...'

Kay hugged Zoe, as her daughter continued to talk. Then she sent her back to bed, unpacked her own case in the room she'd stayed in over Christmas, and went through the rest of the house to take stock.

She could see right away that she hadn't come a moment too soon. Her daughter's normally immaculate house had been left to accumulate dust, the kitchen bore signs of meals prepared and not eaten, and the laundry basket overflowed with dirty linen. In short, the place was a mess and in dire need of a housekeeper or cleaner or both. Well, Kay was here now, and it looked as if she'd have her work cut out to restore order. She'd have no time to brood over what she'd left behind in Granite Springs.

*

Two days later, Kay was preparing breakfast for herself and soft-boiled eggs with toast and vegemite which she hoped the others would manage to eat, when Eric walked into the kitchen.

'You're up! Are you feeling better?' she asked.

'I am. You've been taking such good care of us. I don't know how we'd have managed without you. It's not like Zoe. She's never ill. But this bug caught all of us by surprise.' He ruffled his hair and glanced down at his striped pyjama trousers. 'I'll just take a shower, then I think I could eat breakfast. Zoe's still asleep, Noah, too. I looked in on him as I went past.'

'Good to see you up and about. But best not try to do too much today.'

'No fear. But I need to get into the study and check how a few projects are going. Things don't stop because I'm sick.'

Kay shook her head as he wandered off. She took a few sips of her tea, then set a couple of trays, before taking one into Zoe where she found her just opening her eyes. Zoe groaned when she saw Kay. 'Oh, Mum, I don't think I can eat anything.'

'Try a few bites of toast. You need something in your stomach. I'll come back in for the tray in a bit.'

In Noah's room, Kay was pleased to see her grandson looking better. 'How would you like a nice boiled egg with soldiers?' she asked, taking a seat on the side of the bed and placing the tray beside her.

'Maybe?' Noah said doubtfully, but accepted eagerly when Kay handed him the strips of toast spread with vegemite and dipped in the soft-boiled egg.

'When will I be well again for school?' he asked, when he'd finished.

Kay thought for a moment. She knew it was almost school holidays in New South Wales, but the school terms were different up here. 'I'm sure you'll be right after the holidays,' she said. 'You started school when you came home, didn't you?'

He nodded, but Kay could see his little eyes were closing again. She picked up the tray and left quietly.

Back in the kitchen, Eric was making more toast and had already eaten the remaining egg. 'Sorry, was this your breakfast?' he asked.

'No, I intended that for you. I rarely have a cooked breakfast. Toast is fine.'

They were both seated when Kay's phone buzzed. A quick glance told her it was Nick. He'd called and texted several times since Wednesday, but Kay had ignored all of them, even refusing to read the texts. She wasn't ready to speak to Nick or to read what he had to say; she wondered if she'd ever be ready. Maybe the best thing would be to resign her position at the university. Then she'd never need to see or speak to him again. She conveniently forgot the need to pick up Milly.

'Do you want to take that?' Eric asked. 'I suppose you'll be keen to get back home?'

'No. No to both,' Kay said, trying to smile, but feeling the tears come to her eyes.

'Hey, what's wrong? You dashed up here, coming to our aid at the drop of a hat. We didn't think what it might mean to disrupt your life for us.'

'No. It's all right. I was glad to come. The timing was good for me, actually. It helped, got me out of a difficult situation,' Kay said, hoping Eric wouldn't ask for more explanation but she should have known her sensitive son-in-law wouldn't leave it there.

'How so?' Eric leant his elbows on the table, his desire to work in the study obviously forgotten.

Kay hesitated, then it all poured out – her relationship with Nick, the conference, his children, and the letter. 'So, you see,' she said, 'I'm not keen to go back. I don't think I can continue as his PA given the circumstances.'

'Mmm. Aren't you going to give the poor guy a chance to explain? There might be…'

Kay's lips tightened and she knew her eyes took on a glassy look.

'Well, maybe not,' he said. 'But, from my point of view, it seems there could be a few explanations. However,' he rose, took his mug to the sink and rinsed it, 'I'm sure you know what you're doing, Kay.'

But, as he disappeared in the direction of the study, Kay gazed at her phone and wondered if she did.

*

By Friday, both Zoe and Noah had fully recovered, and Eric had gone back to work. With her return to full health, Zoe had regained her typical brashness, and Kay knew it was time to go home, while dreading what it might bring.

'Let's have a day out before you leave,' Zoe said on Saturday morning when Kay told her she'd booked her flights for Sunday. Kay agreed, so as soon as they'd had breakfast, she, Zoe and Noah – Eric pleaded pressure of work – drove to Mount Coot-tha Botanic Gardens.

At the gardens, and at Noah's insistence, they followed the Children's Hide and Seek trail, despite Zoe's objection that he'd done it so often already. With Kay and Zoe following more slowly, Noah ran ahead, gripping the brochure with the map, and yelling with delight when he found each object in the trail. Kay found his pleasure in this activity almost as enjoyable as the gardens themselves.

Afterwards, they wandered through the gardens admiring the displays till they reached the lagoon where Noah had fun checking out the fish and turtles. While he was feeding the ducks with the breadcrumbs they'd taken along, Kay and Zoe sat on a nearby bench.

It was relaxing, sitting there in the sunshine. Maybe now was the time. Kay took a deep breath. 'I've never asked you this, Zoe. But I've often wondered... And when you took so against him, when you refused to come home after your dad died. Did he ever... Did your dad...?' She couldn't say it.

Zoe looked horrified. 'No, Mum. He didn't... he wouldn't... How could you think such a thing? But with the way he died, the gossip, how could I come back? How could I face people I knew in the street? I know it must have been just as bad for you. I'm sorry about that. But I'd made my escape, I had a new life here. It would have been too humiliating to return.'

'Right.' It was a relief to Kay to have cleared that up. She was about to say something, to reassure her daughter that she understood, when Noah returned brandishing the empty paper bag.

'All gone!' he said.

The two women stood up and hugged, then Zoe decided it was time for lunch.

'What will you do when you get home, Mum?' Zoe asked over coffee when they'd finished lunch and Noah had prevailed on Kay to treat him to an ice cream. 'I think you're right to want to leave the university. I can imagine how difficult it would be for you to see your professor every day, remembering how he treated you. But I don't like to think of you going back into hibernation like you were before.'

Kay regretted having shared her concerns with Zoe, though, once she'd confided in Eric, she knew it wouldn't be long till her daughter found out anyway. Unlike Eric, Zoe had taken her mother's view and condemned Nick, saying, 'Men! Not to be trusted,' which, to her surprise, made Kay want to defend him.

And now Kay had made the move to get herself back into circulation, she doubted she'd return to the hermit-like existence she'd had before.

'I know,' Zoe said, 'why don't you get in touch with Donna? I didn't manage to finish all my interviews because I left so suddenly. You did say it was something you'd enjoy doing, didn't you?'

Kay remembered thinking that. She couldn't remember saying it, but supposed she must have. It was an idea. 'I might do that,' she said.

'Now, the planetarium,' Noah said, taking both Zoe and Kay's hands and dragging them towards the dome-shaped structure just outside the gardens.

Kay enjoyed the displays and the informative talk given while they reclined in comfortable chairs and gazed up at the display of stars moving across the underside of the dome.

'Is Noah able to understand all that?' she asked Zoe as they left.

'It's one of his favourite spots,' Zoe said. 'We've been coming here for years, and he soon outgrew the children's shows.'

'It's my birthday soon, Grandma. Will you be here? Can we come here, Mum? And can the twins come?'

'I think it may be too far for the twins, Noah,' Kay said.

'And your grandma won't be able to come back up so soon, will you, Mum?'

'Well…' Kay would love to be here for Noah's birthday, but Zoe's tone told her she might not be welcome.

'We've had this lovely day with her instead.'

'Okay.'

Noah appeared satisfied, but Kay wasn't. It would serve Zoe right if she just decided to turn up. But she probably wouldn't. There was no sense in antagonising her now that they seemed to be getting along better.

'Home, tomorrow, Mum,' Zoe said as they were driving back. 'I can't tell you how much I appreciate your coming up to help out.'

'That's what family is for.'

And this was Kay's family. Regardless how much Zoe might irritate her, she was family.

Nick Kerr wasn't. He had his own family and she had no part in it.

Forty-six

Kay was gripping her letter of resignation tightly when she met Ann Baird on Monday morning. She'd emailed her from Brisbane on Friday, asking for a meeting and indicating her decision, in an attempt to avoid having to confront Nick.

'Is there any way I can get you to change your mind, Kay?' Ann asked. 'Wendy, the girl who's been taking your place, hasn't worked out well. Professor Kerr's not happy with her performance and Fran should be back in a few weeks' time, so it wouldn't be for long.'

They were standing outside the main office, at the foot of the stairs to Nick's office, and Kay felt too exposed to discuss this in such a public spot. She'd anticipated a private meeting with Ann, but the other woman met her just as she arrived and immediately started to talk.

'I don't...' Kay began, when she sensed a presence behind her – one she knew all too well.

'I need to talk to Mrs Jackson,' Nick said. 'Thanks, Ann. I'll take over here. Come up to my office,' he said to Kay and strode off upstairs.

Tempted to leave the building, Kay threw a startled look at Ann, before following him upstairs, her thoughts racing, her heart beating rapidly. This is exactly what she'd been at pains to avoid.

Once in his office, Nick gestured to one of the two low chairs which sat either side of a rarely used coffee table. He took the other himself.

'You've been ignoring me,' he said.

Kay looked down at her hands. What did he expect her to say?

'I suppose it's because of that letter – the one you opened and left on my desk?'

'I didn't mean to… I didn't read it all… just…'

'Just enough? Kay, I have no idea why she wrote that.' He dragged a hand through his hair.

'You don't deny you know the woman, that you and she…' Kay couldn't put it into words. 'I know I have no claim on you. You're a free agent. I've heard about what goes on at those conferences and it's a bit like *What happens in Vegas stays in Vegas*. I know that, but…' Kay felt her eyes begin to tear up.

She wasn't going to cry, she wasn't!

She scrabbled in her bag for a tissue and when she looked up, Nick wore a more conciliatory expression.

'I can explain.' Nick stretched out his hands, palms up. 'Will you let me?'

Kay nodded. She couldn't imagine what sort of explanation he could give, but she was here, so she might as well listen. She didn't have much choice.

'It's not what you obviously think. I'm disappointed you'd think that of me, but maybe it's understandable given…' He cleared his throat. 'I admit I do know Nadia. Did know her, to be more exact. Back when I was studying in the States. She dated a friend of mine – not me.' He looked away. 'I admit I did see her a few times. I'm not proud of that episode in my past. Her sort never interested me – then or now. I managed to escape her clutches then, too.' He pulled on his beard.

'I was shocked to meet her again at the conference, and when she tried to latch onto me.' He rubbed the back of his neck. 'I can only imagine she hoped to succeed now where she'd failed all those years ago. She was drunk and asked me to drive her home. What was I to do?'

Refuse?

But Kay knew Nick was too much of a gentleman to do that.

'I was in her apartment,' Nick thrust a hand through his hair which Kay noticed had grown since they last met, 'I had to make sure she was all right, wasn't going to be sick. But, I promise you, that was all. Nothing happened.'

Kay saw a dull look in his eyes as if he was reliving an unpleasant experience.

'I made sure I kept out of her way for the rest of the conference. She was part of the organising committee, so it was pretty awkward, especially the last night. Seems she also made a play for a mate of mine from Sydney, and he was more gullible than me. But it did mean I had to make my escape from the conference dinner before the speeches – maybe not such a bad thing. You do believe me, don't you?' Nick pleaded.

Kay didn't know what to think. She wanted to believe him, but…

'Why did she write that letter?' she asked. 'What did she hope to achieve?'

'I have no idea. I'm as surprised as you were. I was shocked when I found it on my desk – and to realise you'd opened it, read her nonsense.'

'The first sentence was enough.' Kay shuddered at the memory, still not entirely convinced.

'So?'

'I need to think about this.' Kay made to rise.

'But you'll reconsider your resignation?'

'For the moment. I need to go home. I need time to digest this.'

'And us?'

'Is there any us?'

'I hope so.' Nick looked penitent. 'I'm sorry you had to go through this. Believe me when I say it was none of my doing. I had no idea…' He pulled on his beard again, and Kay's stomach gave the now familiar lurch. 'Look. Sam and Ryan are with their mum – school holidays. Why don't we get together tonight? Your place or mine?'

Kay thought for a moment, tempted to refuse. But it was a reasonable request. Where would she feel more comfortable? If she went to Nick's she could leave if things became difficult, but she'd feel more secure in her own home.

'Mine,' she said. 'Eight o'clock suit?'

*

By seven o'clock, Kay had managed to get herself worked up into such a state she couldn't sit still. The dinner she'd cooked lay uneaten, her hands were trembling, she was hyperventilating, a tightness in her chest. Even poor Milly, who she'd picked up on her way home from the university and seemed pleased to be home, failed to comfort her. When Kay eventually sat down on one of the armchairs in the living room, the cat leapt onto her lap, nuzzling into her, purring, and kneading Kay's lap with her paws, to no avail.

'Sorry, Milly,' Kay said, rising again. 'Oh, what am I to do? Can I believe him? I want to – so much.' She checked the clock again. Only ten past seven. What had possessed her to say eight o'clock? The phone rang.

'Kay, how did it go today?'

'Jo!'

Kay had forgotten she'd confided her plan to Jo and, of course, her friend was calling to find out what had happened.

'Oh, Jo, I don't know what to do!' Kay related the tale of her meeting with Nick finishing with, 'What should I do? I wish I hadn't agreed to see him again.'

There was silence at the other end of the line for so long Kay thought Jo had hung up, then, 'What would you like to happen – if you could choose?'

Kay had only to think for a moment. 'I'd like everything to go back to the way it was – before he went to that damned conference. Oh, Jo, we were getting on so well. I was even thinking... You know. We talked about it. My only concern was his children.'

'But what's changed?'

'What's changed?' Kay's voice rose a notch. 'Everything. That letter changed everything.'

'Has Nick changed? Have your feelings for him changed?'

'No...oo,' Kay said slowly, remembering the bolt of desire that shot through her in his office. 'But... what if I can't trust him? I can't go through that again.'

'Calm down. You say he wants to talk to you. That's a good sign. But sometimes words aren't enough. I may not have told you how Col came around here and changed my mind when I was determined everything between us was over. I suggest you give your professor a chance. He's a good man, Kay.'

A chance – that's what he was asking for. She could do that.

When she finished the call, Kay felt better. Jo could always have a calming effect on her. She'd helped Kay remember the good things about her and Nick, helped her realise that maybe – just maybe – something could be salvaged from this whole muddle.

She looked around the room – the heart of this house she'd lived in for all her married life with David. It was home, but a home she'd already decided to leave before she met Nick. Only Zoe's precipitous arrival had delayed her making the move.

Kay remembered the conversation she'd had with Jo before Nick left, her joy, her doubts. To her surprise, all of those doubts had disappeared when she read what she now thought of as THE LETTER, to be replaced with a sense of loss, of having lost something she hadn't been sure she wanted. If only she could travel back in time.

The doorbell rang.

'Nick!'

'Kay!'

Nick moved to kiss her cheek, but Kay wasn't ready for that. Not yet. Maybe not ever.

'Come in.'

Nick's expression was unreadable as he followed her into the living room where, seeming to sense the tension, Milly leapt down from the chair where she'd been grooming herself, to disappear through the door.

Kay placed a hand on her stomach as if, by doing so, she could still the butterflies that were racing around. 'Would you like a drink?'

'Thanks.'

'Wine?'

'That'd be fine.'

In the kitchen, Kay stood for a few moments holding onto the edge of the sink. She felt sick. This had been a bad idea. Forcing herself to move, she took two glasses from the cupboard and poured the red wine she'd removed from the wine rack earlier. Taking a deep breath, she carried them through to where Nick was sitting, tapping one foot and drumming his fingers on the arm of the chair.

So, he was nervous, too?

Somehow, that made her feel better.

Nick was the first to break the silence. 'You asked if we were still... if there was still an "us"? I hope so, Kay. I really do.' He took a gulp of wine before placing his glass on a side table and letting his clasped hands drop between his knees. 'I thought about you a lot while I was gone, about how good we are together, how you make me feel. When Michelle left...' He took a deep breath.

Kay could see he found this difficult. Her heart went out to him, but she let him continue.

'...I thought I'd never be able to feel anything for a woman again, never be able to trust one. Then you walked into my office and into my life. It was as if the sun had come out. You can't imagine how you've changed my life, how much you've come to mean to me, how much I want us to have a future together. I wish I'd never gone to that damned conference. I should have refused Aaron.' He thrust a hand through his hair. 'Can we get back to where we were? As I said, while I was over there, I thought about you a lot. I planned to talk with you when I got back, to ask you...'

Nick met Kay's gaze with one which would have melted even the hardest heart. How could she doubt him, how could she question his honesty, his integrity? She'd been right. Jo had been right. He was a good man.

They rose as one, their arms reached out, their lips met, and they were back in their own world, the one they'd made for themselves before any of the Chicago stuff happened. But, this time, it was with the knowledge that their relationship had been tested and had survived.

'I want to spend the rest of my life with you,' Nick murmured into Kay's hair.

She felt her heart leap with joy. Suddenly all the obstacles, imagined or otherwise seemed to disappear. This was the man she wanted to spend the rest of her life with, too.

Nick was what she'd been waiting for. Nick was what she wanted.

She could choose how her life was going to be, and a future with Nick Kerr was the life she was going to choose.

If you enjoyed this book, I'd love it if you could write a review. It doesn't need to be long, just a few words, but it is the best way for me to help new readers discover my books.

Look out for the next Granite Springs novel, *The Life She Wants*, which is Fran's story.

From the Author

Dear Reader,

First, I'd like to thank you for choosing to read *The Life She Chooses*. Having spent seven years teaching university and living in an Australian country town, I've enjoyed writing a series with a rural setting. This is the second book in the series set in the fictional country town of Granite Springs.

If you'd like to stay up to date with my new releases and special offers you can sign up to my reader's group.

You can sign up here
https://mailchi.mp/f5cbde96a5e6/maggiechristensensreadersgroup

I'll never share your email address, and you can unsubscribe at any time. You can also contact me via Facebook Twitter or by email. I love hearing from my readers and will always reply.

Thanks again.

Acknowledgements

As always, this book could not have been written without the help and advice of a number of people.

Firstly, my husband Jim for listening to my plotlines without complaint, for his patience and insights as I discuss my characters and storyline with him, for his patience and help with difficult passages and advice on my male dialogue, and for being there when I need him.

John Hudspith, editor extraordinaire for his ideas, suggestions, encouragement and attention to detail.

Jane Dixon-Smith for her patience and for working her magic on my beautiful cover and interior.

My thanks also to early readers of this book –Helen, Anne, Maggie and Louise, for their helpful comments and advice. Also to Annie of *Annie's books at Peregian* for her ongoing support.

I'm also grateful to my lovely granddaughter, Lara who, while living some distance from me, was only a text away to check that my teenage dialogue was current and provide me with terms with which I wasn't familiar. So much has changed since I was that age

And to all of my readers. Your support and comments make it all worthwhile. I'm thrilled you enjoy my more mature characters.

About the Author

After a career in education, Maggie Christensen began writing contemporary women's fiction portraying mature women facing life-changing situations. Her travels inspire her writing, be it her frequent visits to family in Oregon, USA or her home on Queensland's beautiful Sunshine Coast. Maggie writes of mature heroines coming to terms with changes in their lives and the heroes worthy of them. Her writing has been described by one reviewer as *like a nice warm cup of tea. It is warm, nourishing, comforting and embracing.*

From her native Glasgow, Scotland, Maggie was lured by the call 'Come and teach in the sun' to Australia, where she worked as a primary school teacher, university lecturer and in educational management. Now living with her husband of over thirty years on Queensland's Sunshine Coast, she loves walking on the deserted beach in the early mornings and having coffee by the river on weekends. Her days are spent surrounded by books, either reading or writing them – her idea of heaven!

She continues her love of books as a volunteer with her local library where she selects and delivers books to the housebound.

Maggie can be found on Facebook, Twitter, Goodreads, Instagram or on her website.

www.facebook.com/maggiechristensenauthor
www.twitter.com/MaggieChriste33
www.goodreads.com/author/show/8120020.Maggie_Christensen
www.instagram.com/maggiechriste33/
maggiechristensenauthor.com/